THE FIRST TO KNOW

**Books by Abigail Johnson
available from Harlequin TEEN**

If I Fix You
The First to Know

THE
FIRST
TO
KNOW

ABIGAIL JOHNSON

WITHDRAWN

HHARLEQUIN®TEEN

ISBN-13: 978-1-335-00794-0

The First to Know

For my sisters, Mary and Rachel. You are both my favorite.

CHAPTER 1

The swing was so smooth and effortless I barely felt it. Adrenaline slammed though my body as I hit a screamer into right center, knowing it would find the gap. It had to. I dropped my bat and bolted for first, picking up speed as I rounded to second. I had at least a triple. I made the split-second decision to ignore the stop sign from my coach, kicking up dust as I passed third and charged for home. We needed this run to go to extra innings. From the corner of my eye, I saw the second baseman pivot and rear back to throw home. My heart rate skyrocketed and I slid, taking out the catcher staked over home plate.

She fell onto me in a cloud of orange dust that choked us both. We were still in a heap on the ground when the sound of the cheering crowd shifted from one side to the other—from our team's fans to theirs. The Hawks swooped out of their dugout in a flurry of teal and black and tackled their rising catcher in a massive hug.

Only one of my fellow Mustangs came and offered me a hand up: our shortstop and my best friend, Jessalyn. I brushed her off, despite my eagerness to get away from the celebration going on around me.

"Way to go, Dana."

"I was safe," I told her, yanking off my batting glove to check my nose. I'd hit the catcher's knee pretty hard.

"Actually, you weren't. Otherwise Coach would be screaming at the umpire right now instead of—"

"Dana!" Coach was descending on me with a look that sent Jessalyn retreating to our dugout. His eyebrows were practically touching his hairline and his face was blotchy red from the blood roiling just below the surface. "What are you doing? Huh? What the hell do you think you're doing?"

"I was trying to win."

"For us or them?" He got in my face, so close that I felt exactly what it meant when someone was spitting mad. My own anger receded under his frothing fury. "Are you wearing teal?" He jutted his chin toward my uniform. "Is that the color you're wearing?"

"I'm wearing red," I said, but so quietly he made me repeat it. "I'm wearing red."

"I gave you the stop sign because you were never going to beat that throw. Damn it, Dana!" He turned away, hands on hips, and then faced me again. "You don't get to decide what rules to follow. They—" he pointed at my teammates, who were watching me get chewed out from the dugout "—all know that."

My temper flared again, but I held in my response.

"That's it? You got nothing to say?"

Nothing that would make him stop yelling at me any faster. Silence was my best bet. I'd had more than a little practice getting yelled at by coaches, especially this one.

"You're not starting on Tuesday—"

My head jerked up. "What?"

"—and I'm benching you for the first three innings."

"You can't—" When he walked away, I was right on his heels but skidded to a stop when he rounded on me.

"What? What can't I do?"

It took everything in me to bite my lip. I clamped down so hard I tasted copper. I wasn't responsible for us being down by one with two outs in the bottom of the seventh. And I sure hadn't made a lineup that put Amanda Watson at bat after me. I'd had to take the chance. Amanda was the least consistent batter on our team. She either hit moon shots or struck out, the latter being more often the case when the pressure was on. But I couldn't say any of that, not if I wanted to play at all the next game.

He was in my face again. "You think Selena would have pulled a stunt like that? No. Because Selena listened to her coach."

My eyes stung at the mention of my sister, whose gaze I could feel from the stands. Every time I messed up, he compared me to her. I rotated my jaw and looked at my cleats. Selena had led her team to the state championships as a senior two years ago, something I was determined to do my junior year. And I couldn't do that by risking wins with unreliable players. Why was I the only one who saw that?

"I was trying to win," I repeated, half through my teeth.

"Yeah. All by yourself." He thrust my discarded bat into my

hands and went to join the rest of our pissed-off team as they lined up to congratulate the Highland Hawks on their win.

After the less-than-sincere—at least on my part—congratulations were given and I'd sat through our coach's spiel about how well we'd played—not well enough, or I wouldn't have had to try to save the game—and how we won and lost as a united team, I ducked out before anyone else could yell at me and headed around the bleachers.

"Hey, slugger."

My scowl evaporated at the sound of Nick's voice and became a smile when I turned to see the hulking Samoan guy who'd been one of my closest friends since junior high. Since then, he'd grown a lot bigger, a lot cuter and, frustratingly for me, a lot more shy too. It had gotten so much worse since we got partnered together in biology that semester. I thought he was developing more than friendly feelings for me, but with Nick it was hard to tell, which made it really hard to tell if I was developing any feelings of my own. Still, he'd come to my game, so maybe he was trying to be bolder. He even spoke to me first, though I could tell he was regretting his choice of the word *slugger* based on the way he lowered and shook his head.

"I should have just said Dana."

"Nah, slugger's a classic. So, the first game you got to see this year ended with me losing. Awesome."

"I thought you were great."

"Thanks," I said, not really meaning it. "I didn't see you."

"I had to come late, so I only caught the last inning."

"Even better," I said.

He smiled, ducking his head a little. "It was only the first game, right?"

"Said like a guy who doesn't play sports." I stopped walking when Nick slowed. Then I mentally shook myself in an attempt to beat back my venomous mood. "Sorry. I'm the worst loser on the planet." I also wasn't looking forward to the car ride home with my endlessly disappointed dad and the shining sibling I'd never live up to. At least Selena would have to head back to her dorm eventually. Dad could berate me all night if he wanted.

Nick recovered from my semi-insult and kicked his foot to dislodge a cricket that had landed on his shoe. It was mid-March in Arizona, which, in addition to being the start of softball season, meant the weather was losing its cold bite. That was all the invitation the crickets needed. They weren't at summer-level swarming yet, but the chirping was an ever-present sound outside, and it was already hard to avoid the little hopping bodies, try as Nick might.

"Aren't you going to ask why I was late?" he asked.

I hadn't known he was coming at all. I'd told him in class that I was playing, but that was all. "Everything okay? Did something happen with your grandmother?" Nick's newly widowed grandmother had recently moved in and was still grieving deeply.

"She's actually doing a little better."

"Oh, good." I squeezed his forearm, and he half jumped like I'd touched him with an iron.

"Yeah, so, that's not why." Nick slid the backpack from his shoulder and unzipped it for me to see inside.

"No way." I grabbed the sides of the bag and stepped right

up to him. "Why didn't you text me?" I looked up when Nick didn't answer and found him staring at me.

"I thought it'd be worth it to see your face." He swallowed. "And it was."

Nick's skin was as rich a brown as my glove, but I thought he was blushing. Still, I couldn't dwell on the cute-but-shy thing he had going at the moment. I had eyes only for the white rectangular box he'd brought me. "I'm still pissed about losing, but a lot less now."

"Have you figured out how you're going to do it?"

I nodded. "Selena finally agreed to help, despite her massive reservations." I took a deep breath as I put the box in my duffel bag. "I think this will be the best thing I've ever done, and she's convinced it'll be the worst."

"You know if it doesn't work out, you don't have to tell anyone."

Right. But it had to work out. "I guess tonight's the night." I couldn't help bouncing on my feet a little. "Okay."

"And you can call me if you have any questions or anything." He reached out like he was going to pat my arm or something but pulled back before touching me.

That was fine. I'd need to get used to taking the lead with us, if we ever became us. I hugged him. "Seriously, thank you, Nick. I wouldn't be doing this without you."

It had been only a couple weeks since our biology teacher had started class by sticking his rolled tongue out at his students. A few people laughed at the continued display; the rest waited for the inevitable explanation. When at last Mr. Rodriguez raised his arms and gestured for us to imitate him, he was quick to point a finger at Nick.

"Thank you, Mr. Holloway—no, no. Keep your tongue out. You too, Miss Fields." He shifted his finger to me. "Here we have a perfect display of a dominant phenotype for tongue rolling." He pointed back at Nick. "And a recessive phenotype for tongue rolling. I'm assuming you cannot roll your tongue, Mr. Holloway?"

Nick shook his head while a slight flush marched up the back of his neck.

"Then my original statement stands. Now, what is a phenotype? As you all should know from last night's reading, it's simply the collection of observable traits, like a widow's peak." He pointed to his own hairline. "Or freckles or any number of characteristics that are physically demonstrable, like our tongue rollers here—feel free to close your mouths now," he said, addressing the half of the class who still had their tongues out. "What I'd like you all to do with your partners is complete a chart listing several phenotypes, note which are dominant and recessive, then *felicitaciones!* You're going to have two children and, from your original data, determine the phenotypes of each child." He began passing out packets. "Refer to chapters eight and nine of your textbooks if you need further reminders about phenotypes, genotypes, alleles, gametes and the marvelous process of meiosis. I'll be circulating the room to answer questions. Now learn, students, learn!"

I leaned into Nick, who still hadn't fully recovered from being singled out. "I think our kids are screwed. Between my attached earlobes and your flat tongue, what can they possibly accomplish in life?" I got a pity smile for my lame humor, but Nick made eye contact for more than two seconds. "Though maybe there is something awesome hidden on my dad's side that they could inherit. He was surrendered at a hospital as a baby, so we have no clue about his birth family."

Nick nodded. "I never knew that about your dad but I guess that goes for me too."

Nick had grown up knowing he was adopted—his family had their own mini holiday, Nick Day, celebrating the day they brought him home—and had never shown the least bit of discomfort talking about it. The opposite, really. Score me for bringing it up. I had Nick's full, unguarded attention. He turned to face me.

"Did I tell you I recently took one of those online DNA tests to try to figure out more of my heritage? I'm obviously Samoan, but turns out I'm 8 percent Inuit too. I even found a few fourth cousins floating around the country."

I'd forgotten to care that he'd been holding my gaze for longer than his usual few seconds. "Wait, like actual blood relatives? A DNA test can tell you that?" My heart rate spiked as the possibilities began darting through my brain.

"Yeah. A lot of people are doing them now, so you never know who you'll find. Cool, huh?"

I'd almost kissed him that day in biology class. Instead I'd pumped him for every speck of info on the company he'd used and started planning something I'd hopefully get to finish that night. The knowledge now made me hug Nick tighter despite the duffel bag smashed between us.

From over his shoulder, I saw my mom heading toward us. I pulled back a scant second after he'd worked up the nerve to hug me back, noticing that I'd transferred a good amount of orange dust from my uniform to him in the process. I left him beating dust from his spotless white T-shirt and quite possibly ironed jeans with a promise to text him once I'd succeeded—which I absolutely would. I wasn't about to lose twice in one night.

Mom didn't care about dust and gathered me into a hug while whispering a disparaging comment about the umpire's vision before releasing me.

"Tell that to Dad." He was still in the dugout talking to a couple of the girls before making the final shift from Coach to Dad again, a distinction he and Selena had established back when he'd coached her softball team. Honestly, I never noticed much of a difference.

"Oh, I will."

That made me smile, because she would. My parents often had loud, passionate disagreements that, to an outsider, might seem like fights. But they didn't see the way Mom would goad Dad even after she'd made her point just to watch the heated color infuse his pale skin, or the way Dad would bait her until she slipped into her native Spanish because she had even less of a filter in those moments than normal.

"Who was the boy and when do I get to meet him?"

I tightened the grip on my duffel. "That was Nick, and you've met him a dozen times."

"Not since you started hugging him like that."

I so wasn't having that conversation. "Where's Selena?"

Mom gave me a knowing look at my obvious subject change. "Ask him to come to dinner. He's not a vegetarian, is he?"

To my mom, being a vegetarian was slightly less offensive

than being a Dodgers fan. "He's not a vegetarian. And he's still just a friend."

"Hmm," Mom said, which meant we'd be revisiting the topic later. "Selena's waiting for us at the car."

"Where's her car?"

"She got in early, so we drove together."

Great. I get both her and Dad the whole way home.

As soon as we were within earshot, Selena started. "I can't believe you ran through a stop sign." Her shoulder-length brown hair, a shade darker than mine, swished as she shook her head. "I get that when the adrenaline is flowing, it's hard to stop, but, Dana, you don't get to make that call. When I was playing…"

I tuned her out. Selena had this way of seeming to support and motivate me that undercut everything I did, and it had only gotten worse since she left for college. The University of Arizona was only a couple hours from Apache Junction, so she still tried to make most of my games—largely, I was convinced, to remind us all of her glory days as a Mustang. She was no doubt relaying one of her many victories, where she single-handedly played every position and hit so many home runs that the other team's coach begged her to transfer schools, or my personal favorite, Dad crying when she told him she wasn't interested in playing college ball. Those were all slight-to-gross exaggerations. Dad never cried; he'd just looked like he wanted to.

"Got it. I'll play better next time. Hey, weren't you telling me that you need Mom and Dad to help you with some school project tonight?" I moved my duffel bag in front of me and widened my eyes at her. Selena could be an annoying braggart when it came to softball, but she was also the only person on the planet who could read my mind with only the slightest cue.

"I was," she said, without missing a beat, then forestalled Mom's inevitable question. "It's an extra-credit thing. I'll tell you about it when we get home. I'm sure Dad's gonna want to talk about that last out first."

I groaned. "Can we just not? Let's talk about something lighter, like teen-pregnancy statistics. Besides, it was a bad call."

"You looked out to me," Selena said.

Blood heated my face, but Dad was there before I could respond.

"That's because she was." He unlocked the trunk, not looking at me. "The umpire called it."

I came up alongside him, wishing he could be a little more my dad and a little less my coach the next time a close call cost us a game. "You know, you used to get thrown out of games all the time for arguing when you coached Selena. This would have been a perfect opportunity."

"Not all the time," Selena said, though I was positive she was calling a list to mind same as I was.

"More than once," I said, before turning back to Dad and waiting with raised eyebrows for his response. "There was that game against Chandler. You almost took a swing at the umpire."

"I was never going to hit him," Dad said. "Back then I was more of a..." He searched for the right word.

"*Calentón*," Mom said, smiling.

I thought it was more than Dad being hotheaded, but I didn't get to protest before he went on.

"I told you to stay, you didn't, and we lost. And even if you'd been safe—run through a stop sign again and I'll bench you for more than a few innings." He opened the front passenger door for Mom, a practice he'd apparently started on their first date and was still doing more than twenty years later.

"You're not serious." But the look he gave me said otherwise. "Fine. Am I supposed to apologize to my dad or my coach?"

"What was that?" he asked, though we both knew he'd heard me.

"Nothing."

He sighed, coming around to where I stood. "What is this attitude?"

"Why didn't you fight the call?"

"Because you were out. Hey—hey." He called my attention back when I looked away. "I'd have fought for you if you weren't. Same as I did for your sister." He lowered his voice so that Mom and Selena on the other side wouldn't overhear. "You are one of the best players on the team. You could be as good as Selena if you worked harder."

Except Selena never had to work the way I constantly had to. And she'd never cared enough to see how much better she could have been if she had. That was maybe the one bone of contention between her and Dad. So I worked twice as hard to be half as good, and it still wasn't enough.

"Take the loss and work harder next time. We've got the whole season ahead of us, and you're no good to me or anyone else on a bench. I need you." He clapped a hand on my shoulder and squeezed. I nodded and worked my mouth into a small smile for his benefit. He needed me. I wanted more than that, but I'd settle for *need* just then.

I cradled my duffel in my lap during the car ride home, feeling the shape of the box within. And I smiled for real.

CHAPTER 2

My plan went off without a hitch. Selena was calm and cool, explaining that she needed family DNA samples for a criminology class she was supposedly taking. Selena was still technically undeclared, but she'd expressed enough middling interest in pursuing a sociology degree that neither of our parents questioned this. I think they both took it as a sign that she was finally committing to a career path. Mom happily swiped the toothbrush-like swab on the inside of her cheek. Dad was equally willing, joking about taking Mom on the lam if they connected him to any unsolved murders. They had no idea what we were really doing—what *I* was really doing.

After that, Selena passed me Dad's swab and was officially done with the whole thing.

"I'm officially done with the whole thing," she said, when we were in my room afterward.

"Fine." I didn't even look up from the DNA Detective website open on my laptop. "But don't come back to me when I'm about to give Dad the birthday present to end all birthday presents."

Selena peered over my shoulder, chewing on her thumbnail. "You really think you'll find someone he's related to?"

Arizona's Safe Baby Haven Law allowed newborns to be anonymously handed over at hospitals or fire stations without having to provide personal information, which meant Dad's birth certificate was basically blank. But none of that would matter if we found even a single DNA match. "Yes." I turned sideways in my chair. "Nick found a bunch of fourth cousins when he took his test, and he sent me links about other people who were orphans just like Dad finding half siblings and even parents."

"What if it tells us something he doesn't want to know, something *we* don't want to know?"

I frowned. "What, that he's related to some douchey celebrity? The whole point of doing it as a surprise is that if we don't like what we find out, then we trash it and he never knows." I couldn't believe I still had to convince Selena about this. She knew as well as I did how much it would mean for Dad to find his own relatives. That was part of the reason he and Mom got pregnant with me. They wanted to make sure Selena had a sibling, someone she was directly connected to. Dad didn't have that. There was such a huge contrast between Mom's sprawling Mexican clan back in Texas and Dad's blank unknown. We didn't see Mom's family all that often, but they were still there, and I always felt like I was a part of something. Dad didn't know what that was like. This was a chance to give him a family that consisted of more than the three of us.

"I needed your money and your criminology-class excuse,

both of which you gave me. If you want out now, that's fine. Go ahead and give Dad a tie for his birthday."

Selena dropped her arms in obvious irritation before fishing her car keys out of her bag. "Fine. I have to get back to my dorm." She hesitated at the door. "Just don't tell me if he's 86 percent more likely to get colon cancer or something. Good stuff only, okay?"

I gave her an exaggerated eye roll. "But if it's good?"

"Then, since I paid for half of this, my name better be on the birthday card too."

Under my breath, I said, "A little more than half," before turning back to the computer and filling out the final field on the registration form.

Selena strode back to my side and blocked the touch pad before I could click Send. "I paid more?"

Oh yeah. "I'm a poor high school junior who has to constantly put money into your old car."

"And I'm a poorer college sophomore who gave you that old car for way less than it was worth."

"It was my idea, and I'm doing all the work. Plus, now you're making me go through the potentially traumatic results all on my own." Not that I expected them to be traumatic. When Selena still didn't seem convinced, I glanced at her hand covering the touch pad, then up at her while simultaneously clicking Enter on the keyboard.

She dropped her hand. "Fine. Was that it? Is it done?"

"I mail the sample back in the morning and the results come in six to eight weeks."

"Six to eight weeks. That seems fast."

Not to me. Plus, Dad's birthday wasn't for another two

months after that. Nick told me it could take time to hear back from any potential matches I found and contacted, and longer still if I needed information from any of them to track down closer relatives. Still, I couldn't stop the excitement buzzing through me. Family for Dad. Family that I found—with Selena's help, but that I made happen. That would be worth more than all the softball games she ever won him.

I turned out to be right: six to eight weeks did not go fast. As we approached the six-week mark, it became impossible to focus in Biology, my last class before lunch. Not even Nick working up the nerve to ask me out—something he'd started but abandoned the last three days in a row—could completely hold my attention.

He sucked in a deep breath. "Dana, I was wondering if… I mean…do you…" A sheen of sweat broke out on his forehead and he gave up yet again. "Can I borrow a pen?"

So close, I thought, passing Nick a pen. I could have asked him out, but I really needed him to find that initial bit of courage. Otherwise I'd end up running all over him in a relationship and that wouldn't be good for either of us.

Glancing at the clock again, I didn't have any more time to give Nick in the hopes that he'd try again before class ended. "Hey, so if I leave early, can you cover for me with Mr. Rodriguez?" I was already packing up my stuff and eyeing our teacher, who was helping a student in the back row. "I need to be home when the mail is delivered or else my dad might get it first. Just tell him I went to the bathroom if he notices I'm gone." And then I slipped out the door, mouthing *thanks* to a dumbstruck Nick as I did.

Our house was only a few miles from Superstition Springs High School on the outskirts of Apache Junction, tucked into a development of identical midsize homes that were distinguished from each other only by the cars parked out front. In our case, Mom's red mini SUV and Dad's silver hatchback. We had a corner lot, which meant we had twice as much backyard as our neighbors and could practice a little without having to drive to a park. That had been the number one selling point of the home, the trade-off being that it had only three smallish bedrooms, one of which we converted into Mom and Dad's office because the large bay window afforded it the most natural light. It also gave me a perfectly unobstructed view to spy through. I slowed as I drove by, banking on the hope that they'd both be too consumed in their work to look up and recognize my car. Sure enough, Mom was fastidiously writing code on her computer, while Dad was filling his with design mock-ups for whatever website they were currently working on—I could never keep track. It was a good business, one that allowed Dad to set his own hours and still coach our high school softball team while giving Mom's analytical mind the challenge she craved since she had to code whatever designs he came up with. A right brain and a left brain working together in near-perfect harmony.

Neither glanced up as I drove by, but they would if I pulled into the driveway, so I had to be insane and park around the block, skulk/sprint through neighbors' yards and duck behind the bougainvillea bushes in front of our house. Then I spent the next twenty minutes crouched and pulling pink petals out of my hair while waiting to accost the mail carrier before she reached our house.

I'd never felt more excited in my life.

As soon as I heard the distinctive sound of the mail truck, I started disentangling myself from branches, emerging from my hiding spot just as Dad stepped outside. I didn't know how he missed me diving back into the bushes, and I really didn't know how he failed to hear my strangled breathing as I watched him share a greeting with the blue-clad mail carrier and then slowly walk back into the house with a stack of envelopes. The DNA test results were addressed to me, but I hadn't wanted to risk Dad seeing my name along with the DNA Detective logo in the corner and asking questions—and he would ask questions—so I could only hold my breath and wait while he stood in the entryway, shuffling the first letter to the back, then the second, and on and on while I tried not to have a heart attack. But then he tossed the stack on the table and closed the door behind him. I leaned my head back against the stucco-covered wall, my heart jackhammering in my chest.

After that day, I started leaving Biology earlier and earlier, as soon as attendance was taken, so that I could be home before the mail in case it came early. But the real problem was Dad. Twice more that week he beat me to the mail, which meant two more near heart attacks for me. Not good. Plus, while Nick might have had trouble expressing his feelings for me, he was a lot less reticent when it came to his thoughts on me skipping out early.

Nick had a perfect attendance record. He'd even come back to school after having his wisdom teeth removed during lunch hour. He understood why I was leaving early, but he really, *really* didn't want to be a part of covering for me. So far, Mr.

Rodriguez's move-around-the-room-as-you-will policy had kept my absence from being noticed, but Nick was growing increasingly unsettled by the prospect. It probably didn't help that he abandoned several more attempts to ask me out. Each class, it was worse, the sweating, the nervous glances, the bouncing leg under our shared desk. I made a huge mistake one day when I pressed Nick's knee still with my hand. He made the most insane noise, somewhere between a yelp and a gasp. Needless to say, the entire class—including Mr. Rodriguez—turned in our direction. Nick's face was on fire, and I was too distracted by the need to beat the mail to play off Nick's outburst convincingly. For the rest of class, Mr. Rodriguez watched us too closely for me to slip away. I was almost as agitated as Nick by the time the bell rang and I could race home. Thankfully, the results didn't come that day either.

When the mail truck started down our street on Wednesday, Dad heard it as soon as I did. He looked out the window, pushed back his chair and stood up. Mom was softly head-banging to the heavy metal music pounding through her earbuds, oblivious to anything else. I started counting steps while watching the approaching truck. Five to the hall. Ten to the front door. He was going to beat me again.

I pulled my phone out and called home. Seconds later, I heard it ringing inside and, through the windows, saw Dad head back to the office to answer it.

"Dana?"

"Hi, Dad. I think I left my History homework on my desk upstairs. I can come by before lunch is over if it's there, but could you check for me?" As soon as he moved to the stairs, I slid out of the bushes and waved at the mail carrier while directing Dad to search every random spot I could think of in my room. "It might have fallen behind my desk—can you pull it out and check?"

He put the phone down but I heard his grunt of effort as the mail was placed into my waiting hands.

"I'm not seeing it anywhere. Are you sure you left it? Dana?"

I was only half listening as I sorted through random bills and magazines. "Did you look under the bed?"

He said something about my messy room, but I didn't hear it, because the second letter from the bottom was from DNA Detective.

The envelope shook in my hand along with my voice. "It's here."

"Look more carefully next time. And you're cleaning your room the second you get home today, do you understand me?"

I hurried to put the rest of the mail in the mailbox. "I will. Thanks for checking. Love you, Dad."

"You too."

For once I didn't care that he didn't say it back. Mom always said he had a hard time verbally expressing love since he'd had so little growing up without a family, but just because he rarely said the word didn't mean he didn't feel it. I did know he loved me, and once he opened his birthday present, I'd get to feel it full force.

As soon as I was around the corner, I tore into the envelope. I skipped the geographic-ancestry and health reports as fast as I could shuffle the pages, until I had it: the possible-relative list. At first the onslaught of information was overwhelming. On the left were default symbols indicating the gender of each potential relative; next to that was the percentage of DNA Dad shared with each person, followed by the predicted relationship. Most were listed as third to fifth cousins, but I barely saw them.

The top result had a 47 percent DNA match, with the predicted relationship listed as "father or son."

CHAPTER 3

Fourth period had already started when I got back to school, but instead of spending my study hour in the library like usual, I headed straight for Nick's class. I'd had Mr. Drobitsky for Woodworking the year before and knew he'd be more likely to put me to work than kick me back to my own class, plus, it'd be loud enough that no one would hear me and Nick talking.

Sawdust floated thick in the air when I entered the shop. A few people looked up from their whirring lathes or table saws, but no one stopped me, and Mr. D was in the staining room. After making sure Nick wasn't working with anything that could potentially cut off his finger if I startled him, I hurried up to him.

"Dana?" He stopped sanding. "What happened?"

I didn't ask how he knew something had happened. I could feel that shell-shocked expression still carved into my face. "I found way better than fourth cousins."

"The results came?" Nick lifted his safety gasses to his head and glanced around the room. "Wait, will you get in trouble for being in here?"

I couldn't care less if I got detention for a month, but Nick wasn't going to be able to think about anything else until we moved somewhere. I grabbed his hand and towed him into the walk-in project cages in the back. "Nick, I think I found my grandfather." I laughed and grabbed him in a hug he wasn't expecting, which only made me laugh more. I pulled back. "Look. Just look at it."

Nick took the results from me and I moved back enough to run my hands through my hair, all but twirling in triumph. Whoever he was, he wouldn't be like my *Abue*, who'd died two years before, but he could be a Grandpa or a Pop Pop or… Screw it. I did twirl. Dad was going to meet his dad!

"Wow. It's great, Dana. Really." Nick's voice stopped my spinning. He wasn't exactly frowning at the papers, but he wasn't grinning like I was either. "It's just…"

"*Awesome* is the word you're looking for." I pointed at the results. "Forty-seven percent! Can you believe it? You told me I'd be lucky to find someone who shared a fraction of his DNA."

"It's amazing that you found this guy—"

"My grandfather." My voice broke imagining the reunion to come. Had I ever been this happy in my life?

"Probably, yes."

I laughed out loud. "This is because it says 'father or son'? That's why you're acting like you've got a two-by-four up your—" I bit both lips, holding back another smile and the spot-on observation I was making. "It's okay, you can say it.

The test can't tell father from son, because both relationships share the same amount of DNA. I've been reading everything I could find about DNA testing since we started this thing. I know what it means."

Nick spoke softly. "Then you know you can't assume he's your grandfather."

"He is. Trust me, if you spent an hour with my parents, you'd know there's not a chance that my dad has some secret kid floating around out there. This is my grandfather." I eased the papers from Nick's grip. "The only question is whether or not he's a serial killer or something." I went for a worst-case-scenario example, but the truth was, he could be anything. Probably not a murderer, but something else terrible. He could be a Dodgers fan. I pushed off the wall and started pacing the small area.

A loud voice called out in the shop. "Clean up! Five minutes to bell!" One by one, machines turned off and their noise was replaced by talk and laughter, the sound of running water and finally footsteps.

Nick edged toward the cage opening. "I need to clean up."

I waved him on. "Yeah, go."

He stood there looking anxious, which I normally found cute. "It's just that someone needs to lock these cages…"

I tried not to sigh audibly as I dodged a few people carrying pieces into the cage. Nick was just being Nick. Would it have been nice for him to focus on the monumental news I'd just shared instead of worrying about shutting a door? Yes, but to his credit he was much more at ease once everything was put away.

"Sorry," he said. "But I guess you probably saw it..." He reached into his cubby and produced a small wooden bat with my name carved into the side. "It's a keychain. You know, for keys."

"Nick." I could hardly imagine his large hands making something so delicate. "I love it. But you have to tell me how many you broke before you finished this one." The grip was grooved and barely half as thick as my pinky.

He shrugged and made one of those guy noises that meant it didn't matter. "So what are you going to do about your dad's results?"

"First, I'm going to do this." I rose up on my tiptoes and brushed a kiss on Nick's cheek. He really was a sweet guy. I still wasn't sure if sweet was enough for me, but I wanted it to be. "And then I'm going to see what I can learn about my grandfather."

I walked through floating sawdust and lingering noise, exited into the silent hallway, before pulling out my phone. I logged in to DNA Detective's website, scrolled to the relatives and clicked on the top match. Sadly, I wasn't taken to an expansive profile page complete with photos of an older-looking version of Dad. I knew from Nick's and Dad's reports that all users were encouraged to add their results to a database, but they were under no compulsion to divulge any personal details. The website showed the same default avatar from the mailed report. The option to send a message was available, though. And best of all, there was a first name.

"Brandon." I said it out loud and couldn't stop myself from envisioning a man with Dad's reddish-blond hair—heavily grayed—and hazel eyes. Then I jumped when my phone buzzed. Selena was texting me.

Selena: The results came, didn't they? Is it bad?

I'd been texting her every day after getting the mail, always at roughly the same time. I was an hour late today.

Me: They came.

Then my thumbs hovered over the keyboard. I didn't know anything about Brandon besides his first name. He was probably a normal, noncriminal retiree living in Florida or something, but until I knew for sure that he belonged in Selena's good-stuff category, I was keeping her in the dark.

Me: You were right. It's a bust. There are like two tenth cousins and no option to contact them even if we wanted to.

Selena: So, what, you just weren't going to tell me? I told you this was a bad idea. And expensive! I'm on week three of ramen because of you.

Me: Sorry.

Selena: Sorry like you'll pay me back?

Me: Sorry like I'll wash your car this weekend.

Selena: Because that's the same. I gotta go, my lunch is getting soggy. Because it's ramen :P

I was going to be hearing that for the foreseeable future. At least I could show her this conversation when she later tried to claim she'd been on board the whole time.

I pushed my bangs off my forehead, then went back to the website. Because of Selena's initial "What if we don't like what we find?" concerns, I'd set Dad's profile to private when I registered his test kit, so Brandon wouldn't get any kind of notification for matching with Dad. He wouldn't see the "father or son" relationship prediction even if I contacted him, which meant I was going to have to come right out and say it and pray he didn't freak out. No point in delaying that.

Hi Brandon.
I just got my dad's test results back, and I think I'm your granddaughter. We don't know anything about his family apart from the fact that he was born in Arizona. I don't know what else to say at this point except that I hope you write back.
-Dana

There. Done. Easy. I was the first person in our family to talk to one of Dad's relatives. That was monumental. And when he wrote me back and confirmed what I hoped to be true—that he was a normal guy who maybe made some mistakes in his younger life—it would be the best gift ever. Selena wouldn't even care that I'd had to lie to her.

CHAPTER 4

I made it through the rest of my classes, obsessively checking my phone between periods. I was anxious, but I'd already waited six weeks; I could survive another day. Except good news was so hard to keep. At home, I kept breaking into a grin for no reason. I did it often enough that after dinner, Mom finally commented.

"Okay, what is going on in that head of yours?"

Without prompting, I'd gathered up the plates and was heading to the kitchen. And I couldn't stop smiling as I did it. "I'm just happy, is all." Mom came to join me at the sink. I rinsed and she loaded the dishwasher, waiting for a full explanation. I glanced behind us, making sure Dad was out of earshot. He was, but I whispered anyway. "I got Dad the gift to end all gifts for his birthday. Selena could end up on a Wheaties box and I'd still win."

Mom closed the dishwasher with a hip bump and added her hands to the sink to rinse them. "Tell me, tell me!"

"No way, joy thief. You'll tell Dad so fast." Mom was horrible with secrets, especially good ones, and if Dad was concerned, forget it. Selena and I used to clock her, and her fastest spill time was under a minute. She couldn't hold in good news no matter how hard she tried.

"I promise I won't say anything."

Sure she wouldn't. "Hey, Dad," I called. "What's Mom getting you for your birthday?"

"Diamondback tickets," was his immediate answer.

Mom put a hand on her hip, opened her mouth, then shut it with a smile. "Fine, don't tell me. But, in my defense, he's really handsome."

"What…" I said, laughing, "…does that have to do with anything?"

Dad joined us then, and Mom turned a blissful smile in his direction. "I like your face," she told him.

"Yeah?" His arms went around her waist and he gave her a quick kiss and whispered something I was really glad I couldn't hear into her ear.

"Mmm-hmm." She snaked her arms around his neck. "Thanks for making dinner."

"Thanks for cleaning up."

"Kiss me again."

He did. Then she did. Then I hightailed it out of there before things got even more uncomfortable. I was halfway up the stairs when Dad called me back.

"Hey, hey, hey!"

I turned in time to catch the ball he threw.

"Grab your glove. We've got work to do."

★ ★ ★

The ball hit my glove with a thud. The leather was soft from the lanolin Dad had been rubbing into it each night since I got it, but it didn't feel like part of my hand yet. I threw the ball back.

"Good," Dad said. "How's it feeling?"

"Getting there." I caught the ball, threw it back.

"Tell me about the guy."

My throw went a little wide, but Dad caught it. "He's not *the guy*. He's Nick and we're still just friends."

"He hasn't missed a game." No, he hadn't. Home or away, Nick had been to all twelve so far. He'd kind of become my good-luck charm. We hadn't lost since the first game. I was surprised Dad had noticed. "You like him?" He still held the ball, waiting for my answer before he threw it again.

"I guess." Sure, I liked Nick. He was nice, sweet. Thoughtful. All good things, easy things. The ball soared back to me.

"Your mom wants him to come for dinner."

"I know." Mom hadn't stopped bugging me about it. Dad caught the ball, returned it.

"And?"

"And I'm not sure." If I officially invited Nick to dinner with my parents, that would be a pretty big step, a boyfriend-type step. There wasn't anyone else I was interested in, and I already knew Nick would be a good boyfriend—he wouldn't hurt me or break my heart. But I had this idea somewhere in the back of my head that he should be able to, that I should feel enough for him that a broken heart was a possibility. I didn't think my heart would ever be at risk with Nick, and I kind of wanted it to be.

"You met Mom when you were both nineteen, right?" Dad nodded, turning the ball before throwing it again. I caught it. "And she was your first real girlfriend." Another nod, another throw. "Didn't you ever like anyone before that?"

"Sure," he said, "but no one caught me like she did."

The ball hit my glove, I threw it back. "What do you mean?"

"Some people you meet and it's nice, it's good, but you can walk away. You're okay without them." He gazed toward the house. "I've always been that way, good on my own—it never bothered me until your mom. I knew from our first date that I would never be okay without her."

I was slow to throw the ball back. Dad rarely talked about his life before Mom. I knew pieces, random things he or she let slip over the years. He'd never been adopted, and at least one of the foster families he'd lived with wasn't allowed to have any more kids after Dad was removed. As for the others, he wasn't in contact with any of them, which was telling enough. Mom was his first real family, his only family, until Selena and I came around. I wanted him to have so much more. I started to check my phone to see if Brandon had replied, but Dad barked a warning at me.

"No. No phones. Come on, Dana, do you want this or not?"

I couldn't tell him what I was checking my phone for, so I had to take the reproof. "I do," I said. I liked softball; most of the time I even loved it. I knew I'd never give it up like Selena had, but what I really wanted was Dad nodding at me again, smiling. I wanted him to be proud of me.

"Then start acting like it."

My hand came up reflexively as he released the ball. It sank right into the pocket of my glove. "There," he said. "You ready?"

Our easy game of catch was over. In hindsight, I was surprised it had lasted this long. I sucked in a breath and nodded, knowing he was going to start relentlessly hitting screamers and grounders at me. Dad grabbed the bucket of balls and a bat while I set up the net we used to mark first base, then moved back to the far end of our dirt yard—not the most aesthetic on our block, but that was by design. We didn't host barbecues or have a swing set in one corner; we ran drills. Endless drills.

The bucket of balls Dad set beside him was close to overflowing. "We're going through it three times."

I avoided looking at my legs. Their fate had just been sealed, and sure enough, my shin ate the first grounder Dad hit my way. He'd drilled me enough over the years that I didn't even think to olé out of the way. As third baseman, I was used to taking hits to the chest and shins, and more than one to the face. But I wouldn't trade the hot corner for any other position. I scooped up the ball and fired it at the net designating first base.

It was nine by the time Dad started refilling the bucket, and I still had homework to do. When I mentioned that fact to Dad, he gave a little shake of his head and hit a hard shot to my left so that I had to half dive to catch it, barely snow-coning the ball in the tip of my glove.

"You do some tonight and get up early to finish the rest in the morning. Selena was out here with me every night." He picked up another ball from the bucket. "Nothing else took priority, not boys or needing to be on her phone constantly, just this." The ball stung a little when it hit my glove, reminding me how close Dad had come to playing professionally before a torn rotator cuff in college ended that dream for him. He'd had hopes for Selena, but now all those hopes rested heavily on me. I wasn't as good as my sister, and no amount of drills in our backyard was going to change that, but I was willing to work that much harder because of it.

I put more heat on the ball I threw toward the net, hitting the target dead center and earning a little nod from Dad.

"Again."

CHAPTER 5

My shoulder was still aching when I woke up the next morning. It was dark out, and my textbooks were waiting for me exactly where I'd left them the night before. I missed breakfast, but in between checking my phone for Brandon's reply, I got my homework done in time to grab a few pieces of cold bacon from the kitchen and a kiss from Mom before racing to school.

I half slept through my first hour, rousing every few minutes to check my phone under my desk. Still no response. My disappointment was palpable. I had to keep reminding myself that it hadn't even been a full day since I'd written to my grandfather, but I really needed this to work out. I rubbed a freshly formed bruise on my shin while I waited for the bell to ring.

I repeated that process until sixth hour—practice. Superstition Springs had recently approved a new policy that not only allowed participation in extracurricular sports to count as PE credits but let us practice during school hours. I couldn't wait to be outside. The weather was perfect, not a surprise for Arizona in the spring, but the clear, baby blue sky and the hint of a breeze to temper the warm sun were the distraction I needed while I waited for Brandon's reply. I met Jessalyn in the locker room and plunked down on the bench beside her to change my shoes.

"Don't you look pretty?" She started lacing up her cleats. "Not everyone can pull off bloodshot eyes, but you?" She nodded, grooving a little and causing her braids to swish against her back.

I dropped my head on her shoulder. "My dad had me taking grounders until eleven last night, and then I had three hours of homework after that. Every night I feel like it gets later. In a month I won't be sleeping at all."

"So that's why you were late." She raised the shoulder I was using as a pillow. "You know Nick waited for you before first period."

I lifted my head. "He never said anything." Though now that she mentioned it, Nick had been waiting by my locker most mornings for a while now.

"He wouldn't, would he?"

Probably not. Nick would never risk saying something that he thought might make me feel bad. Jessalyn did that for him. She was taller than most of the guys in school, and even without the conditioning that she got from playing softball, she sported totally natural lean muscle definition. I would have swapped arms with her in a second, but there had been more than one idiot boy who was less than impressed with her by-all-rights-impressive physique. Nick had always been a notable exception, which in turn made Jessalyn fiercely protective of him, even with me.

"He stayed until the last second and then had to sprint so he wouldn't be late."

My stomach gave a little lurch. "I never asked him to wait for me. I would have texted him that I was running late if I had."

"The guy follows you around like a puppy dog waiting for any scrap of affection you throw his way."

I pulled on my T-shirt over my sports bra. "Come on, that's not fair or true. You've been friends with him almost as long as I have. You know how he is."

"I know what he was like before you became the sun in his solar system. He can barely talk when you're around now. So I can hang out with either him or you, but not together. It kind of sucks."

It did suck. A lot. "Then help me. I haven't changed—why did he have to?"

"Ask your boobs."

I tried not to laugh, but I failed. "I'm seriously asking you for help right now. You know he's been helping me with the DNA thing for my dad, but even when we're talking about that, he's Nick, so he's super sweet, but he's still...I don't know...uncomfortable around me." That admission wriggled in my stomach. I hated that I was inadvertently doing that to him.

"Anything back yet from Secret Grandpa?"

My phone was faceup on the bench beside me so I could glance at it constantly. "No, and I'm failing miserably in my attempt not to obsess over it." I pulled my gaze away to look at Jessalyn. "So what do I do with Nick?"

"He's got that job interview at my parents' café after school today. He told you, right?"

I nodded. Nick was trying to save up for a new car. According to Jessalyn, his current rusted jalopy was made of Lifetime movies and people who take their cousin to prom and therefore too sad to drive except under the direst of circumstances. I had to agree it was pretty rough, and it died more often than it ran. Our friend Jill worked as a mechanic at her dad's garage and had been keeping it alive for him, but she'd recently started begging him to let her put it down.

"I promised to give him a ride and help him with his totally unnecessary nerves," Jessalyn went on. "I could talk to him a little and maybe subtly hint that his solo silent game around all of us might not be the best way to get a girl to like him."

I hugged her tight. "Thanks, Jess."

She gave me a long, considering look when I released her. "Just don't be that girl, okay? Nick is a sweet guy who really likes you. If you know he'll never be more to you than he is right now, then save him from worse heartache and cut him loose."

I appreciated Jessalyn's concern for Nick, but I did like him, a lot. I just needed to give my heart enough time to catch up to my head. Then there wouldn't be any heartache at all.

"I'm not going to hurt him," I said. "But Coach will put the hurt on us if we're late to practice, so…" I nodded at the cleat she still needed to tie. I checked my phone one last time before putting it in my locker. Most of the girls were already outside, but a few were still here.

"Dana," Ainsley said, drawing my attention to the far end of the bench. "Will you please tell Sadie that your sister pitched two no-hitters in a row her senior year?"

Technically, it had been her junior year, but I kept that clarification to myself and just nodded my answer.

"Wow," Sadie said, leaning back and looking sort of dazed. Sadie was our starting pitcher and had, to my knowledge, never pitched a single no-hitter in her life. Ainsley knew that too. She could be petty like that. It was almost as exhausting as fielding grounders for four hours after dinner.

"Don't sweat it, Sadie," I said, gathering my hair into a ponytail. "Selena was awesome, but your curveball is nasty." I looked at Jessalyn. "You're hitting .400 right now." Then, to Ivy, "And you're a vacuum cleaner at first base." I turned to each girl in the room, naming a unique strength she brought to the team. Even Ainsley, hoping she'd remember we were a team and needed to be strong together. "And your speed."

Sadie brightened; so did everyone else.

"Nice," Jessalyn said to me in a low voice as we followed the rest of the girls—all smiling—to the field. "Your dad needs to see you like this. What you do for our team off the field is just as important as what you do for us on."

With one last thought about the phone inside my locker, I said, "Hopefully, he will soon."

Practice was grueling, and my shoulder was screaming by the time I got back to the locker room. It was like my *coach* had no idea how hard my *dad* had made me work the night before. I was dreading what Dad would have in store for me after dinner. It was all I could think about as I opened my locker and pulled out my clothes.

My phone was on top of my shirt, and the screen was lit up. I grabbed it…and it was like taking a bat to the gut when I read Brandon's reply.

Sorry, I live in Arizona too but I think you've got the wrong guy. I only just turned 18.

CHAPTER 6

"Hello? Earth to Dana." Ivy waved a hand in my face, breaking my stare at my phone screen.

"What?"

"A bunch of us are going for ice cream. Are you in?"

Half a dozen pairs of eyes were on me, including Jessalyn's.

"Something wrong?" she asked, and then started to smile. "Wait, is it..." Her gaze flicked to my phone, and her grin grew. She lowered her voice so that only I could hear. I hadn't told anyone else on the team what I was doing, because I hadn't wanted word to get to my dad/our coach. "Is it something from your grandfather?"

I fought to keep my hand steady as I shoved my phone and cleats in my bag, not bothering with anything else. "No, I just need to go. Sorry." Then I was pushing open the heavy locker room door and bursting into the now-empty quad.

He can't be eighteen.

He's my 65-year-old grandfather.

No.

It was a tiny word, so I said it out loud. "No." A million times no.

No, no, no.

There was no way that Dad had an affair.

There was no way that he fathered a son.

There was no way that I had a brother less than a year older than me.

Dad would never cheat on Mom.

Dad would never do this to us.

It had to be a mistake.

My steps picked up speed as I headed for the parking lot. I broke into a jog as I reached the blacktop, then sprinted to my car. As soon as I was inside, my phone was in my hand and I was typing.

Brandon,
I must have read the results wrong. I do think we're related somehow. Maybe you're a cousin? Would you be willing to meet me? I have so many questions and I think you're the only one who can answer them. Name the place, name the time.
Dana

I dropped the phone in my lap the second I hit Send. My message sounded hella creepy, but I couldn't take the time for anything more composed. His message had been sent only twenty minutes ago, so there was a good chance he was still online and would—

He wrote back.

Dana,

You should try to get your money back. I'm the third Brandon McCormick, and before that there were five Davids. We are from Arizona though, going back at least four generations. I'd have to check with my dad to confirm that. I'm not really sure how the family side of all this DNA testing works—I was interested in my geographic heritage, not finding relatives—but my family tree is full up, no unaccounted for branches. But, hey, I work at the Jungle Juice in Mesa. Feel free to stop by if you have any more questions.

Sorry I can't be more help,

Brandon

My breath came out in a rush. The third Brandon McCormick. As in his dad was also Brandon McCormick. As in his dad was not Dennis Fields. Brandon seemed very confident in his family tree. Could it be a mistake? Had the DNA company messed up the samples? People were fallible; it could happen. I did a quick search for DNA-testing failure rates, and pages of results came back. Something loosened in my chest. A mistake would make more sense than Dad having an affair, which made no sense at all. And mistakes had happened before—not often, but more than once. I needed only once. There was an option to send in another sample for a retest, but I couldn't swing that without Selena's help, and there was no way I was waiting another month and a half for the results. I wasn't waiting a day.

I looked up the address for the Jungle Juice in Mesa. It was only a thirty-minute drive.

I started my car.

CHAPTER 7

Jungle Juice was decorated like a jungle, complete with massive plaster trees sprouting from each table and along the walls, and fake wild animals prowling through the immense branches that stretched overhead and covered the entire ceiling. There were birdcalls and cat growls playing in the background, and every time the door opened, a monkey scream spiked. I definitely would have lost my mind working there. But it smelled great, fruity and sweet, like sugared mangoes.

There were a number of small round tables scattered about, along with padded bench nooks in the corners. And people—more than I was expecting. Close to a dozen chatting and sipping from tall foam cups or eating sandwiches. I was glad for the people. They gave me cover to slip in relatively unnoticed.

Ignoring the noise and the people milling around me, I zoned in on the three employees behind the counter.

Two I dismissed right off: a girl with gorgeous ombré teal hair and a guy with coal-black skin whom I heard her call

Zere. The last guy wasn't as easy to exclude. Instant nausea was my involuntary reaction at seeing him. He was cute. But he didn't look anything like my dad, which helped settle my stomach. Not a single feature was familiar to me, and his olive coloring was the antithesis of Dad's light skin and hair. He was also big, I'd guess a full foot taller than me, and he looked strong enough to crack a coconut with his bare hand. I drew closer to the counter only to discover that he wasn't wearing a name tag. But the next second, it didn't matter.

"McCormick!" the girl called, holding up a blender and bringing it down a little too hard on the back counter. "This thing is sticking again. I'm gonna chuck it."

"No, you're not. Let me see it." He walked to his coworker and pried the blender from her reluctant hands. He rinsed it out with a handheld sprayer and fiddled with something on the bottom. "Here, look."

The girl moved to his side, sweeping her teal fishtail braid over her shoulder.

"Someone's been jamming it on the base and bent—"

"And of course you mean me, 'cause it couldn't be Zere or your cousin or anyone else with half a brain. Fine." She started to walk away with an expression on her face that made the next customer in line back away from the counter, but he stopped her with a hand on her back.

"I didn't say you."

She snorted.

His voice was calm, patient, completely at odds with his I-could-squish-you-like-a-bug physique. "Ariel, I'm not saying you. I'm saying someone, probably a few people. It's an easy fix." And he straightened whatever had been bent. With his hands. I was impressed from ten feet away; Ariel was right there and looked at him with disbelief. "See? No problem."

I watched him show her how to twist the blender onto the base a few times. Her pinched expression smoothed as it clicked easily into place, and dissolved completely when the blender whirled to life. Still, all she said by way of gratitude was, "Huh."

The conversation was too quiet, or the screaming monkeys were too loud—either way I couldn't hear what they said after that, but I watched him. Brandon. Every fiber of my being said no, said there was no way this guy was related to me. He couldn't be. I felt that confidence more keenly as he drew closer to me.

"Sorry about that. What can I get you?"

For the first time in my life, I had no words, nothing. I just stared at him until reality and the slight raising of his eyebrows at the extended silence reminded me that I couldn't let myself stay silent. It was now or never. Somehow, I didn't think I could come back here if I left without talking to him. And I definitely couldn't go home and face Dad with this sword of doubt still dangling over me.

"I'm Dana."

His brows didn't smooth back, but they didn't draw tighter either. "Hey, Dana. Ready to order?"

There wasn't a single spark of recognition at my name. Now my brows furrowed. He'd typed it, told me where he worked and that I could drop by barely thirty minutes ago. There should have been some kind of recognition.

Behind him, Ariel walked past.

I extended a finger in the direction she'd gone. "I'm sorry, I thought I heard her call you McCormick earlier."

The guy that I was suddenly convinced wasn't Brandon nodded. "Yeah, she calls me and my cousin by our last name."

My stomach twisted in two different directions. "What's your first name?"

He wasn't frowning at me anymore; he looked concerned. "Are you okay?"

"Low blood sugar." I gave him the first excuse for my sudden pallor that I could think of. "I think I thought you were someone else."

"I'm Chase," he said.

I nodded and tried to smile. "My mistake." I turned and left in a cacophony of monkey screams. The door didn't shut all the way behind me. From inside, Ariel caught it and stuck her head out to talk to a guy sitting at the table outside.

"Break is up in ten. Also, your cousin just bent metal in front of me with one hand—one freaking hand. If that's how he flirts, tell him it's scary and that I get off at nine." She paused, eyeing his hands. "Do you think you could...?" When he didn't respond, she shook herself. "Forget it."

I didn't watch her leave, but the guy did with the kind of smile that said he'd be trying to bend metal with his hands in the very near future. The hairs on my arms stood on end as I watched him return his attention to his phone.

It wasn't just the cleft chin or the sprinkling of red in his otherwise brown hair. It wasn't the way his brow lifted higher on the left than the right in response to whatever he was reading on his phone, or the height he couldn't conceal even sitting down. It was all of that and nothing. I knew him.

Forty-seven percent shared DNA slammed into me, and I couldn't find a breath to say even that tiny word of denial. I was twenty feet from my brother. *My brother.* He was my brother. I couldn't doubt it for a single second more. Dad had had an affair. He'd cheated on Mom and had a kid—*this* kid— guy—the one who looked so much like Dad that I couldn't blink, much less turn my head away from him.

I stopped beside his table, waiting for him to look up. "Brandon?"

"Yeah?"

"I'm Dana."

CHAPTER 8

Brandon recovered from his initial confusion quickly, returning my bleak stare with a smile. "Oh, hey." He stood up right
away, considered extending his hand but moved his drink to
his side of the table instead. "I didn't realize you were going
to come right away." He indicated the chair across from him,
but I couldn't sit or even move. My skin prickled, waiting for
him to see me and *know*, to make the connection the way I
instantly had. But he didn't. He sat there, still smiling Dad's
smile. "Like I said in the email, I don't think I'll be able to
help your dad, but whatever you want to know." He spread
his hands. His smile started to slip the longer I stared at him.
"Wow, I'm sorry. I guess this was kind of a big letdown."

"Dennis Fields," I said, my eyes unblinking. "We don't
know who his birth parents were, but that's the name his first
foster family gave him."

Brandon slowly shook his head. "Doesn't sound familiar."
He paused. "Are you okay? You look a little…"

I was shaking. I could feel the blood draining from my face, and there was a buzzing growing in my ears. I'd never fainted before in my life, but I knew I was seconds from blacking out. I gripped the back of the chair, locking my elbows to keep me upright.

"You wanna sit? I really think you should sit." He moved to pull the chair out for me, and I lowered myself into it as he returned to his. Both our arms rose in tandem to rest on the metal bistro table. The movement was identical, and for a heartbeat, he froze too. Then he looked at my face, really looked at it. "Do I know you from somewhere?"

"Do you?" My blinking was now sporadic, and apart from my lips, my eyelids seemed to be the only part of me still capable of moving. I watched a pink flush creep up his neck, but then it stopped and started to recede.

"No, I guess not. I mean, how could I? Eighteen is a little young to be a grandfather." He tried to laugh but saw how incapable I was of joining him and sobered. "I'm really sorry I'm not him."

"It's a mistake," I said, my voice echoing in my head.

"Don't worry about it," Brandon said. "I'm sure those DNA places mess up all the time, right?"

Right. A screwup. A mistake, that's all. Earlier I'd been confident I'd reach the same conclusion as soon as I saw Brandon—it was why I'd rushed over. But I knew—*I knew*—even if he didn't, that there was no mistaking who he was.

Sitting, I was still shaking, but the dizzy light-headedness was dissipating. "I needed you to be someone else," I whispered. "I don't know what to do." It felt like a huge confession to be making, especially to him.

"Well, hey, you're welcome to take a look at my family tree, but honestly, I know you won't find anything. The Mc-Cormick line is extremely well documented."

But you're not a McCormick, I thought. *You're a Fields, just like me.* My hands covered my mouth, but they couldn't contain the sudden full-body sob that choked free. Brandon drew back in his chair, as far as it would let him, but I couldn't stop, and when Brandon came around to pat me on the back in an awkward gesture, I cried harder.

"I'm sorry," I said, leaning away from his touch. I needed to leave, to get away from him and everything that reminded me of Dad. I pushed back my chair and stood.

"Don't give up, okay? Just 'cause I'm a dead end, doesn't mean the next one will be. I'm sure you'll find what you're looking for."

"I don't want to find anything else." The words tore out of me, my throat trying to choke them back along with the sobs I was holding in. Brandon was right in front of me, and something made him move back, frowning just a little. His gaze moved slowly across my face. Taking in the slightly squared jaw and full bottom lip, the dark hair that sparked copper in the fading sunlight, just like his. And it stopped. In that moment, I wasn't sure if I wanted him to see the connection or not. If he saw it, I wouldn't be alone—and I had never felt more alone in my life—but then he'd feel like me too, stripped and cored and irrevocably severed from the thing that made me *me*: my family. It was gone—worse, it had never been.

I looked back at Brandon, not seeing the knife that cut me or the cliff I'd been hurled from. I saw my brother. I had no concept of what that word meant; I only knew instinctively that I didn't want to hurt him.

He backed up again, swallowing. "You—"

I broke the stare, brought my gaze down to where he'd inadvertently kicked over my bag, spilling its contents everywhere. I dropped to my knees, grabbing keys and sunglasses, reaching for a tube of lip balm that was rolling away. Brandon knelt too, but he wasn't handing me an errant pack of gum. The top of the paper I'd stuffed inside had unfolded, the DNA Detective logo clearly visible. "Don't!" But it was too late. Brandon was already pulling it free from my bag, his eyes scanning. And then they stopped.

His name. Forty-seven percent shared DNA. Relationship prediction: father or son. It took half a second, and he could never go back, never not know. I felt just as alone watching him, seeing the page tremble in his hands, except worse, because I was the reason he knew.

"What is this?" he asked, but he knew. The way he'd looked at me... His eyes rose to meet mine. His lips kept pressing together, opening for a breath, then closing again when I didn't answer. I didn't want to say it, to make it more real than it already was. "You said *grandfather*." His eyes were wide, like he was pleading with me. I was silently pleading with him just as much.

"I didn't want to believe it either, but you..."

Brandon's eyes narrowed at me.

It came out in a whisper. "You look like him."

He shot to his feet. "Bull. Shit."

I wanted his conviction so badly that I reached for him.

"How can you be his son? My parents are happy. They've always been happy. I don't understand how you—"

The muscles in his neck and arms were clenched tight, but he was making an effort to control himself. He didn't yell. "You said grandfather."

"I didn't know how old you were. I hadn't seen...you."

"Then it's a mistake."

Except it wasn't. Seeing him, I knew it wasn't. We both did. "My dad is... And my mom never..."

"Mine neither," I said.

His movements were jerky as he crumpled the paper into a tight ball. "I'm not your brother, okay? I can't be. It's a mistake. I'm sure if you talk to your dad or the website, you can figure it out, but I'm not your guy, so..."

I tried to match the calm tone he was striving for, but I could hear the desperation strangling my voice. "My parents have been married for more than twenty years, but we're not even a year apart in age, which means..." I couldn't say it out loud. The idea that Dad had had an affair was unbearable.

"It's not possible." His lips were barely moving, but I heard him perfectly. "My father is Brandon McCormick Jr. His father was Brandon McCormick Sr. His father was David McCormick V. I can go back another ten generations if you want. I know their names and their families. Dennis Fields—" he practically spit Dad's name "—is nothing to me."

In that moment, he felt like nothing to me too. I wanted to cry for Mom and Selena. I wanted to cry for our family. I wanted to cry for everything that had been stripped away from me in an instant, for the brother I'd never known who was looking at me with fear-mingled contempt. "I'm sorry."

"Are you? Is that why you showed up like this and tried to tell me my mom slept with your dad?"

"No." Tears stung my eyes. "You weren't supposed to be him. I was supposed to see you and know. I was supposed to be able to go home and not feel like my whole life has been a lie."

He took a couple steps backward. I panicked and grabbed his arm.

"Wait, please. I didn't know. I came because I needed it not to be true. You're the only other person who knows, and I— Please don't go." I forced myself to release him. I had to calm down, to think. "I can't go back home and forget you aren't...who you are. I can't look at my dad and pretend he didn't have an affair." The word hurt to say. "I don't even know if he knows you exist." Brandon hadn't moved, but he was pulling farther away, shutting down with each thing I said. I started nodding before I spoke. "Okay, okay," I said. "Everything—" my chin quivered "—hurts. Talking, breathing." Looking at him. "I'm going. I'll come back when—"

"No."

I started, both at the word and the flat tone. "Then I'll message you."

"No. Don't come here. Don't message me. Don't anything."

"But...you're my brother."

His hard-won composure threatened to snap, but he didn't deny it.

"Okay," I said. Neither of us moved. "Will you...when you're ready?"

He looked at the crumpled paper still clutched in his fist. "No. It doesn't matter."

My eyes bulged as I leaned forward. "It doesn't *matter*? How can you say that?" The fear and anger I understood—they were both still roiling under my skin—but indifference played no part in my emotions, and I didn't believe it did for him either. "How can you look at your mom and not scream?"

"I don't have to," he said. "She's dead."

CHAPTER 9

Brandon didn't look back as he went inside, and I walked slowly to my car, only to stop in the act of unlocking my door. Where was I supposed to go? Back home so I could watch my parents cuddle on the couch? I couldn't make Brandon exhume a past that was truly buried in his case, but neither could I ignore what had already been dug up.

I dropped my forehead on the hood and let the sunbaked heat from the metal seep into me, but it couldn't thaw the ice inside. I couldn't face Dad or Mom. I looked at my phone, but I couldn't call Selena and do to her what I'd inadvertently done to Brandon, my brother. That word crashed horrifically into my heart. I had a *brother*. I could almost have been happy about that, except it meant Dad had committed adultery. He'd cheated on Mom.

I didn't understand it. How could he have cheated on Mom? How could he have had another child? How could they still be together, happy? Did he know about Brandon? Did anyone? Had Dad loved Brandon's mom? Had he planned on leaving Mom for her? Did he know she'd died? When did she die? Brandon was as devastated by the DNA test results as I was, but who else knew? Just his mom? Her husband? Dad? Mom? Did Selena know? I dismissed that thought immediately. She would never have helped me test Dad if she thought it might lead to this.

I turned around and gazed at the darkening sky. At home we'd be getting ready for dinner. Mom cooked occasionally, but Dad usually ran the kitchen. Lasagna, I decided. He made that every week, and we were due. There'd be a salad and maybe ice cream after that. My eyes flooded, blurring the sky overhead.

"Hey, Dana, wait up."

My head snapped straight and I saw the guy from Jungle Juice—Chase, the wrong McCormick. He'd ditched his uniform polo shirt, revealing a plain white T beneath it. He didn't look pissed, like he was coming to add to his cousin's stay-away warning. Instead he glanced at the tall foam cup in his hand before jogging toward me. He slowed when he saw my face, but he didn't stop. I was very obviously crying, so I didn't rush to wipe the tears from my cheeks as he drew nearer. What did it matter if he saw me cry? What did any of it matter?

"This seemed like a good idea from across the parking lot."

"What?" I asked, only half seeing Chase and not caring even that much. He held out his cup and an unopened straw.

"Might help the low blood sugar."

I looked at the drink, then at him.

"You looked like you were ready to pass out when you

left," he said, not lowering the drink. "Take it—make one of us feel better."

I took the cup and automatically ripped off the straw's wrapper before I jabbed it in to take a sip. The drink was fruity and cold, adding to the numbness I felt inside. My gaze went past Chase to Jungle Juice. Brandon was hidden inside. My breath hitched.

"So did you find who you were looking for?"

"No." What I'd found was so much worse. My eyes pricked again. "I was supposed to be meeting my grandfather for the first time. Turns out I got some bad information."

"Oh, wow. That sucks."

There was something about him being a complete stranger that made it harder to lie, so I didn't. "It really does." I brushed away the last of my tears. "I don't know what I'm supposed to do anymore." I was frozen, stuck. I couldn't go back, and without Brandon's help, I couldn't go forward. I couldn't even leave the parking lot.

Chase's gaze lingered on me, like he was considering something. I must have looked pretty unstable. "I'm fine. I just needed a minute to…" I stopped. I couldn't sell *fine* with my red eyes and damp cheeks. "Thank you for the smoothie— that was nice of you. I *will* be fine. You don't have to stay or anything."

He glanced down at the keys he withdrew from his pocket. "I didn't have the greatest day either, and I was thinking about doing something—" he huffed out a sound somewhere between a laugh and a breath "—the opposite of crying in a parking lot." His gaze rose to mine and held. "You should come with me."

That was the last thing I'd expected him to say. I stared at him, and then an unguarded laugh overtook me. "I can't believe you just said that."

"Which part?"

I shook my head slightly. "All of it." I couldn't get my brain to work right after that conversation with Brandon. And in that moment, I didn't really want it to. "You're serious?"

His answer was immediate. "Yeah."

"Where?"

He smiled.

I parked my car beside Chase's, sent a text to Mom that I was hanging out with Jessalyn, got out and looked at the location I'd followed him to.

We'd driven no more than ten miles from Jungle Juice to an area that looked like it might have once been a nice neighborhood but had long since deteriorated due to neglect. The highlights consisted of a strip mall, empty save for a single payday-advance place, and a seemingly abandoned gas station on the corner covered in graffiti. Chase and I were in the parking lot of a six-story tan brick building flanked on either side by empty lots overgrown with weeds so tall they would have reached my waist.

There wasn't a single person in sight and I hadn't seen a car drive past since we pulled up. It wasn't full dark out yet, or I'd have already been back in my car. As it was, I kept my phone in my hand and my car between me and Chase, just in case.

"What is this?"

"This," he said, "is the Desert Breeze apartment building, and it's scheduled for demolition in two weeks." He nodded his chin toward a white sign covered in warnings like Condemned and Do Not Enter in big bold letters and stared at the building like he was seeing a lot more than I was.

"What exactly are we supposed to be doing here?"

"I used to live here a long time ago. It's empty and they're blowing it up, so it doesn't matter, but this was the last place I saw my dad before he took off, and smashing it is the closest I'll ever get to—" He inhaled through his nose, paused, then looked at me. "I figured you might need to break something too." Then he sighed. "I didn't really think this through. I don't have anything to use to even break a window."

I let my gaze drift back to the building, taking in the caution tape and the boarded-up windows. I slipped my phone back into my pocket, then headed to the trunk of my car. I popped it open and pulled out a wooden baseball bat.

Chase watched me the whole time, not smiling exactly, but something close to it. "You keep a bat in your trunk?"

"I keep multiple bats in my trunk." I offered him the wooden bat. "This one's for you." Then I pulled out another. "So which window looks good?"

Getting in didn't turn out to be a problem. There was a garden-level unit with large—for me and possibly somewhat tight for Chase—windows that were no match for my bat. At that first tinkling sound of breaking glass, I felt shockingly alive, and even more shockingly detached from anything having to do with my family.

After kicking out the remaining shards, Chase slipped through the broken window first. As I'd guessed, it was a tight fit around his shoulders, and he did get cut a little on one arm, but when he looked back at me, I followed him without hesitating. I didn't get sliced—unlike him, I wasn't built like a superhero—but the feel of Chase's hands on either side of my waist helping me down was unexpectedly jarring on the bare skin below my slightly bunched up shirt. His hands didn't linger, though, and neither did my sudden awareness of him.

There was no power, which meant no lights, so we used our phones to see. The glass crunched under our feet as we crossed the dark room and entered the hall. Chase led us up four flights of stairs and down another hall until we stood in front of a door that no longer had a number on it.

"This was yours." I wasn't asking a question, just saying something to break him out of his stare.

"Yeah." He reached for the doorknob, but it didn't turn.

"Good thing we don't need a key, huh?" I tapped the door with my bat, reminding Chase of the one he held in his hand.

"Yeah," he said again, still staring at the door.

He'd said he hadn't planned this out, and I was beginning to wonder if he was having second thoughts. If not about dem-oing his old apartment, then at least about inviting a perfect stranger to do it with him.

"I'm going to try one farther down," I said, already moving.

"No, sorry. I was just caught up for a second." Chase shook his head, then smiled. "My mom is a photographer, so she took a lot of photos." He tapped the doorknob with a fin-ger. "I was only like a year old when my mom and I left, so I know it's just from seeing pictures, but it's weird."

"There are tons of other apartments. It's really fine if you want this one to yourself."

"I'm up for the company if you are."

He said it with such easy sincerity that I had to believe

him. And if I was being honest, I wasn't sure I'd actually follow through with breaking anything on my own. I knew the place was getting blown up and there was nothing of value left behind, but it still felt a little off to just start smashing walls. Chase's childhood claim to his apartment made it easier—allowable, somehow.

"Okay." We stood for another second facing his door. "I guess we just...?" I pressed against the door with my palm, trying to get a read on how secure it was. "Why don't you..." I turned but Chase was already stepping back, having reached the same conclusion. "Yeah, go for it."

He kicked hard. I heard wood crack from the force, but the door held.

"Let's do it together, ready?" I stood closer to the door than Chase needed to, but we timed it right, landing a double kick that knocked the already injured door clean off its hinges. We both laughed, though mine was partially to cover how much that kick had hurt. I was wearing flip-flops, and I wasn't built like a Terminator. Chase seemed fine as he walked over the door.

I gave him a few minutes to look around and deal with any more memories on his own and took the opportunity to rub my knee until it stopped throbbing. I wasn't going to be doing that again anytime soon.

"Dana?"

"I'm here," I said, walking into the mostly empty room. I didn't know why I'd expected it to be furnished. Obviously it wouldn't be. And the few things left in the apartment wouldn't have belonged to Chase anyway. There could have been a dozen tenants since he'd lived here. There was a moldy-looking love seat, a small table and a couple boxes that had seen their fair share of water damage. I looked at the ceiling and saw water spots and even a large brownish-yellow section that had broken through. That explained the smell.

I tried to envision the space clean and with a family, but my imagination wouldn't stretch that far. I wondered if Chase's memories were serving him any better.

"Does it feel familiar?"

"I don't know. Maybe. That was my room." He pointed with his bat. "It's so small."

"You must have been then too."

His mouth lifted. "I'm glad I don't really remember living here. And I'll be gladder still when it's a pile of rocks."

That answered my next question, whether he still wanted to do this. We set down our phones in the center of the room and took up positions in front of the largest wall. I lifted my bat and Chase did the same.

His bat punched right through the drywall like it was cardboard. "Come on," he said, freeing the bat.

The first swing was hugely satisfying. It was so much better than crying. I smashed windows and door frames. I busted rotted floorboards and broke through cabinets. We didn't talk much, which was fine because I didn't want to. I wanted to break things and not think about how broken I felt, and I did. I swung again and again for what seemed like hours until my arms were shaking and I couldn't grab the bat anymore. Then I sat in a corner and watched Chase until exhaustion finally claimed him too. He lifted the bat to swing once more, then lowered it, breathing heavily as he let it slip through his fingers and clatter to the floor. Then he turned to me. His white

T-shirt wasn't so white anymore, and he was covered in the same sweat and dust that coated me.

"Feel better?"

He looked around and nodded. "You?"

Somehow I did. "Yeah." I watched him kick through the debris, feeling warmer than the weather and exertion alone could account for. "So what made your day suck so bad that you needed..." I glanced toward the car-sized hole we'd put through one wall. "You never said."

Chase wiped the sweat from his forehead with the back of his arm. "Ask me again sometime. This is the best I've felt in a really long time, you know?"

"Tired, sweaty and probably covered in asbestos?"

"Yeah," he said, not making a joke out of it at all.

I traced a piece of window frame near my hip. Other people, other families, had lived in this apartment since Chase and his parents, and he'd told me he'd been very young when he and his mom moved, but he still felt connected to it and the father who'd deserted him. I was suddenly reminded that we barely knew each other, and yet he'd let me be a part of something incredibly personal to him.

"Hey, why did you help me today?" I waited until he looked at me. "The smoothie, bringing me here? I wouldn't even have seen you if you hadn't called out."

"Why wouldn't I?"

"I was a girl crying by herself in a parking lot. I'm cute, but I'm not that cute," I said, smiling a little, letting him know I was kidding.

Chase walked toward me, holding my gaze. I was so used to the way Nick couldn't maintain eye contact for more than a few seconds that I felt my face heating even before he said, "You are that cute. Plus, you needed something to break, and I needed not to do this by myself."

I was the one to break eye contact, dropping my head to look at the bat I had resting across my lap. "Well, thanks. I never knew how cathartic it could be to raze a building to the ground. Part of one, anyway."

"You too. I would have brought my cousin, Brandon, but people keep flaking at work. I can't find a shift for us to both be off."

A different kind of tingling drifted over my skin at the mention of Brandon, overtaking the former. I closed my eyes for a second and leaned forward. All the thoughts I'd pushed away for the past couple hours raked over me. That ache, that empty dysphoria, settled heavy in my chest.

Chase sat beside me. "You okay?" His hand barely brushed my back.

I leaned away from his touch, speaking before I really thought about what I was doing. "You two are close?"

"He's more like my brother. We grew up together."

I glanced around the room we'd demolished, seeing it with new eyes.

"Not here. Our parents, they're siblings. They bought houses here in Mesa only a couple blocks away from each other after my dad left and his mom died."

"I'm sorry."

Chase leaned his head against the wall. "I'm not. His dad was a better father than my own ever was. I don't remember his mom, but mine loves him like he's her own. We had it all right." I felt Chase's eyes on me and I met them. "Sometimes your family isn't what you want them to be, but you end up with something better. I did."

I pushed to my feet, dusting myself off as much as I could. Chase stood too and we started picking our way out of the apartment and back down the stairs.

"Sorry, I shouldn't have said anything."

"No, it's fine." If I'd been crying over a lost grandfather earlier instead of a philandering father and secret brother—a brother Chase was deeply connected to—his words might have had their desired effect. "Maybe you're right. Either way, this helped." I looked up at him when we reached the broken window in the basement. "Really."

"Anytime."

I smiled a little and looked away. Just like with Brandon, I needed to stay away from Chase. If he knew who I was, he wouldn't be offering me anything.

"Or not."

"It's just that between school and softball, I don't have a ton of free time." *And you have no idea who I am, and the brother I just found wouldn't want me and the bomb I represent anywhere near you,* I added silently.

"Ah."

"And I live in Apache Junction." It was a lame excuse considering my house in AJ was only thirty minutes away, but I wasn't able to tell him the real reason I was blowing him off.

"Dana, it's okay."

"Sorry." And I meant it. I took the bat he held out to me and slid it and mine outside. Before I could consider the best way to get myself up and out, Chase knelt down and laced his hands together for me to step on.

"Don't be. It was a fun night. For what it's worth, I hope you get to meet your grandfather sometime."

"Yeah. I'm rethinking that. I don't think I want to know the answers to the questions I have." What I really wanted was to go back and undo that whole day, the results, meeting Brandon, all of it. But I couldn't.

Chase boosted me easily through the window, then pulled himself through, being careful to avoid the glass that had cut him the first time. We walked toward our vehicles, which were mostly wrapped in the shadow of the apartment building. There were streetlights, but they'd either been broken or else forgotten along with the rest of the neighborhood, because they failed to turn on. The moon was shining, though, and it illuminated more than I wanted to see of Chase because I still had to walk away. I already knew I'd have liked to see more of him, which was all the more reason not to linger. Standing beside my car, this time under a star-pricked sky with my heart still hurting but my body no longer consumed by it, I reached for my door and looked one last time at Chase approaching his.

"You kind of saved me tonight."

Chase stopped, keys in hand. "Well, I'd have been screwed without your bat."

I laughed a little and opened my door.

"Take care, Dana."

"You too."

I got home and went upstairs to my room with an excuse over my shoulder that I had a headache. The farther I'd driven away from Chase and the apartment building, the more real the day had become, until my head really was pounding. It got worse as I lay on my bed, sleep not even remotely attainable. I curled onto my side. Every part of me was aching to act, to do something, but for once I couldn't bring myself to move. There was pain in every direction, and nowhere to retreat. I could hear my parents downstairs, working late, their voices dancing around each other with dips of occasional laughter. The sounds, so normal and carefree, spurred me from my bed. I stopped inches from my bedroom door, my hand wrapping around the knob, but I didn't turn it. I couldn't go downstairs and look Dad in the eye and tell him I knew. I couldn't watch Mom's face, because I knew, as much as she loved me, she wouldn't believe it. I'd seen the results and stared into my brother's face, and part of me still wrestled with disbelief.

Underneath all the horror and denial, Brandon and I had said basically the same thing to each other: how could this be true? The facts went against everything I knew, everything he claimed to know too. So how?

I'd told Chase I didn't want answers, and I didn't, but my insomnia meant I needed them. My insides were tearing themselves apart, flinging emotions at me faster than I could process. I had to talk to Brandon again. He had to be feeling the same emotional schizophrenia, he just had to.

I opened my laptop on my bed, logged back on to DNA Detective and clicked on Dad's results. Brandon's match was gone. Dad's highest match was now a predicted fourth cousin. My brows pinched together as I checked again, then a third time. There was no record of Brandon at all. I dove for my purse, upended the contents on my bed, then froze, remembering that Dad's results weren't there. Brandon had left with them still crumpled in his fist. My only hard copy. And he'd deleted the rest.

CHAPTER 10

Wednesday morning I slept in for maybe the first time in my life. And by *slept in*, I mean hid in my room waiting for Mom to drag herself down the stairs and into the steaming mug of coffee Dad always had waiting for her.

It was hard hearing him up and moving around downstairs. Most days, I'd be up with him—at least, when I wasn't frantically finishing homework from the night before. We'd always been the early birds in the family, while Mom and Selena were the night owls. Dad and I never did much in the mornings. We never had deep father-daughter conversations, but we'd make breakfast and we'd sit together at the kitchen table grumbling at whatever ESPN was talking about. Eventually, Mom would stagger in like she'd just woken from a coma and Dad would start her coffee IV. Halfway through her second cup, she'd blink at the pair of us as though seeing us for the first time and join our grumblings. It was nice, routine. And I didn't know if I'd ever have that again.

I waited until the last possible minute to go downstairs. Mom was mostly awake by then, not enough to articulate words, but she pointed vaguely in the direction of the toaster when she saw me. I grabbed an English muffin and a paper towel, acutely aware of Dad's back as he refilled Mom's swimming pool–sized coffee mug.

"That headache knocked you out, huh?" Dad's voice made my eyes prick. It was normal, completely normal.

"Yeah. It's fine now. I gotta get to school."

"Hang on." Dad turned and faced me, causing my stomach to plummet into my feet. I started backing out of the room. "I need you to come straight home after practice today. Selena is driving down and she has some news she wants to share." He could barely contain his grin. Dad thought it was good news—which for him meant something softball related. For once I didn't squirm with resentment that he'd never have beamed like that over me. Whatever it was, I knew she wasn't reconsidering playing again. I also knew I wouldn't be coming home right after school.

I found Nick outside the door of my first class when it let out. He smiled as soon as he saw me, which layered guilt into the slurry of emotions sloshing inside me. "Nick. Oh, I'm sorry. I should have texted you not to wait for me this morning." I remembered what Jessalyn had told me the day before about him having to sprint to class. "I hope you weren't late?"

"It's fine. I just wanted to make sure you were okay."

"Yeah, it was just one of those mornings." I started walking, Nick keeping pace beside me. He had to slow his stride so as not to outstrip me.

"And everything else is...okay?"

He meant with my nonexistent grandfather, but Nick would never come right out and ask. I could have shown up carrying a severed head, and the most direct thing he'd ask was if I'd had a tough night. He was trying to be thoughtful by not prying, I knew that, but I wished he'd just say what he was thinking so I wouldn't be able to dodge him. I'd gotten too good at doing that with him.

"Yep." I half turned and took a few steps sideways. "Oh, you had that job interview at Mostly Bread after school yesterday, right? Did you get it? You did, didn't you?"

Nick shifted the bag on his shoulder and dropped his eyes to his feet. "I think so. I'm supposed to hear soon." He swallowed. "But did you—"

"Jessalyn probably gets to tell you in person. Have you seen her yet?"

"Um, no, but—"

"I bet she tells you at lunch." We reached the end of the hallway. It split left toward my next class and right to his. I turned without stopping. "I'll see you then, okay?" Our lunch group consisted of half my softball team—no way he'd be able to ask me anything then even if he worked up the nerve. I didn't doubt Jessalyn's ability to help Nick loosen up more in mixed company, but I didn't think one conversation was going to do it.

"Dana." Half the people in the hallway along with me turned to look at him. Nick could be heard when he wanted to. Whatever he was going to say to me withered under all the eyes trained on him. "I was just— I mean—"

"Tell me at lunch, okay?" Then I disappeared into the crowd of students around me.

I met Jessalyn in the pizza-cart line in the quad outside. I'd made better time than she had, and I let a couple people cut in front of me so that we could stand together.

"You were supposed to let me cut in line with you, not the other way around." She smacked her palm lightly against my forehead, but she smiled. "Ugh, I despise cold pizza." The pizza was never piping hot since Barro's delivered it ten minutes before lunch started and the insulated delivery bags they were kept in could do only so much. Two people ahead of us weren't going to make much of a difference, but Jessalyn enjoyed complaining, even when she didn't have a reason. I thought it had something to do with her being an only child, and a late-in-life one at that. I wouldn't call her spoiled, but I wouldn't call her *not* spoiled either. She leaned toward me, frowning, and pointed at my eyes. "I'm guessing you didn't get to sleep much last night. Damn, did your dad make you cry? Because you know there's no crying in baseball."

"Or softball," we said together.

I smiled a little. "No drills last night. I had a headache."

"Is it better?"

I opened my mouth to tell her about Brandon, but the words stuck in my throat. I didn't want to say them out loud yet to anyone. "I'm fine today."

She swept her braids over one shoulder. "So where's your boy?"

I rose up on my toes and glanced around for Nick but

didn't see him. "He's probably grabbing food from the cafeteria. Also, please don't."

"What did I say?"

I eyed her sideways.

"Fine, but don't you want to know if he got the job?"

"I already know he got the job or you wouldn't be smiling."

She stopped immediately, though that might have been because we'd reached the front of the line and the cheese had visibly started to de-melt on the pizza. She pointed two fingers at her eyes, then at the pizza-cart guy, and kept repeating the gesture until I pulled her away.

We took our slices of slightly warm pizza and made our way to the grass knoll by the far end of the auditorium. Some of the other girls from our team were already there—Ainsley, Ivy, Monica and Sadie, along with a couple boyfriends and guys who fell into the want-to-be-boyfriends category. Nick was there too, having very obviously saved me a spot on the ground beside him. My steps slowed, but Jessalyn came right behind me, urging me ahead.

"If you like him, don't stop now."

I sat next to Nick, tugging Jessalyn down with me. Nick glanced at me, then looked away. I bumped his shoulder with mine. "Hey. You don't have to sit on the grass," I told him. There was a bench right next us, and though most of our group preferred the grass, I knew Nick didn't. He'd risk being late to his next class because he'd need to pick off every stray blade of grass from his jeans. "Come on." I started to stand to move to the bench with him, but he shook his head.

"I'm fine. You like the grass."

I did, but I liked it even more that Nick said so outright

instead of shrugging and looking away. He did look away, but the words still counted. I smiled at his profile. "Thanks, Nick."

Beside me, Jessalyn was mopping grease from her pizza with a napkin, almost like she was angry at it for not being steaming hot. I bit into my own slice—lukewarm, but pizza was pizza.

When she got to the crust, Jessalyn dropped it and leaned around me. "So, Nick, you've been to all our games this season. Are you really into softball or are you just really into Da—"

I tackled her to the grass. She laughed around the hand I used to smother her mouth. "What is wrong with you?" I hissed in her ear. "You can't corner him like that!"

One of the guys asked Nick a nonmortifying question, distracting him enough for me to let Jessalyn up.

"Why not?" she said, savagely tearing off a chunk of pizza crust and chewing it. She gestured with the remains at Nick's back, then at me. "He says how he feels, then you're forced to face how you feel. Rip-the-Band-Aid-off relationship advice—it's the only way to go."

"Thanks but no thanks." I returned to my own pizza, which had gone completely cold. We both knew Nick wasn't a rip-anything-off kind of guy. After yesterday with Brandon, I wasn't either. Slow and steady was the way to go, especially when there weren't any other options.

"Fine," Jessalyn said in my ear, then louder, "By the way, Nick, you got the job."

CHAPTER 11

I was used to seeing my coach and not my dad when we were on the field, which was the only thing that got me through practice that day—that, and he kept us so busy that there was rarely time to think about anything besides how exhausted we were.

Coach was big on conditioning drills during practice. Beyond baserunning, hitting, bunting and rundowns, that day we did running lap tosses, where we paired off and ran while throwing a ball back and forth. Next was Z drills, where we lined up in two facing rows and threw one ball as fast as possible, zigzagging down the line until it ended with me. And we finished with dirty drills, which again paired us off to throw ground balls that forced the other player to drop down or even dive to catch.

Normally, practice ran only a little longer than sixth hour for the rest of the school, but we had a game the next day against a team that had solidly beat us the year before. No one wanted a repeat performance, so it was after four when I waved bye to the other girls and lowered my exhausted body into my car in the school parking lot. I was glad for the physical weariness, because it helped distract me from how weary my heart felt.

It had been barely twenty-four hours since my world imploded. I checked the website on my phone, but I wasn't expecting Brandon's account and results to be back. They weren't. There also weren't any messages from him. I did have a text from Selena, though.

Selena: What time will you be home? I can't wait to tell you what's going on!!!!!

I rocked my head back against my headrest. Five exclamations points was excessive, even for Selena. If she was already trying that hard, it couldn't be good.

Me: Dad thinks your big news is joining the softball team.

Selena: Did he say that?

Me: He didn't have to. So?

Selena: So...what?

Me: What is it?

Selena: I'll tell you at dinner.

Me: That bad?

Selena: No.

Me: Are you okay?

Selena: I'm fine.

Me: You're starting to freak me out.

Selena: I'm fine. It's good news.

Me: You are so full of it. Just tell me.

Selena: I will. Tonight.

Me: I still like my idea of telling me now.

Selena: Don't be cute.

Me: Since when do you keep secrets from me?

Selena: It's not a secret. It wasn't ready until now.

Me: Did you join a cult?

Selena: Yes, Brother Todd is taking me to Vulcan on his magic Pegasus.

Me: That sounds like one of the better cults.

Selena: I comparison-shopped before getting the forehead tattoo.

Me: I need you to tell me because I can't come tonight.

Selena: Why not?

Me: I just can't. Can you put it off a night?

Selena: No, I planned for tonight.

Me: Please?

Selena: What is with you?

Me: I met this guy named Brother Todd.

Selena: Now who's keeping secrets?

Me: I just have to do something tonight. If you want me there for whatever bomb you plan to drop, pick another day.

Selena: I can't switch.

Me: I can't tonight.

Selena: @%#!

Me: Do I win?

Selena: &*#@ ^$# @!%!

Me: Thanks, Sel.

I was halfway to Jungle Juice when Mom texted.

Mom: Selena can't make it home tonight, so we have to wait to hear her news. Do you know what it's about?

Me: Not a clue. If tonight's off, is it okay if I go study at Jessalyn's?

Mom: Sure, sweetie. Be home by eleven.

CHAPTER 12

I shifted into Park outside Jungle Juice. I'd driven there because I had no other options, but once I was actually facing Brandon's work, I couldn't make myself get out of the car.

I hadn't thought it was possible for another desire to compete with the one currently shredding its way through my heart, let alone eclipse it, yet, as much as I needed to know how my seemingly loving dad had fathered a secret son, every part of me recoiled at the thought of hurting the brother I'd just discovered. But I couldn't see how to do one without the other. I couldn't.

I didn't even know if Brandon was working today, and besides that, he'd told me to stay away and made it impossible for me to even message him back. He couldn't have made it any clearer that he didn't want to hear from me, and in his situation, I might have done the same thing. But I still longed to talk to him again, so badly that I convinced myself that it was okay just to watch for him.

I hadn't parked close, and Brandon didn't know what kind of car I drove. With my baseball cap and sunglasses on, he wouldn't recognize me even if he glanced my way. I wouldn't be hurting him, and it might help me just to see him, somehow.

That was the extent of my plan: sit in my car and stalk my half brother. Hope that he changed his mind about talking to me, and pray that I could survive until he did. It was a terrible plan. Every part of me chafed against the inaction of it, but every time I reached for my car door, I'd remember Brandon's face when he read Dad's results, and I couldn't bring myself to open it.

Outside, the sky grew hazy orange and purple. The lights in the parking lot blinked on, growing brighter as the day dimmed. The crickets started up their nightly symphony, singing the sun to sleep. At eight o'clock Jungle Juice officially closed, but it was another hour until the remaining employees trickled out. With a sinking heart, I realized Brandon wasn't one of them.

But Chase was. He was the last to leave. He came out carrying two large trash bags and stopped to lock the doors before circling around the building to where I presumed the dumpsters were.

That same first impression struck me: he was cute, and it hit me harder seeing him the second time. Maybe that was because when he'd seen me crying, he hadn't fled. Maybe it was because he'd offered me a much less pathetic outlet for the emotions I hadn't been able to handle the night before. Maybe it was because he'd let me see a little of what was hurting him so that I wouldn't feel so alone with my own hurt. And it might possibly also be because he uprighted a knocked-over wrought iron table with one hand like it was made out of cardboard without stopping on his way to the dumpsters.

A minute later he was strolling toward his truck. His big white truck that I'd somehow failed to notice in my single-minded search for my brother. Too late, I realized that, unlike Brandon, Chase knew exactly what my car looked like. He wasn't halfway across the parking lot when he saw me, and he didn't miss a step, just changed course to walk just as casually in my direction.

I got out of my car as he reached me.

"Hey," he said.

"Hi."

"I wasn't expecting to see you again."

"I wasn't expecting to be here again." The unspoken question lingered between us, waiting for an answer I couldn't give him. I should have gone with an obvious excuse, claimed I was there looking for a lost earring or something, but I didn't.

I hadn't technically lied to Chase yet, but I had deliberately misled him, whereas he'd been open and honest in return. I couldn't tell him the truth—that had to be Brandon's decision, just like it was mine with my family, but I didn't want to lie to Chase either.

I wanted to squirm under the weight of Chase's brown eyes, which were a deep honey color. I was waiting for him to realize that that was all I was going to say and then make the decision I seemed incapable of making. He'd be nice about it. I'd spent only a few hours with him, but I already knew he'd be kind but direct. Maybe borrow my brush-off line from the night before about being too busy.

"You like black olives?"

"What?"

"Black olives. I was going to go grab a pizza," he said. "Do you want to come with?"

"That's not even close to what I thought you were going to say."

His mouth lifted in the promise of a full smile. "Well, I'd offer you another smoothie, but we're closed."

I bit the side of my lower lip so I wouldn't smile back. I'd given myself a pass with Chase the night before. I hadn't known how close he and Brandon were, and I'd been too heartsick to focus on the reasons I should keep my distance. I didn't have the same excuse anymore. I was still hurting, but I was thinking more clearly too. Brandon had told me to stay away from him, not anyone else, but I couldn't imagine him loving the idea of me hanging out with his cousin.

Then again, that was part of the problem. I couldn't imagine what Brandon would feel, because I didn't know him. Most everything I knew about my half brother had come from Chase, and it wasn't a lot.

"It's just pizza." Chase pointed a few stores down. "And it's literally right there."

It was as though I'd just needed to see the neon-red-and-green sign for my nose to register the mouthwatering mix of garlic and cheese beckoning me toward LJ's Pizza. My stomach loudly expressed its approval.

Chase's promised smile showed up. "Hungry?"

"Apparently." My cold pizza from lunch was a distant memory, and the thought of one fresh from the oven with the cheese still bubbling all golden brown on top was enough to have me half swaying toward the restaurant. My appetite wasn't the problem; it was the potentially illicit company. I knew I was giving him all kinds of mixed signals, which I didn't want to do. I'd shown up at his work with no explanation, my stomach had outed how hungry I was and I wasn't retreating back to my car.

He took a step backward toward LJ's. "I know it's not smashing up a building, but I swear it's the best thin crust in the state."

I laughed. Maybe it could just be pizza. With effort, I kept my gaze from moving back to Jungle Juice as I fell into step beside Chase. "You ever try hamburger?"

"On pizza?"

"It's the best," I said. "My sister and I tried it a few years ago when we were home alone and broke, and now we make it all the time. Before she left for college, I mean."

"You say it's good, I'll try it."

We reached the pizza place and Chase grabbed for the door, pausing when it was only half-open. I'd already stepped forward, expecting to go inside, but when he held the door, I was forced to stop right next to him. "Where did we land on the black olives?"

My breath came out as a laugh—I was relieved he hadn't asked anything serious. "They go great with hamburger."

When he pulled open the door, he leaned toward me as I walked in. "I'm glad you came back."

Right or wrong, I felt that way too.

"So," I said, fiddling with the parmesan shaker. "Do you like working at Jungle Juice? You said your cousin works there too. How'd that happen?"

"No story there." Chase rested his forearms on the table. "I told you Brandon and I grew up together. Our parents are siblings and all—"

"Wait, yesterday you said your coworker calls you both McCormick. How do you guys have the same last name?" I knew there was no way Chase and I were related, but I couldn't help blurting out the question.

"Easy." Chase pulled the pepper-flake shaker toward him and wrapped both hands around it. "The day I turned eighteen, I legally changed mine to my mom's maiden name."

Oh. "Oh." I felt stupid for bringing it up considering we'd spent the previous night smashing his childhood home in effigy of his dad. If I'd been thinking less about myself, I'd have kept my mouth shut.

"No, it's okay," he said, picking up on my discomfort. "It was a great day." Great maybe, but something in his voice told me that wasn't the same as happy. "His last name was the only thing my father left me when he took off, and I waited a long time to give it back to him." He pulled out his wallet and handed me his driver's license. The name read Chase William McCormick. "Now I can look at that without thinking of him."

I handed him back his license.

"Best birthday I've ever had." Chase put away his wallet and a few seconds later reclaimed the pepper-flake shaker. I could tell, despite his words, that it was just shy of okay.

"You look like a McCormick."

He smiled before lifting his gaze to me. "Dana…?"

"Fields."

"You like your last name?"

Chase's question caught me up short. I used to. I'd thought it was perfect, given how much my family liked baseball and softball. But everything was different now.

"I used to," I said, frowning at nothing in particular. "I don't think I can anymore."

"Why's that?"

Chase asked his follow-up question so casually that I almost gave him an equally unguarded answer. "Stuff with my dad," I said, after I took a moment to refocus.

"Your grandfather, the one you were supposed to meet yesterday, was his father?"

I nodded. "My dad never knew his family, so I thought I was doing this amazing thing by finding his father, and it all blew up in my face."

"You didn't get to meet him, though."

"I didn't, because he doesn't exist. Or, I'm sure he does somewhere, but I didn't find him. My sister kept warning me not to go looking because I might get hurt or I might hurt our dad." I pushed the parmesan shaker away. "But I'd rather talk about anything else right now. You didn't finish telling me how you and your cousin started working together." When I lifted my gaze to his, I found Chase staring at me so intently that I had to run back through what I'd just said to make sure I hadn't inadvertently mentioned my connection to Brandon.

The pepper shaker rolled in Chase's hands before he set it back in the middle of the table. "I started there in high school, became manager after I graduated last year and hired Brandon. He's a good guy, not to mention he's in love with Ariel—she's the girl with the blue hair—and she detests him less than anyone around here, so it works."

"Do you still live near each other?"

Chase nodded. "I told you his mom died right after he was born, so Brandon lived with me and my mom for a few months while my uncle... I guess it was hard for him, losing his wife. I know he really loved her. He didn't blame Brandon or anything, but, yeah, it was hard for him."

My brain froze, imagining a much different scenario than the one Chase believed. One where a husband found out the child his wife had borne wasn't his, only to lose her and be faced with raising another man's child or walking away altogether.

"When he got himself together, Brandon was still a baby and he needed help, and with my mom raising me on her own, she did too. We all lived together until I was seven and Brandon turned six. Uncle Bran got his own house then, a couple blocks away. Growing up, I spent half my life at his house and Brandon spent half his at mine. We're cousins, but we're brothers too."

Our pizza arrived before I was forced to try to respond to him.

Chase wolfed down three slices in the time it took me to finish one. I slid another onto my plate, and he added two to his.

"So you're a senior?" he asked.

"Junior. And you're a freshman? Where at?"

"Mesa Community College. I'm planning on transferring to Arizona State next year. And you're...seventeen?"

I nodded. "You?"

"Nineteen. Last month."

"Happy birthday. I'd buy you a pizza, but..." I gestured to the empty pan in front of us.

His mouth lifted on one side. "I could go for more."

"Really?" I was uncomfortably full and still had crust left on my plate. Then again, I was basically half his size. I started to push back my chair, intending to make good on my offer, when his hand shot out and covered mine.

"Dana, I'm messing with you. I'm good."

My hand grew warm under his. I slid it free, then took another bite of pizza and chewed it slowly. What the hell was I doing? I hadn't stopped to think about that question since I'd sent my supposed grandfather that first message. I'd reacted with little to no thought, first with Brandon and then with Chase. I was still just reacting. The longer I sat there with Chase, the more I realized that just seeing Brandon wasn't enough. I wanted to know him, to figure out if he was allergic to cinnamon like I was, or if he loved french fries dipped in ice cream. I wanted to know if he was a Diamondbacks fan or rooted for another team, or if he even liked baseball. I wanted to know which movies had scared him as a kid and which ones had made him laugh until he cried. I wanted to know if he'd ever imagined having a sister, and if she was anything like me. I wanted to know *him*, and Chase might be the only way I ever could.

"So," Chase said, walking me back to my car. "Still think AJ and Mesa are too far away from each other?"

I had to blink at the directness of his question. "I have softball practice every day till four or four thirty, games three nights a week and tournaments most Saturdays. I'm betting you work a lot too, besides the classes you take."

He nodded, still looking at me in that unnervingly direct way. "When's your next game?"

"I have tournaments all day tomorrow."

"I work on Sunday. What about the day after?"

I would have laughed at his persistence if the question hadn't made me feel so warm. "Just practice."

"And I get off at five. I'll even come to you and save you the drive."

That time I did laugh. "You don't give up, do you?"

"You want me to?"

I should, but I didn't. "How do you feel about batting cages?"

"If you're asking, pretty damn good."

The smile on my face lasted me halfway home. It was way too easy to spend time with Chase. I'd also discovered more about Brandon and possibly learned that at least one other person besides Brandon's mother knew about his paternity. Those were things I wanted to know, but I couldn't completely shake the scummy feeling that accompanied me the rest of the way home because of how I'd learned them.

CHAPTER 13

Tournament days were good. They required complete focus, which was exactly what I gave. In the dugout, I was just another player getting the same speech from our coach as the girls on either side of me. He wasn't my dad on game days, and I made sure to remember that. I did nothing that would single me out for correction, nothing that would necessitate a private talk after the game or later at home, good or bad. I played well, but my heart wasn't in it the way it usually was. I didn't know if I expected Dad to notice or not, but he didn't seem to, and we still won the game.

I saw Nick afterward, but I made sure to dominate the conversation so as to avoid the chance he'd ask any more follow-up questions about my dad's DNA results. I left him and Jessalyn talking about work and joined my sister.

Selena beat a drum solo on my shoulders as we walked to the cars. "You guys are killing it this season. You have a real shot at state, which, you know…" Her pause was unnecessary. Of course I knew. And just in case I forgot, my sister was there to remind me at every opportunity that she'd won two in a row.

I didn't feel like enduring Selena's thinly veiled bragging the whole way home, but anything was better than riding with my parents. "Are you coming home for a while or do you have to head back to U of A right away?"

"I can hang out a bit. Ride with me?"

I got into Selena's car. And actually, she wasn't that bad. With Dad out of the picture, we could talk about the game and not have the conversation be tainted.

"Sadie's pitching really well." She laughed to herself. "I think her curveball is better than mine."

"It is."

Selena's eyes swung to me. "You're supposed to say we're both good."

I canted my head against the window. "You already know you were the best, but Sadie's curveball is sick. When she's on, no one can hit it."

"I know. Maybe she'll give me a few pointers."

"You don't care about softball anymore." I didn't say it to be harsh; it was true, as far as I could tell.

Selena scoffed a little but kept her eyes on the road. "I care."

Yeah, she cared enough to turn down an impressive athletic scholarship after Dad worked so hard to make sure colleges knew about her. I didn't want to think about Dad, though, so I let it drop. But Selena didn't.

"Do you know how many hours a week I spend in this car so I can drive to your games? It's a lot, like a stupid lot, but I'm here. Okay, fine, I'd probably still be here if you were on the basketball team, but I'd enjoy it a lot less. I love watching you play this game. Don't forget I'm a Fields too. Baseball is in our blood."

Dad's blood, she meant, but I ignored that for the moment. It was a drive, usually four hours round-trip even when our away games brought us closer to Tucson. I knew that; I loved her for that, even more because I'd thought she hated softball. "Then why did you quit? You don't play at all anymore."

"I play," she said. "Intramural."

"You turned down the chance to play for a Division I school so you could play intramural?" When she'd turned down the scholarship, she'd said it was because she was done with softball. I'd assumed she meant entirely. I couldn't fathom why she'd choose to play intramural over college level. I couldn't stop shaking my head, whereas Selena nodded and smiled.

Glancing at me, she sighed like she shouldn't have to explain something that was so obvious to her. "How many hours a week do you spend on softball?"

Still feeling gobsmacked, I answered. "I don't know, twenty-five?"

"For me it was forty, minimum." She nodded at my widening eyes. "Yeah, I was good, but Dad made me work so much harder because of it. For four years, every day of my life revolved around softball. Apart from my teammates, I had no friends, no boyfriend, no job. I couldn't go out for choir or school plays. I missed dances and trips and everything. And it would have been so much more intensive playing in college. I know girls who leave the dorm at six a.m. and don't get back until ten, and I didn't want to be one of them."

I wanted to be able to contradict her, but the more I

searched my memories, the more they matched what she said. Her whole life had been softball. I guess I'd always thought that was what she wanted.

"It was at first," she agreed when I said as much. "And Dad was so proud of me, which felt great too, but it kept getting bigger. It wasn't enough to practice every day with the team—Dad wanted me working at night too. There was no off-season. In the winter I played club ball. Every weekend I was at another camp. I don't know how I kept my grades up, I really don't. I barely remember anything from high school except softball, which was reason enough not to surrender another four years of my life." Her hands had grown tight on the steering wheel, but with an effort, she relaxed them. "But it doesn't mean I don't care. I love softball. I love it more now than I ever have, because it's fun again. Watching you, playing at school without committing every waking minute of the day to it—I love that. And I love that I'm getting to do new things and try some of what I missed in high school, you know?"

Selena looked at me expectantly, waiting for me to understand. I did, to a degree. But I couldn't imagine walking away and disappointing Dad like she had, no matter the cost. Maybe I'd feel differently if Dad pushed me as hard as he'd pushed her, or if playing well came half as easily to me as it had to her. But he didn't, and it didn't, and I couldn't completely quell the resentment toward my sister that lingered just below the surface because she'd given up what I'd never have.

I opened my door when we pulled into our driveway, but Selena didn't follow. "Aren't you coming in?"

She hesitated, then shook her head. "I guess I'm more tired than I thought."

She didn't look tired. "What about your big news?"

"It'll keep."

It had barely kept the other night when I'd had to beg her to hold off. I was getting a bad feeling. "Are you okay?" I asked. "Because the cult comment was supposed to be a joke."

Selena smiled, but it looked a little sad to me.

"Hey." I pulled my door shut again. "You'd tell me if something was wrong, wouldn't you?"

"Yes, Dana," she said, in a tone that implied an eye roll even without one. "I was just thinking about old stuff that I don't have to anymore." She grinned. "I get to think about new stuff, really awesome new stuff. Stuff that will blow your cap off." She leaned over and flicked my ball cap up. "Now get out so I can get back to my dorm. Tell Mom and Dad I'll see them on Tuesday for your game, and then I'll spill."

CHAPTER 14

Jessalyn was right behind me as we reentered the locker room after practice on Monday afternoon. We both lifted off our sweat-drenched T-shirts and let them hit the ground with a wet smack. We grinned together.

"We are beasts," she said, slapping the hand I raised.

"Super-hot lady beasts." I flexed in my sports bra. Then I collapsed onto the bench. "And I'm done."

"Oh, get this." Jessalyn opened her locker. "Ryan asked me out during fourth period."

I opened my own locker. "What a tool."

She scoffed, nodding. "He broke up with Sadie, what, a week ago?"

"Not even. So what did you do?"

"I told him to blow me."

"Did you really?"

Jessalyn and I both turned to see Sadie standing behind us. Their breakup had blindsided her. Most days her eyes were still red from crying, but she almost looked like she could smile as she waited for Jessalyn's answer.

"I have the detention slip to prove it."

Sadie did smile.

"He's a turd of a human being," I said. We'd all told her the same thing over and over again, but she said it helped each time she heard it. I had no problem reminding her as often as I could.

"Thanks, guys."

"Hey, why don't you come over?" Jessalyn said to Sadie. "We can all swing by Mostly Bread and grab food, say hi to Nick, then binge watch something at my house."

"Yeah, okay."

I slipped on my flip-flops, avoiding eye contact. "I can't this time."

"Why not?" Jessalyn frowned at me. "I know you were sick yesterday, but you said you felt better."

I'd claimed another headache as an excuse to hide in my room Sunday and avoid my parents. "I feel fine. I just can't, okay?" I turned to Sadie. "Ryan never deserved you. Never. Not for one tiny second. He's a skid mark."

"Skid mark," Jessalyn echoed, but she was still frowning at me as I pulled on a clean shirt and grabbed my bag.

"I'll catch you guys tomorrow."

At home, I tried to slip in unnoticed, but Mom had bat ears. She probably heard me walking up the driveway. She came around the corner just as I was closing the front door behind me.

"Hi, honey. School good? Practice?"

"Yep. I learned all the things." I craned my neck to peer into the office and saw a mountain of empty Hershey's Kisses wrappers on her desk. "Tough design?"

Her lips pursed. "He gets these ideas—" and by *he*, she meant Dad "—and they look great, but I have to figure out a way to make them work. This morning he drops this brilliant design for a website we are already overdue on." She sat on the armrest of the sofa and pulled out another Kiss from her pocket. "Triangles. In pure CSS." She crumpled the wrapper in her fist. "I mean, right?"

I was supposed to be upset by triangles, but I didn't know anything about coding, so I went with, "Triangles, those bastards."

Her chin dropped to her chest. "Thank you." Then it snapped back up. "And don't swear."

"Sorry." I backed toward the stairs behind me, knowing I needed to hurry up if I wanted to be gone before Dad came home, which I did. "Can't you just tell Dad that he's asking for something you can't do?"

"Oh, I can do it." She opened another Kiss. "I might go insane trying to get the angles right, but I can do it." Her eyes lost focus, and I knew that look well enough to know she was already imagining how she would succeed.

"Fine." She stood up and set the empty wrappers on the corner of the coffee table. She slipped her earbuds back in and her voice rose to compensate for the deafening music she liked. "YOU AND DAD ARE ON YOUR OWN FOR DINNER. I'LL HAVE HIS TRIANGLES BY MORNING."

I went upstairs just long enough to drop off my books

and shower at lightning speed before dashing back downstairs into the kitchen. On the message board by the fridge, I wrote a note.

Dad,
Mom is working on the triangles (?) you wanted. I'm going to Jessalyn's to work on homework. I'll eat dinner out.

I started to write *sorry*, but my nostrils flared and I erased it, leaving only my name. I dropped the marker, letting it swing in a wide arc from its string, and left.

I got to the batting cages a good half hour before I was supposed to meet Chase, so after sitting for a few minutes in my car, I did something I hadn't been able to bring myself to do at home.

I Googled my brother.

I checked every social media site I could think of. And there he was: Brandon McCormick III. I found pictures going back to middle school, where he looked so much like Selena, all long limbed and skinny. His awkward phase had been short. Between seventh and eighth grade, his skin had cleared up and he'd filled out. He looked the way I remembered him from a few days ago.

I read up on his hobbies (video games and swimming), the movies he liked (he was really into Asian films) and his favorite books (big fan of Robert Jordan).

I found out he'd broken his leg skiing when he was fourteen.

I found out he wanted to be an astronaut, and not like a

little kid wants to be an astronaut. He was planning on joining the air force.

I found out that he and his dad—and Chase—went deep-sea fishing in Alaska every summer. There were pictures of the three of them on different boats, holding high their catches.

His dad looked like an average guy. Shorter than his son in recent photos, but with similar coloring. They weren't so different that people would notice and wonder.

That was something I hadn't had a chance to ask Brandon. I could see my dad so clearly in him. I hadn't seen the man Brandon thought was his dad, but I thought Brandon could have wondered why the resemblance between him and his supposed father wasn't stronger. Then again, what kid really did that? Seeing the man now, dissimilar from Brandon but not startlingly so, I could see how love might have blurred the differences between them. And if both Brandon and his dad had been truly ignorant of the affair—though I was less convinced about his dad—they might never have thought to scrutinize each other. I believed Brandon had been blindsided by my paternity claims, but I still didn't know about his dad. Pictures online could tell me only so much.

Still, I kept looking. It was a compulsion.

I found out that Brandon still mourned the mother he never knew. He posted about her every year on her birthday and on his—April 18. He'd said he'd just turned eighteen; I hadn't realized he'd meant literally the week before. He was only five months older than me. Selena would have been barely a year old when Dad was with his mom and then back with Mom not even half a year later. I lowered my phone and tasted bile.

How could he have left her with one baby to go off and make another only to return and make me? What kind of man could do that?

I forced my eyes back to my phone, my only hope for answers in that moment. Brandon always shared the same photo—apparently, he had only one of the two of them together. It was in a hospital and he was lying on her chest wrapped in one of those newborn blankets with a tiny blue baby cap. She wasn't really holding him—she clearly didn't have the strength—but she was smiling at him. My stomach churned. Had Dad known about his son? Had they picked out his name together? Made plans to leave their spouses and start a new family? Had her death devastated him so much that he'd lied to his first family all these years, or was he as ignorant about Brandon as I'd been?

I couldn't imagine Dad abandoning his son for someone else to raise, doing to his child what had been done to him, but I couldn't have fathomed his cheating on Mom either, so my shattered faith in him wasn't a litmus test for anything anymore. On top of that, I knew nothing about Brandon's mom. Had she been in love with my dad? Happy to discover she was pregnant with his child? Or had she viewed the affair as a mistake and the paternity of her unborn child as something to conceal from both his father and her husband?

I banged my head against my headrest again and again. It was either that or cry. Maybe Dad knew, maybe not. Maybe the man who raised Brandon knew, maybe not. I had no idea what I was supposed to do. I no longer had any proof of Dad's connection to Brandon. The DNA results were gone, the website didn't even list the match since Brandon had revoked and removed his information, and it wasn't likely that he'd be giving my one printed copy back, assuming he hadn't destroyed it when he deleted his account. I had next to nothing to corroborate my claim, if I decided to make one. And that was a big if. The destruction that would rain down on my family, on Mom in particular... Tears pricked my eyes, blurring the face of my half brother as a newborn. He looked round and swollen like every other newborn. The resemblance to Dad didn't show up until later. I blinked, noticing something else in the photo of Brandon with his mom—a man's hand resting on the bedrail of the hospital bed. The rest of him was out of frame. I pinched the image larger, trying to see every possible detail of that hand. I scrolled back to the last fishing-trip photo, trying to make out any distinguishing marks on the hand of Brandon's dad, but the sun was glaring and I couldn't tell. Back to the hospital pic. My nose was practically brushing my phone screen. Whose was it? My dad's or his? If he'd been there, then he knew, he—

I jumped as a figure approached my window. Chase.

I dropped my phone. The image was so zoomed in it wasn't recognizable, but I didn't want him asking about it either. Mentally, I was still thinking about the hand. It was a man's hand, of indiscernible color, and it was strong, like say from playing baseball or years spent reeling in monstrous deep-sea fish. It could be either of them in that photo. But if it was Dad's hand, if he'd been at her bedside when their son was born, bile or not, Mom had to know.

My best shot of finding out was standing right outside my window, smiling and happy to see me. I swallowed a wave of guilt and smiled back.

CHAPTER 15

Once we'd claimed our cage, Chase wanted me to go first, but I was still preoccupied by the hand in the photo. I let him start while I tried to sever myself from everything that picture might mean.

Fortunately for me, Chase was not as proficient hitting balls as he was smashing walls. He missed his first swing. And his second.

And his third.

The rest of the round didn't get any better. He tipped a few, but that was about it. He stepped back and shook his head before meeting my eye. "A little help?"

I joined him in the cage, widened his stance slightly and used my hands over his to line up his knuckles on the bat. At that first brush of contact, warmth pulsed through me, heating my cheeks down to my toes and everywhere in between. I'd come up behind him, but he was so much bigger and taller than me that I'd had to go up on my toes and lean into him to see over his shoulder. "If you grip it like this, it'll help you turn your wrists when you swing." My arms were around him as we practiced the motion. It was almost like a dance, slow and focused. Pressed up against him, I was feeling the muscles I'd only ever seen before, and they made me go a little light-headed. That close, it was impossible not to breathe him in. He smelled like the ocean, fresh and inviting. I swallowed and moved back.

"You ready to go again?" I stepped clear as soon as he was in position, and I fed more tokens into the machine. He swung again, and the solid hit elicited a whoop from me. I held both hands up for the double high five he gave me through the net.

"You're good at this coaching thing."

"I was raised by one, plus my dad has been coaching me and my sister since T-ball." Chase made another solid hit to the back of the net. "And you're picking it up really well. Did you ever play as a kid?"

"Not much. Little League for a year or two with Brandon, but—" *crack!* "—we were never really into it. My uncle isn't a big sports guy, so he never pushed us one way or another."

Chase was the kind of guy you looked at and immediately thought *athlete*. He was strong, and there was something about the way he moved, a sense of complete control. I watched him hit again, and there was enough power in his swing to rival the sound of a gunshot when it connected. "You had to have played something."

"I played some football in high school, and now I do Cross-Fit."

That explanation fit almost as well as his T-shirt. I got lost watching the way the muscles in his back and arms shifted each time he swung. It was…impressive. I was almost disappointed when Chase lowered his bat once his second round ended.

He looked at me on the other side of the cage. "You're up."

I was conscious of Chase's eyes on me as I took his place, aware that he was likely looking at me as intently as I'd studied him. Once I started hitting, though, I forgot everything but the ball and bat in my hands. Half my life had been spent in a batting cage or on a field with Dad pitching to me and Selena, cheering our wins and helping us to improve when we lost, lifting me on his shoulders the first time I hit a home run. How could I reconcile the pain of what he'd done with the happy memories that came unbidden now? I missed the next pitch and only tipped the one after that. Chase couldn't see my face or my rapidly blinking eyes to know that anything was wrong. I twisted my toe into the ground, trying to focus only on the ball. *Crack!* And another, until my pitches were out. Then I turned to Chase with a smile I didn't feel.

"Up for another round?"

We hit for a long while. The crack of the bat sounded good—it always did—but somehow it was extra cathartic now. My mind would no sooner drift than my body would swing, and the impact would bring me right back to the present.

When we were both too spent for another round and my mind had stropped trying to stray, we made our way to the parking lot and sat on the open tailgate of Chase's truck.

"This was fun."

"It's not smashing a building, but yeah." I smiled, glancing at Chase. Like the night we first met, his shirt was damp with sweat, and I could feel a furnace of heat coming from his body. We were close enough that our arms kept brushing, and once or twice our knees. Everywhere we touched, it was like little fireworks went off and shot straight to my erratically beating heart.

Chase laughed. And then he did something that knocked my smile right off my face. He slid his hand into mine, lacing our fingers together and resting them on his thigh. His hand was as warm as the rest of him, and calloused, even more than mine. He didn't act like it was a big deal, taking my hand, but it felt big to me. And nice. Really, really nice. My skin was darker, more tan than the sun had made his, but it was possible he'd catch me by summer. His closely cropped hair might lighten then too, but I hoped not too much—I liked the dark brown on him. I wondered if the color came from his mom or dad.

"Can I ask you something…kind of random?" I said, keeping my eyes on our linked hands.

"Sure."

"Do you ever see your father?"

I felt the muscles in Chase's arm contract. "No, I don't see him."

"Your choice or his?"

"Both. He's never come back and I've never gone looking." I nodded.

"Why?"

I turned our hands over, revealing more of my skin, a mix of Dad's and Mom's. I could hide from the sun for the rest of my life and the color would never fade. "Were you ever curious about that side of your family?"

"No. I don't want anything that's connected to him. And

I don't need anything from him either. I have a father in my uncle Bran." He squeezed my hand. "Are you thinking about looking for more of your dad's family?"

"No." My answer was immediate. "I'm still reeling from looking the first time." I suddenly decided to be as honest with Chase as I could, maybe as a way to balance everything I had to conceal. "Part of me wishes that I hadn't done it at all. I didn't find what I was looking for, but I did find out things about my dad that I can't reconcile with my life."

"What things?"

I shook my head. "He did something...really awful and painful." I took a deep breath. "But there's something else that he might have done that is infinitely worse, something I don't think I could ever forgive him for." If he knew about Brandon and had hidden him... "The possibility alone is enough to make me feel sick every time I look at my dad, but if I keep digging and discover it's true..."

"You can't ever go back."

"I can't." I looked up at Chase. "The worst part is that I found something good too, something completely amazing," I said, thinking about the fact that Sel and I had a brother. "But it's all tangled up in something that will hurt a lot of people, people I care about, possibly in ways we can't ever recover from. I can't tell them about the good without revealing the bad." Chase's gaze never left my face and under his stare, warmth started to spread through my body, hitting but not thawing the knot of ice in my stomach. He was one of the people who might get hurt. I started to pull my hand free, but he stopped me.

"Would you want to know?" Chase asked. "If it was someone else in your position right now, would you risk the bad for the good?"

Initially, I'd have said no, that it was better to be ignorant than in pain, but that was before I'd met Brandon. Whatever else had happened, he was a good thing. My voice was soft. "I would."

"Then you have your answer."

I smiled, but it didn't reach my eyes. I wanted to tell him the whole truth and see if he still felt the same way, but for Brandon's sake, I couldn't. And I wasn't ready to risk losing Chase when I'd only just found him.

Before I could slip my hand free, I heard my name from across the parking lot.

"Dana?"

My breath froze. I turned to see Jessalyn and Sadie walking over. This time Chase didn't stop me from pulling my hand free, though my friends were close enough that they had to have seen us holding hands. Jessalyn was going to give me so much crap. Not only had I blown them off—blown Sadie off when she could have used all the support she could get—to be with a guy that I hadn't told her about, but I was giving her further proof that I didn't have even potential feelings for Nick. I'd have to talk with Nick. I really didn't want to hurt him, but based on how things were going with Chase, wise or not, I needed to be honest with Nick. I'd have preferred to do that without Jessalyn looking at me like I'd cheated on him—I hadn't—but she and I were going to have to talk too. Just not in front of Chase.

"Hey." I pushed off the tailgate to stand when they reached us, glancing quickly at Chase when he moved to stand beside me. "Guys, this is Chase. Chase, these are my friends Jessalyn and Sadie from my softball team."

"Hey." He shook their hands in turn. "I hear you guys are really good. What positions do you play?"

"Pitcher," Sadie said.

"Shortstop," Jessalyn said, eyeing Chase without any of the subtlety Sadie had used. "And how do you know Dana?" She was annoyed and didn't bother to hide it.

"We just met the other day," I said. "He helped me out with a low-blood-sugar situation, so I thought I'd return the favor and show him how to hit."

Jessalyn slid her eyes to me. "Yeah, Dana hits hard when she wants to."

I pleaded with her silently to be nice, and she did dial it back a little. She stopped frowning, but I could tell by the tight way she held her mouth that she wasn't just mad at me; she was disappointed too.

We chatted another couple minutes before they went in. Alone with Chase again, I worried that he'd comment on the semi-awkward meeting or the way I'd dropped his hand as soon as I'd seen my friends, but he didn't. In fact, the last thing he said to me before I got in my car was, "When can I see you again?"

Mom was still working when I got home that night and Dad was in the shower, so I was able to slip into my room and turn the lights off, ostensibly to go to sleep. They'd be able to see my car in the driveway, so I didn't even need to give the cursory "I'm home!" shout-out.

I didn't drift peacefully to sleep. I lay in the dark staring up at the glow-in-the-dark star stickers Selena and I had put up when we were little and shared a room. They barely glowed. I'd been gone almost the entire day, and they'd had no light to absorb. I felt just as dim.

It'd been easy to avoid Dad today, but tomorrow would be different. We had another game, and afterward Selena would sit us all down and share her very-likely-not-good news or she would have told me already. I'd be expected to talk to him, civilly, as though he hadn't cheated and possibly done the unforgivable.

I decided to think about Chase instead, and the warmth of his hand in mine. When I closed my eyes, I could still feel him on my skin. Without realizing it, he'd given me permission to hurt him...but he'd also given me every reason not to.

CHAPTER 16

Jessalyn did not do cool and composed. She did loud and in your face—or more specifically, my face.

"Seriously, Dana? Seriously?"

She hadn't even bothered to get in the pizza line for lunch the following day. She was standing next to it in the quad when I saw her. She also didn't wait for me to get close enough to keep our conversation private. I was still twenty feet away when she started.

"Who even was that guy last night?"

I didn't answer until I was within grabbing distance of her arm. I tugged her away from the faces turned toward us in the pizza line. "I told you who he was. Chill out, and I'll tell you the rest."

"It's not me you need to tell." She wasn't even trying to keep her voice down.

"Enough about Nick. You're not his personal bodyguard. And we're not dating!" My voice rose to match Jessalyn's. "He and I are friends, and don't you give me that look. It's true. He's never asked me out. We've hung out and he comes to our games, but you see him more than I do now that you're working together. I never said 'Nick, I like you' or 'Nick, I want to be your girlfriend.' Yes, he's a nice guy and a great friend, and yes, I thought I might get to the point where I'd want something more between us, but you're right, I don't. I met this other guy, and I already feel more for him than I ever will for Nick. So, there." Suddenly exhausted, I let my arms fall to my sides. "Are you happy? Is that what you've been waiting for me to say?"

Jessalyn did this thing. It was so much worse than yelling at me across the quad or lecturing me in front of the pizza line. She didn't say a word; her eyes slid just slightly to my left, and all the animosity fled from her face.

I knew what I'd see before I turned, but when I met Nick's gaze and saw him there, close enough to have heard every word I'd just said, close enough to see that not even Jessalyn had known how deeply I'd been capable of hurting him, few things had ever felt worse.

CHAPTER 17

I looked for Nick the rest of the day but he was a ghost and what I needed to say to him couldn't be done over text. Jessalyn, on the other hand, couldn't have avoided me if she tried. I was waiting at her locker at the start of practice.

"What did he say?" I asked when she reached me. She and Nick had American Government together for fifth period.

"Nothing, so either he's in love with me now too, or he doesn't want to talk to either of us."

I sank onto the bench, and a second later Jessalyn joined me. Quietly, I said to her, "You could have just talked to me, asked me instead of yelling in front of half the school." *In front of Nick.* I braced my head in my hands. "Did you see his face?"

Her voice was soft too. "Yeah, I saw it."

"That's it?" I opened one eye to glance at her sideways. She was staring at the closed lockers in front of us. "You don't have anything else to say to me?"

"I don't feel like yelling anymore."

I closed my eye again, then braced my hands on my knees and straightened up. "Fine. Chase. Yes, he's a guy I like, and yes, I didn't tell you about him. I didn't know for sure if there was anything to tell until last night. It's complicated, but I would have told you. And Nick," I added.

Other girls were filing into the locker room, preventing me from telling Jessalyn exactly how complicated things were with Chase. She waited for me to elaborate, and when I didn't, her brows pinched ever so slightly together in genuine hurt. "I asked you not to be that girl and you did it anyway. It was a sucky thing to do, Dana."

And with that, she finished changing and headed out to the field.

I'd lingered too long in the locker room after practice hoping to catch Jessalyn alone and finish the conversation we needed to have, but it didn't happen, so both my parents were home when I let myself in. Mom was emerging from the office in the same clothes she'd been wearing yesterday, looking tired, but her smile was triumphant. I guessed she'd figured out the triangles. Dad lowered the tablet he was holding and was the opposite of smiling.

"Where'd you go last night?"

"I left you a note," I said, avoiding all but the briefest of eye contact as I made my way to the kitchen.

"You had a homework thing?" he asked.

"That's what I wrote in my note."

Even Mom's smile dimmed a bit at my less-than-respectful response.

Dad followed me, leaving Mom in the living room. "Right, with Jessalyn. You get it all done?"

I grabbed a banana from the bunch in the bowl. There was something off in his tone that didn't jibe with the routine question he'd asked. Rather than looking up, I focused on peeling my banana. "I'm all set."

"That's not all you are."

My eyes flicked to his and I halted midbite. His arms were locked and he was resting his palms on the kitchen island. My respect for him had been demolished in the past few days; otherwise I might have been more concerned at the you-are-in-big-trouble vibe radiating from him.

"Jessalyn is close to failing History. Her teacher talked to me after practice today, because Jessalyn missed another extension on some report she's supposed to turn in."

My mouth opened automatically, a lie coming easily to my lips without me even breaking a sweat. "Right, that's why—"

"If you lie to me again, Dana, it won't end well for you."

"Lie to you? Lie to *you*?" I mirrored his pose on the other side of the island. I'd barely looked at my father since finding out about Brandon, but standing across from him while he prepared to lecture me about honesty was more than I could bear. I almost said it, right then, almost screamed out what I knew. My mouth was opening again, the truth ready to pour out, when the only thing that could have stopped me in that moment entered the kitchen behind Dad.

Mom looked between me and Dad. "What is going on in here?"

Dad's eyes never left my face. "She lied about where she was last night."

"Dana?"

"And she's gonna tell us where she went right now."

Both my parents were staring at me, though with polar-opposite expressions. Mom looked confused, like she was waiting for me to explain away a misunderstanding. Dad looked pissed, like he was waiting for—demanding—an explanation that he'd already decided he wouldn't accept. I was torn right down the middle. I was so angry with him, but I still didn't know how deep his betrayal went. Laying into Dad the way I burned to would shatter Mom. It was going to hurt enough when I did; unanswered questions would only make it worse.

So I beat the words down. But that did nothing to cool my temper. "Fine. I lied."

Dad's expression wavered. He hadn't been expecting me to come right out and admit it.

"I didn't go to Jessalyn's, and I didn't do homework. I went to the batting cages with a guy. I didn't tell you because I thought you might say no. So I lied." I drew out that last word, making sure to hold Dad's eye as I did. I couldn't help it. If I'd felt more guilty over blowing off Dad, I might have tried to lessen my lie by pointing out that Jessalyn and Sadie had shown up too, but I didn't feel guilty enough to want to try. I didn't feel guilty at all.

"A boy?" Mom said. "You lied to us over a boy? What's wrong with him?"

"Nothing," I said, eyeing Dad and his inexplicable silence.

"I lied because I never do anything besides softball and homework. But don't worry, Dad." I shifted my eyes and only my eyes to him. "I hit better than I ever have. I'm good for the game tonight."

It would have been cool to toss my banana peel in the trash can on my way out of the kitchen after that, having left both my parents speechless in my wake, but I didn't get to be cool—I got to be yelled at, tag team–style.

Lying was wrong, ninth commandment–level wrong, and let's throw in breaking the fifth commandment about honoring parents too, since I obviously hadn't done that either. I didn't know that I'd ever been yelled at so thoroughly and for so long before in my life. Not because lying was the worst thing I'd ever been caught doing, but because I wouldn't apologize. I was defiant and obstinate at every turn. I didn't express remorse. I didn't promise never to do it again. I was like a kid possessed, one who was too stupid or too far gone to see that every willful and barb tongued response was only digging myself deeper and deeper into a hole of my own making.

It might have gone on indefinitely had it not been a game day. Like matching Pavlovian dogs, Dad and I both turned to the kitchen wall clock the second it hit five o'clock.

Games were sacrosanct. Not even a knock-down, drag-out fight could delay them.

Dad and I left the kitchen to change and gather our stuff, then met back downstairs in the garage.

"Adriana, are you coming with us?" Dad asked Mom, who was still in the kitchen where we'd left her. She tossed the sponge she'd been using on the island countertop into the sink and shook her head.

"So our daughter can complete her transformation into Pete Rose, ready to charge the mound the second she gets

on the field? No. I'll text Selena to pick me up on her way."
With one last head shake of disgust from her in no particular
direction, Dad and I headed out.

I simmered during the entire drive, ready to boil over
again at the slightest comment from Dad, almost hoping for
it. Without Mom's presence, I might not be able to hold back.
But he was as silent as I was. We didn't exchange a single
word until we were walking to the field from the parking lot.

"This is over now. You play, I coach—"

"We win," I said, my gaze locked ahead.

"Win or lose," he went on, "everything about last night is
over. Next time you want to make other plans, fine, tell me.
Do not lie to me or your mom—do you understand me?"

I glanced at him. He was squinting into the setting sun,
not looking at me. "I understand you better than I ever have."

"Good. And you're grounded next week."

Play ball!

CHAPTER 18

We won the game. Jessalyn and I didn't talk, but I hit the crap out of everything that came my way, fielded like my life depended on it, and yelled and cheered so much that my voice was gone by the end of the night. Not that I needed it. Dad kept his word about dropping the argument. We didn't mention it driving back from the game or once we got home. Mom must have said something to Selena, because she refrained from commenting about the total lack of bragging— on my part—and game analysis that we all usually shared in after a win. Rather than winding me down, however, the atypical quiet only added to my resentment toward Dad. Here was another thing he was taking from us.

If I'd been Selena, I'd have taken one look at the faces around me once we spilled into the living room and kept my mouth shut about anything even remotely contentious. But Selena could be a huge dumbass sometimes, and she couldn't leave well enough alone.

She strode into the center of the room as the rest of us were heading toward our respective corners and, with her arms spread wide, said, "I guess now is as good a time as any to share my exciting news. Sit, sit!" She directed us to the couch in front of her. It was telling—or it should have been to Selena—that none of us moved with any kind of enthusiasm.

Mom went first, raising her chin and determining that she was about to hear something good. I followed after, frowning in warning at my oblivious sister. Dad remained standing behind the couch, his expression somewhere between Mom's and mine.

With her arms outstretched and her palms down, Selena smiled full-out. "You have to promise to hear me out. This is good news."

Which, of course, meant it wasn't. Not even Mom could keep her chin up after that opening.

"I'm leaving college."

Mom shot to her feet. "No. Nope." She blinked at her daughter. "Selena, no."

"Mom, you're supposed to let me finish—"

"If you are starting with dropping out of college, then no. I'm not supposed to do anything." She turned to Dad, arms slapping against her sides. "Dennis, back me up."

It was beginning to dawn on Selena that her exciting news was exciting only to her—and even that was being thrown into question by our parents' reaction. Dad wasn't yelling yet, but he was gearing up.

"What happened?" he asked.

Selena's laugh lacked conviction. "Nothing happened. I just figured out what I want to do and I don't need college to do it. Really, you guys should be happy. Think of all the tuition you'll save!" She bounced her gaze between our parents, her face falling more and more each time she settled on one. "I was really hoping you guys would be more supportive. Isn't this what I was supposed to be doing at college? Figuring out what I want to do for the rest of my life? Some people need all four years—or more. I only needed two."

"When you put it that way, you're kind of a prodigy." I waved my hand in a flourish.

Selena glared at me. "Shut up, Dana."

"Hey, I'm just here for moral support, which you are clearly going to need once you drop out of college."

Mom made a sound in her throat that drew every eye in the room.

"I'm not dropping out!" Selena said. "I'm moving forward!"

"Where exactly are you moving?" I asked, knowing it couldn't be good or she would have led with it.

"Well, you guys have always encouraged me to dream big and work hard toward whatever goal I wanted. I'm taking your advice." She filled her lungs with fortifying air. "I want to move to Nashville and become a singer."

"No, you don't." My face scrunched both in disbelief and annoyance. We sang in the car, and she'd sung in the choir at church before, but singing as a career, no way. She'd never shown any interest in that. But when Selena didn't respond, my expression fell as flat as our parents'. "Since when?"

Selena turned more fully to face me. "Since kind of a while. I've been learning to play the guitar, and I've even sung at a few coffee shops. I'm writing my own songs, and Gavin thinks—".

"Ohhhh," I said, just as Mom started shaking her head.

"A boy? This is about a boy?" She looked at Dad. "Both of them in the same day."

Selena had no way of knowing Mom had asked me almost the exact same question earlier that day.

"Gavin is not a boy."

Mom stretched her five feet two inches to an imposing height. "He better be, because if you say the word *teacher*—"

"He's only a couple years older than me, Mom. And he's really talented. He's worked with a ton of great people and knows basically everyone in Nashville." Ignoring the escalating hostility in the room, Selena let her obvious enthusiasm flood her voice. "And get this, he thinks he can get me a record deal within six months. Six months! Can you believe it?"

Nope, I really couldn't.

"Brother Todd, was it? Does he also have plans to ride off into the Vulcan sunset with you?"

Selena snarled in my direction. "Shut. Up. Dana."

Sitting back on the couch, I crossed my arms. If she wanted to fly solo with our parents, that was fine by me.

"What's the timeline here? Is your plan to finish the year or just the semester?" Dad asked through his teeth, a sign he was attempting to maintain self-control.

"Well..."

"You already dropped out, didn't you?" I mimicked Mom's head shaking. "Wow."

"Hey, I wanted to tell you guys the other day, but Dana texted me that she had these unbreakable plans, and—"

"Whoa, whoa!" I held my hands out at the glare my parents had shifted to me in eerily precise unison. "*Tell*, she said

tell, which means she'd already done it. The other night was
going to be her notification of an already occurred event,
right?" I looked at Selena for confirmation. "When precisely
did you drop out?"

"It's not dropping out if—"

"Before or after you were going to tell us? It's a simple
question."

"I don't really see how that matters." Except she totally
did, based on the wobbly quality of her voice. "I withdrew
my enrollment last week."

"Oh, okay," Mom said, in a too-normal voice. She shrugged
in Dad's direction, then turned back to Selena. "I mean, you're
going back, of course, but I'm thrilled to know Gavin is so
connected. Good for him." And with that, she strode into
the kitchen, calling over her shoulder, "Who else is hungry?"

Selena stood agape for maybe half a second before following
her. A minute later, Mom was yelling in Spanish and Selena
was yelling back in a mix of both Spanish and English, the
whole thing punctuated by banging pots and slammed cabinet doors. Dad and I were left alone to listen from the living room.

"Did you know?" he asked.

"*—how will I know if I don't at least try!*"

"About her dream to become the next Taylor Swift? No."
But I had to give it to her for timing. Mom and Dad were
both still spent from fighting all afternoon with me. I hoped
she knew how easy she was getting it.

"*—try after college. What's two more years?*"

"Aren't you going to wade in?" I asked, inclining my head
toward the kitchen.

"—everything! I'm ready now."

Dad shook his head. "They can yell tonight—we'll talk in the morning. Your mom is better with her anyway."

"Oh, no, you're not!"

The implication being that he was better with me. Maybe that was true, once. He and Selena got on well enough when things were going well—which they almost always were with Selena—but whenever they butted heads, it was Mom who intervened. I guessed it was more often the opposite with me. I'd never really thought about that before.

"—the big deal if I use a stage name?"

"It was a good game tonight. You played well."

My skin itched at Dad's compliment. I would have loved hearing it even a week ago. "Yeah." But a week ago I didn't know about Brandon.

"—you'd spit directly on your grandmother's grave?"

"Did you ever wish you'd had a son instead of two daughters?" I started at my own question. Between Mom and Selena arguing in the kitchen, the exhaustion from my own earlier fighting and the game, the filter that had been blocking questions like those failed.

"—you say that when you don't even know him!"

"Instead of you and Selena? Never." He didn't pause before answering, which told me everything and nothing.

"—he your boyfriend?"

"Not instead, then—in addition to."

"—and Dad met at this age, and you're still together!"

"I'm happy with the family I have." Then after a particularly loud bang, he added, "Most of the time."

"—think it was always easy? No!"

Dad's last comment was supposed to be funny, but I didn't smile, and he didn't say anything else.

"Fine!"

"Fine!"

CHAPTER 19

The one bright note from Selena's college-dropout bomb was that our parents were way too distracted to bother enforcing things like a weeklong grounding for me. When Chase invited me to go see his friend's band play the next night, it was as simple as leaving a note in the kitchen and driving away.

My under-twenty-one hand stamp hadn't fully dried before Chase and I spotted each other. I couldn't not smile watching him weave his way toward me through the crowd, or quell my fluttering heart when his arms came around me and he brought his mouth to my ear.

"I missed you."

"Me too," I said/shouted, holding him to me a second longer when he started to pull back. He still smelled like the ocean. The smile I gave him was embarrassingly big, but he seemed to like it based on the one he gave me back. His hands glided from my back to my waist, down my arms to my hands, leaving a trail of goose bumps in their wake. My breath caught when his fingers slid into mine, holding my hand the way he did everything, with no hesitation or uncertainty. I probably should have pulled away. I could have softened the rejection by tucking my hair behind my ear or checking my phone or something. I doubt that he would have made a big deal about it. But I didn't. Being with him that night without being able to ask about Brandon even if I'd wanted to felt like letting air out of a balloon I'd swallowed. That overwhelming constant pressure to *know* abated somewhat. It was almost too loud to think, and he felt good. I felt good being with him. Just for this one night, I decided to let the world stay away.

The band, Laughing Gravy, was pretty good. They did a ton of covers from the '70s, but the arrangements were modern, and a few of the more melancholy songs were murder on my at-the-moment-tender heart. At some point during the set, between songs whose lyrics I'd never remember but whose melodies were indelibly imprinted in my mind, I realized Chase was a guy who could break my heart, and the happy little masochist in my chest only beat harder at the prospect.

Reality intruded enough that I remembered to check the time, and when I could no longer ignore how late it was getting, I rose on my tiptoes to reach Chase's ear and leaned into his side. I was going to tell him I needed to go, but he slid his arm around my back, bringing me even closer. Our eyes met and I knew he was going to kiss me. Worse, I wanted to let him.

And just like that, the metaphorical balloon I'd swallowed inflated back to twice its size. I stepped back and turned my head. "I have to go soon!"

"What?"

Between the thunderously loud music and my still-mostly-gone voice from my game the day before, I wasn't surprised that he couldn't hear me. "Curfew!"

"What?" He shook his head.

I gave up talking and pointed at myself, then the door. That he understood. I led us through the crowds that time, and instead of holding my hand, Chase rested his palm on my lower back. I didn't know if a guy had ever done that with me before—if he had, I'd never realized how intimate it felt until Chase did it.

The air outside wasn't much cooler than inside the bar, but it was cleaner and quieter. The pulsating music inside was still audible, but muted enough that I didn't need to yell for Chase to hear me.

"You okay?" Chase asked.

"Yeah. I just have to get going soon."

"What time is your curfew?"

I told him. I was actually grateful for the curfew, for once. I needed to get away from Chase and clear my head, refocus.

"We still have time. We could grab ice cream—might help your throat." He stepped closer and reached for my hand again. "I don't want to let you go yet."

I didn't want to let him go either. The problem was, I knew he wouldn't feel the same way when he found out who I was.

We ordered our cones—butter pecan for him and cookie dough for me—and started walking toward an empty bench outside. The ice cream felt amazing on my abused throat, and it wasn't long before the rasp smoothed out.

"I really needed this," I said.

"Good?"

"Hmm." I caught a drip that was running down my thumb. "I don't eat ice cream enough. My dad is severely lactose intolerant, so we don't keep any in the house."

"That's my cousin too. He can't even eat pizza without wanting to die the next day." Chase laughed a little. "You'd think that would stop him, but Brandon still eats the stuff a few times a year."

Another drop of ice cream trickled down my wrist and I left it there. My stomach bottomed out at more proof. Another connection to the father Brandon and I shared.

"Yeah, that's commitment right there," I said, my rasp back. I tried to swallow the sudden dryness in my throat, but it didn't work.

"You need a drink?" Chase asked.

"No, my voice is just trashed from my game. It's getting better."

"How are you guys doing?"

"My team? Good. I told you we won last night, so we've only got the one loss. We have a really good team this year." It was easy to slip into softball talk, safe, so I did. I kept waiting for Chase's eyes to glaze over, but they didn't. He asked about my teammates and how long I'd been playing. He asked a lot of questions, and I answered, finding them easier and easier each time. And even though I shouldn't have squandered an opportunity to learn more about my brother, it was all too easy to let my self-consciousness over Brandon fade and my growing awareness of Chase take its place.

Had I thought him just cute the first time we met? That was such an inadequate word for Chase. The way his mouth pulled a little to the side when he smiled and talked at the same time was more than cute. The way he focused completely on my face when I said something, the way he took my hand when we walked and kept asking me about a sport he didn't play or watch because I liked it. Being with him, I could have melted like the ice-cream cone I kept forgetting to eat.

"So what's it like having your dad as your coach?"

I stilled. People had asked me that question my whole life and I normally answered the same way Selena did, saying it was the best of both worlds. But it wasn't like that at all. Rather than give Chase the well-rehearsed line, I told him the truth. "I don't really know. He's not my dad on the field."

Chase frowned. "What does that mean?"

I didn't answer right away, covering my silence by getting up to throw my cone away. "It's this thing he and Selena came up with...or maybe just him—I don't remember. Basically, when we're playing, I'm not his kid and he's not my dad. He's the coach and I'm a player. We don't drag anything from home onto the field, good or bad."

Chase's gaze never left me when I returned to the bench. "You never call him Dad during a game?"

"Nope." I wished I hadn't thrown my cone away, because I had nothing to do with my hands. I picked at a piece of rust on the arm of the metal bench. "My dad...he's never been super affectionate." I rushed through the explanation of him being a foster kid and how it was hard for him, even with Mom, to show his emotions, at least the softer ones, because he was never shown how. "So the coach role on the field isn't all that different from the dad role everywhere else." My voice trailed off as I heard my own words. "I mean, it is, obviously, but he's been a coach since before I was old enough to be on a team. I think it's easier for him to...coach." I fell silent, and so did Chase. "I'm not explaining this right."

"It's fine. I was just curious."

I was grateful when Chase went back to asking about softball instead of my dad, but part of my mind hung back. I felt this need to defend my dad even in the midst of discovering I had a brother. I didn't want Chase thinking my dad was this cold, unfeeling figure in my life. He wasn't really... Like Mom always said, he was trying to show us love the only way he knew how. It didn't always feel like love—the constant scrutinizing focus, the push to work harder and show him I could be good enough...worthy. But I did feel it, even as I wished I didn't have to try so hard. Or I used to, until these nagging thoughts wormed their way into my brain. Until now I'd never had a reason to wonder if the love I craved from him was worth it.

"When do I get to come see you play?"

"Oh, um..." My nerves jangled to life. He couldn't. One look at Dad, and it would be over. Brandon and I shared some traits, sure, but not all, and our genders blurred the resemblance even further. But Brandon and Dad? I wouldn't be able to hide the relationship. I would lose everything.

"To be honest, I think having you there might make me nervous."

"I've seen you hit, Dana. You don't seem like the nervous type."

"Games are different," I said, inventing as I went along. "I've only let one guy come watch me, and the first time he showed, my team still lost."

Chase turned his head. "So it's a superstition thing?"

Okay, sure. "Yes."

"What about the guy?"

"Nick? We've been friends since eighth grade." I started to smile, but my mouth had barely lifted when it died. Based on the way he'd fled from me on Tuesday and hid from me all that day at school, I didn't know if I could call him my friend anymore. That thought made the ice cream in my stomach sour. I still hadn't talked to Nick. His new job had him working after school, and me showing up at the café where he'd be forced to wait on me... No, I wouldn't do that to him on top of everything else. Remembering his face the day before... He'd looked at me like I'd ripped his still-beating heart from his chest and crushed it in my fist. My own heart constricted at the memory. "You'd like him," I told Chase, trying to distract myself from a situation I couldn't even try to fix until tomorrow at school.

Chase angled himself toward me. "This is new, you and me, but I like *you,* Dana."

My heart, already hurting over Nick, lurched at his words. We'd gone out only a few times, but I already liked Chase way too much. I'd liked him too much that first night, and every time I saw him, it got worse...because it got better.

"So do me a favor and tell me, okay?"

There were so many ways that question could be interpreted, and sweat prickled my skin thinking of my options. "Tell you what?"

"When you're ready for me to see you play."

CHAPTER 20

Nick had been at school on Wednesday, but he skipped Biology, so I only caught a glimpse of him between classes. For the first time all year, I was the one tracking him down and waiting outside his classes. I'd never thought about what a pain in the butt that was. Apart from our first period and Biology, the distance between our classes was almost comically far. On Thursday, I had to run, full-out, to be in place by his second-period class before him. Shame hit me anew as I rubbed out a stitch in my side waiting for him. He'd done this for me all the time, in fact most days, and he'd never complained or suggested we take turns.

I realized then, panting and slightly sweaty in the hallway, how much I'd taken our friendship for granted. Not just Nick meeting me between classes or cheering at my games. He'd been there to help me with all the DNA Detective stuff, from fielding my endless questions about the process to helping me brainstorm a covert way to test my dad. That whole week before the results came, I'd put Nick in a situation that made him uncomfortable over and over again because I knew he'd let me. And when I'd insisted I'd found my grandfather and he'd raised totally legitimate reservations, afterward I'd frozen him out rather than admit he was right. All this time, I'd convinced myself that I had to wait for Nick to make the first move so that I wouldn't trample him in a relationship, when, in reality, I already was.

I slumped into the wall at my back, ignoring the people brushing past me, unable to escape the heavy, slimy rocks that had taken up residence in my gut. I'd been so wrapped up in my own stuff that I'd barely asked him what was going on in his life. I didn't even know if he liked his new job, or if Jessalyn was letting her supervisor position go to her head. For months I'd cared only about things that directly connected to me, and that made me scummier than the slime coating my stomach.

Nick saw me as soon as he rounded the corner. I was used to him singling me out in a crowd, and usually he smiled and/or blushed the second we made eye contact. But not this time. This time, he actually shuffled back a few steps, as if being thirty feet away from me was too close. I couldn't blame him, even though the sight added spikes to the rock inside me.

Nick hesitated as the throngs of students around us began to thin, until at last he started walking forward. Closer, closer, his gaze fixed just above my head, until he was near enough for me to realize he was going to walk right into his class without stopping. My eyes stung, and my throat became so thick that I could barely get his name out.

"Nick."

His eyes lowered that fraction of an inch until they met mine. I flinched, cringing inside. He looked so...so...miserable.

"The bell is about to ring. I can't be late." There was no life in his voice, none. I wanted to sink into the floor.

"I'm sorry."

"It's okay—I get it. You don't have anything to be sorry about." He glanced into the classroom, practically twitching to get to his seat—or away from me. My throat closed so completely that I had to swallow twice before I could talk again.

"I do," I said, more than he knew. "Can we—can we talk at lunch?"

He wouldn't look at me. "I can't. I have to make up that Biology quiz I missed yesterday."

He'd skipped class, probably to avoid sitting next to me for an hour. My heart sped up, reaching a lurching gallop in my chest. "Then after school, after practice. I'll come anywhere."

"I work right after school."

"Then I'll meet you at Mostly Bread. I'll—"

For the first time ever, Nick cut me off. "It's always really busy."

I fought to keep my eyes from welling up. The hall was nearly empty by then. One kid was running past us to make it to his class on the opposite end. The bell would ring any second. "I should have told you about a lot of things," I said in a rush. "And the only reason I didn't is because I'm selfish and I'm a coward. Our friendship has been one-sided for so long, you giving, me taking. I've been awful to you and I'm so, so sorry."

"In or out, Mr. Holloway?" his teacher called, reaching for the doorknob.

I looked at Nick, my eyes wide and pleading until his lowered. I knew my fate before he said it.

"In."

My legs were as leaden as my heart as I walked away from his class. That was it. Over. Nick had literally shut the door in my face. I could keep trying, hound him at lunch or trail him between classes. I could follow him to work, where he'd be forced to take my order, if nothing else. I could wear him down, force him to hear me out, but that would just be me asserting my will over his again. I wouldn't do that to him anymore, even as the thought of losing him for good had my chin quivering.

I was already late to my class, so I didn't care that snails could have outstripped me as I pushed open the door to the stairwell.

"Dana?"

My heart shot into my throat at the sound of Nick's voice. I turned my head and saw him jogging toward me.

"What about your class?"

He held up a yellow slip of paper. "My first bathroom pass of the year. I have three minutes."

I wasn't going to waste a single second. "Nick, I'm sorry. I'm sorry for not listening to you, for lying to you, for treating you like you needed to be more than you already are." Pain was blossoming in my chest as I went on, realizing I'd done to him what my dad had done to me—set these arbitrary goals for him to complete, before I...what? Bestowed my favor on him? I looked up at the ceiling, blinking away tears that pounded to be set free before turning back to Nick. "I'm sorry I made you feel like less. You are completely and wonderfully amazing. And I'm not half the friend you are to me, but if you'll let me, I really want to try."

Nick didn't respond. Just as fear that he was going to turn me down sent the rocks in my belly spinning, he did something so much worse.

Where my hand still rested on the door lever, he slid his over top. The movement was jerky, like he had to fight his innate shyness for every inch to reach out and touch me. And it wasn't a commiserating kind of touch either. His fingers tried to wrap around mine.

My eyes lowered shut, blocking out the hopeful lift of his mouth. How had I screwed this up too? My stomach bottomed out as I drew my hand free. "Nick…" But he was already leaping away.

"I'm sorry!"

I hurried after him. "No, it's my fault. I didn't say it right. Wait!" I darted in front of him. "Please don't go. I want to talk to you about this. I should have before now, but I…was being selfish." I lowered the hands I'd held up to stop him. He looked like he was willing to split himself in two to get around me. The acid sloshing in my stomach showed me exactly what that would feel like. "Actually, I'm still being selfish. If you want to go, you should go. But I'm the one who's sorry. *You* don't have a single thing to apologize for."

When he didn't immediately bolt, I pressed on.

"You might be the best person I know." *Might, nothing.* "And you're smart and kind, and I want to feel the same way back—I want it so bad…" I couldn't blink fast enough to keep the tears from welling in my eyes. "Please don't hate me, not for that."

Nick's face was as blotchy as a Samoan guy's could get, but he wasn't hiding from me. And he wasn't running. "I could never hate you. And I knew that you didn't—that you don't—I know. I knew before I heard you say that there was someone else."

I already feel more for him than I ever will for Nick—that's what he'd heard me say about Chase. My heart stopped in my chest and seemed to refuse to start again.

A small line of ants abandoned a sticky puddle of soda someone had spilled in the hallway and marched their way over the toe of Nick's sneaker. He didn't kick them off or jump away or anything; he just lowered his head. "It's okay."

It wasn't remotely okay. My chin was quivering again, and I wanted to bend down and flick every last ant off for him. "I should have told you."

Still ignoring the ants, he said, "Yeah."

"Can we—can we still be friends?"

Nick flinched at the *f*-word. "Is it okay if I say no?"

The air whooshed out of me.

"Maybe not forever, but for now, okay?"

I nodded frantically. It was either that or cry. He'd feel like he had to stay if I cried. The ants had made their way to my shoes now, flip-flops. "Sure."

"It's just that—"

"You don't have to explain."

He looked up, met my gaze for half a second before lowering his again. "I should get back."

I tried to smile. "Yeah, no. Go."

I watched him trudge back to his class, then disappear inside.

I stood there until the last ant left.

CHAPTER 21

Selena was sitting on my bed watching TV with a bowl of popcorn when I got home. Mom and Dad were sequestered behind their office doors, and from the snippets of conversation I'd heard, they were still trying to figure out what to do about Selena.

She didn't glance away from the TV when I came in. "Hey."

"Hey," I said. I didn't feel like talking to anyone, and it was another sister perk that I knew Selena wouldn't make me. I stretched out my legs as I joined her on my bed, then added another "Hey!" when I saw the boxes and luggage piled on the floor. "What the fresh hell is this?"

Selena rolled onto her side, glanced at her stuff, then rolled back. "Oh yeah. That's my stuff."

"Okay, but what's it doing in my room?"

Trickling a fistful of popcorn into her upturned face, Selena said, "I think you mean *our* room."

I slid off the bed and backed toward the door, not taking my eyes off Selena. "Mom. Mom! Can you come up here?" Selena picked up the remote—*my remote*—and raised the TV volume. "Mom!" I called again.

"What?" Slow footsteps trudged up the stairs. "And no more yelling in the house ever." Mom stopped in the doorway of my room, looked in, saw Selena, then looked at me. "What is the problem?"

"She's moving home? She's moving into my room?"

Mom rubbed her eyes. "They don't let nonstudents stay in dorms." She extended an arm toward Selena. "Nonstudent."

"Yeah, but—" Selena was still munching popcorn on my bed and dropping the occasional kernel on the bedspread. "That's it? No warning? No conversation? I just come home and find that you guys have moved all her stuff into my room?"

"When you go out despite being grounded, yeah, pretty much." She kissed my cheek. "Don't you girls stay up too late."

I gaped at her retreating back, then turned to my sister. "This is part of your big dream to make it as a singer? Moving back home and sharing a room with your little sister?"

Her response was monotone. "Yeah, Dana. It's a real fairy-tale kind of moment for me—can you try not to ruin it?"

I let my knees buckle as I groaned up at the ceiling. "Come on. What did you think was going to happen? They'd be happy, excited, offer to pay for your apartment in Nashville?"

Selena didn't say anything.

"No way. They don't let people that dumb into college."

Flicking off the TV, Selena moved to sit on the corner

of my bed. "Hey, I'm good. And despite what they—" she pointed down to where we could hear Mom and Dad's muffled conversation "—think about Gavin, he knows his stuff and he's not playing me. If you guys would listen to me sing my own music, you'd see that."

"Fine, but why now? What is so urgent that you can't get your degree first? You'd have a good shot of them supporting you then—better than good."

Selena pulled up her legs. "I'm ready. Singing and writing— I'm good at this, and I don't want to waste more of my life and tuition on something I'm never going to pursue." Her eyes were glassy. "I don't want to be or do anything else—why should I have to wait?"

I joined her on the bed and placed a gentle hand on her shoulder, since she looked ready to cry. In the most understanding voice possible, I said, "But what if you're really crummy and everyone in Nashville hates you?"

She burst out laughing, all trace of impending tears gone. "I forgot how much I hated sharing a room with you."

In that same soothing voice, I said, "I didn't."

She laughed again. "This is just temporary. I am going to Nashville. Maybe not right away, but I am going."

I sighed. "Good, because sharing a room was bad enough when we were little. Wouldn't you rather have the futon in the office?"

"Seriously? Mom and Dad are in there constantly. And besides, your bed is huge."

"Yeah, but I like to do cheer routines in my sleep. What if I accidentally reindeer-kick you in the head in the middle of the night?"

"What if I shave your eyebrows off while you sleep? We're both taking a risk here."

I half laughed. "Fine, but if you sleep with gum in your mouth and it gets stuck in my hair and I have to get a girl mullet, Mom won't be able to save you again."

"That was such a bad look on you, but deal!" she said, leaning back when I semijokingly reached for her throat. "No gum, I promise."

"And you can't be a slob."

"How would you even notice?" She wrinkled her nose as she glanced around the room.

"Everything is exactly where I want it. Here." I toed the bottom drawer of my dresser. "You can have this one, and I'll make some room for you in my closet."

She offered me the popcorn bowl. "Thanks, Dana. And it's only for a little while. I have to get a job and start saving. That's the condition Mom and Dad set for me staying here. If I'm not going to school, I have to work and pay rent."

"Those bastards."

"Ha ha. It's not a lot of rent, but it'll take longer before I have enough to get to Nashville and find a little place. Gavin thinks I have a good shot, and I can get a job once I'm there until..." She raised her shoulders and grinned.

"Yeah, so Gavin." We both scooted until we were leaning against my headboard. Selena had never been the type to get excited over a guy. She'd had boyfriends, some for longer than others, but they were never the center of her universe. I was already getting the impression that Gavin was different.

Selena grabbed my arms. "You are going to love him. He's really funny and so talented. And he's got these eyes." She fell sideways on the bed with a bounce. "You'll die. I still do every time." She sat up just as suddenly. "And he really likes me— *likes me*, likes me. We're talking about the future and things I've never wanted to seriously talk about with another guy."

"Wow, Sel. I had no idea." I couldn't help but feel hurt that she'd kept all that from me. She had a serious guy that she had serious guy feelings for and hadn't told me. I'd told her everything about Nick, and I'd only ever had lukewarm feelings for him. And if the circumstances had been different, I'd have called her after that first night with Chase and spilled too.

"I don't get why you waited to tell us about singing and Gavin," I said. "Why not ease us into a new boyfriend and make this radical life shift...less radical?"

"I don't know. At first, I was too nervous. I didn't tell any of my friends the first time I sang in public—outside of church—and I barely got through two songs before I wanted to drop my mic and flee. But there was this one guy who kept eye contact with me the whole time until I forgot about the nervous-about-singing part and just thought about the nervous-over-the-cute-guy part. We ended up talking afterward, and then I saw him the next day, and the next, and I don't think I've gone a day since without talking to him. He's so it for me, you know?"

"Uh-huh."

Selena rolled her eyes. "Don't give me that. Sometimes people just know and they don't want to pretend otherwise. Look at Mom and Dad. They met when they were both freshmen in college, and Mom said she knew she was gonna marry Dad after the first date. Here they are, two kids and twenty-two years of marriage later, and they still go to the movies and make out. I want that too."

Three kids later was what she should have said. I slunk off the bed. "It's not like they have a perfect marriage."

"Um, yeah, they kind of do."

Turning my back to her, I worried my lower lip. "Wasn't Mom just telling you the other night that they went through some problems?"

"Obviously not big problems. We exist, and they're still married."

"Yeah, but what if they just never told us? What if it was so bad they couldn't? Did she say if they ever thought about splitting up?"

Selena laughed. "And you just accused me of being the dumb one. Of course not."

"But how would we even know? I've never heard them talk about problems early on in their marriage. Maybe that's because they wanted to keep something from us—something one of them did."

"What, like maybe Mom held up a liquor store or Dad shot a man just to watch him die?"

"I'm being serious."

She threw a piece of popcorn at my head. "You're being dramatic. They had no money when they got married. Dad had to get a second job once Mom got too pregnant with me to keep hers, and they were both in school. So, yeah— I think it was probably hard, especially when Mom moved back home for a while to help take care of *Abue* the first time he got sick, but—"

"Mom moved back home?" My hands curled at my sides. "Dad didn't go with her?"

"Between work and school, he couldn't. It was just for a few months. I was barely a year old, so I don't remember. It doesn't matter—they had normal problems and they solved them. Together. End of story." She shook her head at me. "Now are you going to give me the remote or do I have to chuck something harder than popcorn at you?"

I didn't move beyond letting her reclaim the remote. That had to be it. Mom had taken one-year-old Selena with her to Texas while Dad had stayed here. I didn't know if they'd fought about her leaving or what, but I did know that Selena was almost exactly a year and nine months older than Brandon.

CHAPTER 22

I had more softball tournaments on Saturday, which kept my mind and body distracted during the day, but the evening at home would have been hard if not for Chase. His text was waiting for me as soon as I checked my phone.

Chase: So?

Me: win, Win, WIN!

Chase: You have to let me come see you play one of these days.

Me: What about you, are you winning at work?

Chase: Only had one guy not show up. What does that count as, a tie?

Me: Seriously?

Chase: I was getting ready to fire him anyway.

Me: Did he at least call?

Chase: Hold on, I can't text while I'm laughing.

Me: I would have been pissed.

Chase: I was.

Me: I would still be pissed.

Chase: Come by. I guarantee I'll be the opposite of pissed.

Me: Who was it that bailed? Not your cousin?

Chase: No, Brandon's here. He's who I called in to replace the no-show. Can you come? I'll ply you with free smoothies and you can tell me about your games.

Me: I'm pretty beat. It's taking all my energy to move my thumbs right now.

Chase: My loss.

Me: Mine too.

Chase: Should I let you go?

Me: Not unless you have to.

Chase: Never.

On Sunday it went back to being hard. We went to church as a family, sat in our normal pew as a family and drove home afterward as a family, but we didn't do anything else that day as a family. We didn't talk much at all. Everyone was nursing hurt or angry emotions. We normally cooked lunch together on Sundays, but that day we just didn't.

Instead Selena and I disappeared into my bedroom. She job-hunted online while I lay on my bed, tossing a softball toward the ceiling over and over again, hoping Chase would text and trying not to think about Mom taking care of her sick father while Dad was here with another woman.

"Anything promising?" I asked.

"Oh yeah. My dishwashing skills are highly in demand."

"No openings for spoiled princesses with no work history?"

"You want to apply too?"

Neither of us had ever worked. Between school and sports, we didn't have the time. I kind of liked the idea of getting a job, though, especially now that I was trying to avoid being home with my parents as much as possible. I'd suggested Mostly Bread, but either Nick was doing such a good job that they didn't need anyone else, or they'd only ever had the one opening.

An hour later, Selena had a list of places she planned to apply to. She read them off to me and we narrowed the list further.

"I think I'll put in for Lava Java, Name Brand Exchange, AJ's Grocery and Jungle Juice."

The softball I was throwing hit me smack in the face. "What—which Jungle Juice?"

She continued typing. "Whichever one will have me. I can put in for all the ones in the area and then see who responds."

I was overwhelmingly glad she was looking at her laptop and not at me. If I looked half as paranoid as I felt with my eyes bugging out, I would never have gotten away with the lie I told.

"Why would you want to work there? Have you ever been?"

"It's a smoothie place. I like smoothies."

"Do you also like screaming monkey calls every time the front door opens?"

She swiveled in the chair to face me. "Do they really do that?"

"Yep. My friend Ariel works at one. She says most people quit within a month and the management structure is horrible. People flake on shifts all the time," I said, using Chase's story from the night before to lend my semi-lie the ring of truth I needed to really sell it. "Whoever is there ends up doing the work of, like, three people without extra pay. She's planning on quitting herself."

Selena wrinkled her nose. "I guess that's a no to Jungle Juice." She turned back to her laptop, and I breathed for the first time in a full minute.

What would I have done? There weren't that many Jungle Juice locations in Arizona. Chase knew I had a sister named Selena, and we looked enough alike that people often mistook us for twins. On top of that, I *knew* that Selena would recognize something in Brandon if she saw him. She might not put together that he was our brother, but she'd know something connected them. I still hadn't decided what I was going to say or even really if I was going to say anything at all. Right now she and Mom were happy; they didn't know that Brandon existed. And maybe Dad didn't either.

I went back to throwing my softball until my equilibrium returned, but once I started thinking about Brandon, I couldn't stop. And thinking about my brother while our dad was downstairs was unbearable.

I eventually escaped to Jessalyn's. We still needed to talk, and not just the few sentences we'd been exchanging during games or practices since the fallout with Nick. We weren't exactly fighting, but we weren't not fighting either. I was mad at her and she was mad at me, but I'd also screwed up and couldn't claim I was the only injured party. I think she felt the same way.

Jessalyn lived only a few blocks away from me, but I still drove in case things didn't go well and I needed to go somewhere else to avoid my family. Unaware of any rift between us, her mom let me in when I got there and sent me upstairs.

Jessalyn's room looked like it had been designed for a ten-year-old princess, which was exactly what she was to her parents—the princess part, anyway. Everything was pink and fluffy or pink and gauzy or pink and...pink. There was nothing that reflected the self-admitted tomboy who lived there, and it was Jessalyn's favorite place in the world. She was particularly in love with the pink toile canopy surrounding her bed that was currently obscuring most of her body.

The door was open, but I still knocked on the door frame.

Jessalyn rolled onto her side, saw me, then returned to her stomach and the laptop she was using. She finished whatever she was typing, closed the laptop, then sat up and faced me. "Hey."

Relief hit me at the way she said that word. I hadn't been sure if she was still angry—I hadn't been sure if *I* was still angry—but there wasn't a trace of hostility in her voice.

"Hey back." I didn't flop onto her bed like I normally did. I claimed a corner, pushing the heavy canopy back so that I could sit. We didn't say anything else. I felt like I had the grievance, but I knew she felt that way too. If we both weren't so stubborn, we might have been able to talk it out. Instead we waited for the other to do the thing we couldn't or wouldn't do ourselves.

So I deflected.

"You didn't tell me you were close to failing History. You know we don't have a shot at making the finals if you get put on academic probation."

Jessalyn's back stiffened. "Who told you that?"

I wasn't touching that question. I knew only because I'd lied to Dad about hanging out with her so that I could see Chase. "Is it true?"

"It's a stupid report." She flopped back on her bed with enough force to communicate her feelings perfectly. "Who cares about a bunch of kings who died half a millennium ago?"

"If it means the difference between you playing with us or not, *you* need to. Come on, I'll help you." I reached for her laptop, but she covered the lid with her hand before I could open it.

"Is this really why you came over? Homework?"

I drew my hand back and broke eye contact. After a moment, I said, "No."

"Okay, then, what? 'Cause last I checked, we were both pretty pissed at each other. And I know you talked to Nick and...it didn't go great."

I let out a sound halfway between a laugh and a sob.

"So are we fighting? What are we doing?"

"We're not fighting," I said. "We're just..."

Jessalyn spun away from me and stood, taking her laptop and setting it on her dresser across the room. When she turned around and leaned her hands on the dresser, she just shrugged her shoulders. "Feels like fighting."

"You want to fight?"

"No, I want to talk. I've wanted to talk for a long time. You're the one who won't tell me anything."

"That's because it's awful! Everything!" A tear that I hadn't even felt forming escaped from one eye. "My supposed grandfather, the one I was so excited about finding? Turns out he's my brother. Yeah," I said when Jessalyn's jaw dropped open. "He was even more horrified by me than I was of him. He won't talk to me or help me figure out how this could have happened. I mean, my parents... You know them... You know my dad... How..." I was drawing in each breath faster than the one before it. "I don't understand, and I can't tell anyone, because then they'd feel like this too...like I can't breathe, and I don't know what I'm supposed to do and it hurts all the time and—" I finally choked off as Jessalyn wrapped both her arms around me.

"It's okay. It's okay."

But it wasn't. I didn't know if it would ever be okay again.

I told Jessalyn everything. About Chase being Brandon's cousin and his having no idea who I really was. I told her about the picture I'd stumbled upon and how I still didn't know if my dad knew he had a son. She listened, but there wasn't much she could do besides offer a shoulder to cry on, which she did—both of them. When she'd asked me what I was going to do, I could only shake my head. I left sometime before my eyes completely swelled shut from crying and after Jessalyn promised she'd let me know if she really did need help with her report.

Despite Jessalyn's best efforts, I still felt too miserable to go home, so I drove past Jungle Juice instead, hoping Chase might be working and Brandon wouldn't. I was wrong on both counts.

I parked out front and watched my brother through the windows, the lights inside making the interior visible against the dark outside. Ariel was working with him. Every time he thought she wasn't looking, he was staring at her. It was almost pathetic the way he watched her, but the expression on his face—even from thirty feet away in the parking lot—was so nakedly adoring that I found myself smiling at his complete lack of girl game. Ariel knew he was staring—of course she did. He couldn't see the small smiles on her lips each time she caught him and he looked away. I wanted to shake him and tell him to just ask her out already. If we'd grown up together

like a real brother and sister, I would have. Selena would have
helped. My chest tightened at that thought.

The three of us. Brother and sisters. Selena and I had a
brother. Nothing else I found out about our parents would
change that.

I'd never pined for a brother like some kids. It had never
been an option. Mom's pregnancy with me had been hard, and
it was never a secret that she couldn't have more kids after me.
We'd always known Selena and I were it. But watching Brandon, I could imagine what it might have been like. Learning
to ride bikes, hitting our first ball, catching our first fish. And
then there were all the memories he would have been a part
of: Christmases and birthdays and visits to Mexico and body
surfing and learning to make Tía Magdalena's refried beans
and camping and road trips and playoffs and putting up post-
ers when our dog, Slammer, ran away. I didn't even realize
I was crying until the first tear dripped onto my collarbone.

We'd missed all of that. And we were missing more, every
day. These were memories we couldn't have. And the more
I thought about them, the more the idea of them shifted and
faded. Even if we could go back, knowing about Brandon,
it wouldn't be as simple as reliving life with him in the picture. He wasn't Mom and Dad's son. He was the son of Dad
and another woman. It would never have been the five of
us singing carols around the Christmas tree or squished together in the back seat during a family road trip with Mom
and Dad yelling at us from the front. It might not have been
Mom and Dad at all.

Inside Jungle Juice, Brandon and Ariel were doing one
of those awkward two-steps where they both kept moving

in the same direction trying to pass the other. Finally, Ariel stopped and slapped her hand on the counter. Whatever she said to Brandon made his eyes go wide. He said something short back to her, and she responded with a quick nod before grabbing the front of his shirt and kissing him. My brother might have been weak in the warm-up department, but he wasn't lacking in follow-through. I could almost hear her squeak of surprise when his arms circled her and he kissed her back. I joined her in laughing at the look on his face when they broke apart. I looked the same way every time I won a softball game. Selena and I both did. All three of us had inherited the same expression from our dad.

I made it home just before curfew and ducked into the office to say good-night when I saw that Dad had already gone to bed.

"Wait, wait, wait. How was studying?" Mom asked, her head turned in my direction but her eyes still locked on whatever she was typing on her computer. "Did you actually do homework this time?"

"We talked about homework—does that count?"

With a dramatic mouse click, Mom turned her full attention to me. "There, I—" Her smile was replaced by a frown. "Honey, what happened?" She was at my side in a moment, her voice matching the softness of her hands as she cupped my face. "You look like you were crying."

She let me pull away. "Oh yeah. Jess and I—we kind of had this fight, sort of. It was dumb, but it's fine now."

"Yeah?"

I nodded. "Yeah."

She tilted her head to the side, holding my gaze as she brushed her thumb over my cheek. "Wanna talk about it? I'll share my Kisses with you."

I hugged her. Mom didn't like sharing her chocolate.

"Is that a yes?" she asked when I held on too long. I could hear the smile in her voice.

Not yet, I thought, *not yet*.

In my room, Selena was snoring on the side of the bed I usually slept on. I changed into shorts and a T and slipped into the other side as quietly as possible. After a minute, I whispered, "Sel?"

No answer. I looked over at her. Not so much as a twitch in her eyelid moved.

"Sel?"

Still nothing.

I took a breath. Saying it out loud was so bittersweet. "We have a brother. His name is Brandon, and I think you'd like him. I think we both would."

CHAPTER 23

Between his work and class schedules and softball, I had to wait another two days before I saw Chase again. I met him in the parking lot outside Jungle Juice after practice on Tuesday. He'd told me just to come in when I got there, but I'd caught a glimpse of Brandon through the window and knew that couldn't happen. Just being in the parking lot when Brandon was working was a risk, but I was too eager—for a lot of things—to care.

"Hey," Chase said when he reached my car and rested his hands on my open window. Every part of me lit up seeing him. I nearly bounced in my seat. Nearly. "I thought you were coming in. You can meet my cousin."

The bouncing urge vanished in an instant and was replaced by a desire to slink to the floor. "Oh yeah. I had to call my sister." I held up my phone as if I needed to offer him proof. "Did you tell him you were meeting me?"

"No, I thought I'd just let him meet you." He inclined his

head back toward Jungle Juice. "We can go in real quick and say hi." He considered me. "Does it bother you that I didn't tell him about you?"

"No!" I probably answered too fast. "I mean, I haven't mentioned you to my sister either, so I'd be kind of a hypocrite if I said it did."

"Come in with me and meet him."

"Um, I'm actually starving. Another time?" I busied myself with putting my phone back into my bag so I wouldn't see if Chase was confused by my reticence. That was twice now that I'd turned down a chance to meet the guy he considered a brother. So far my excuses had been tired and hungry. What was I going to say next time? Feign an illness? Based on the way my stomach was squirming, I might not be lying.

"Okay. Where do you want to eat?"

I picked a taco place nearby—close enough that he wouldn't think to question my starving claim, but far enough from Brandon that my stomach settled enough to let me actually eat.

We found a shaded table outside after ordering and I was beginning to relax again when Chase said, "So how come you haven't told your sister about me?"

The question caused my hand to jerk and topple my drink. The lid held, but I felt as flustered as I would have had it spilled.

"Sorry."

"Low blood sugar again?"

"Must be." I took a huge gulp from my drink. "This is helping."

He was still eyeing me a little askance, though I couldn't

tell if it was due to physical concern or him picking up on the fact that I was delaying answering him.

"So?"

It wasn't that I didn't want to tell Selena about Chase; I did. But she'd want to know everything about him, and she'd 100 percent end up telling Mom, who'd insist on having Chase over. With Nick, Mom already knew him, so she'd given me a little leeway on the meet-the-parents dinner front. But she'd never even seen Chase, which meant I wouldn't have a say in the matter. Which also meant he'd meet Dad, which…no.

"I guess it's just been kind of hectic for a while, what with her dropping out of college and trying to become a singer. Every time we talk lately, it's about that or softball." I had to put my drink down and hide my shaking hands under the table when I returned the question. "What about you? You haven't mentioned me either."

Chase smiled at me. "Brandon's got his own girl problems going on. Didn't feel like rubbing it in how good things are going with mine."

One corner of my mouth lifted. "Good, huh?"

He leaned toward me, resting his forearms on the table. "Great."

The other corner lifted and my heart rate sped up. The table was too big for me to lean forward and…meet him… but the idea had me tingling all the way down to my toes.

When our food came, Chase sat back against his chair. "And anyway, Brandon's never been great with…"

"Girls?"

"That too." He laughed, picking up his carne asada taco. "More just relationships. His dad never remarried after his mom died, never even dated that I know of. So the idea of being with someone or even really hearing about it second-hand…not my cousin's favorite thing."

"Your uncle must have really loved her." My voice sounded so far away in my ears. It wasn't strained or shaky. I almost felt like I was in a trance, watching myself calmly ask questions about the woman my dad had had an affair with. "What was her name?"

"Maggie—Margaret McCormick."

Maggie. My mom's name was Adriana. It always sounded so nice in my head along with my dad's: Dennis and Adriana. I liked them together. Dennis and Maggie clashed with a physical pain in my chest, a throb that I half lifted my hand to press away.

"And yeah, he loved her," Chase went on. "My mom must have taken thousands of photos of them, and it's impossible to miss, but I don't think Brandon has seen half of them. Uncle Bran can't bring himself to look at them, so they're buried in boxes somewhere in the abyss that is my mom's garage…"

"What?" I asked, my hand sliding toward him, distracted from all the info Chase was giving me by the way his voice fell off.

He bit into his taco and chewed a long time before swallowing and answering me. "I told you my mom is a photographer. What I didn't tell you is that she's also kind of a hoarder." He lifted his taco again but stopped it an inch from his mouth and lowered it back to his plate. "I hate that word. You immediately think of those TV shows with people buried under newspapers and broken toaster collections or something. She's not like that."

She was like something, though. The muscles along the side of Chase's jaw tightened.

"She has a hard time letting go of things. After my father left, she tried to keep everything."

"I get that."

Chase didn't smile, not exactly. "Yeah, well, it's a problem. I had an apartment with a few guys right after high school, but I had to move back home recently. I brought my last box the day we met."

I'd been pretty well consumed with my own issues that night, but I remembered him saying he hadn't had the greatest day. When I'd asked why he'd felt the need to smash something afterward, he'd told me to ask him later. I guessed it was later.

"There are three bedrooms, but hers is the only one you can still get into. I don't even know if there's still a bed in my old room."

"Then where do you sleep?"

"On the couch."

I made a face. Chase was the opposite of small. Even if it was a massive couch, I doubted it was comfortable.

"Apart from a suitcase I keep by the couch, everything I own is in the garage right now, piled up in boxes next to I don't even know what—back issues of magazines, old Christmas decorations, clothes that fit no one and so many photo albums."

My blood pressure spiked at the mention of more photo albums, maybe photos from when Brandon was born, from the hospital, but I didn't have to fight myself to stay focused on

Chase and the sadness in his voice. "That's why you needed to revisit your old apartment."

"I love my mom, but she can't let go of anything. She hid how bad it had gotten from me, but when I moved home and tried to get into my old room…yeah. I needed to break something, and it was the closest I could get to him."

I'd kept my hand stretched toward him, and at this I inched it the rest of the way to his. There was no joking lilt or smile from Chase. Like everything else he said, he laid it bare. My hand tightened around his, another ache joining the one already in my chest.

"Chase, I'm sorry."

"Me too. She's willing to let me help her. She doesn't like seeing me squeeze onto the couch each night any more than I like doing it. If I could clear out the garage, I could relocate everything in my old room out there."

"And she'd be okay with that?"

"She wants to be, but I need to do it when she's not home—otherwise she'll have a harder time with it than she already will."

"That's good," I said. "I mean, it's a start, right?"

"It is." He started in on the burrito he'd also ordered. "It's just hard right now between work and school, and wanting to see this girl I can't stop thinking about."

Not even a blink of hesitation at the last remark. I smiled and picked up my taco. I so didn't need the hot sauce I'd dumped on it. Chase was making me feel more than warm. "Maybe that girl would understand and be happy to get you off the couch as soon as possible. Maybe she'd even be willing to help with the garage."

"Yeah?" His smile grew.

"Yeah." But then a thought brought me up short. "Unless you already asked other people for help? What about your cousin?"

Chase took another big bite, swallowing before he answered. "Brandon is…" He paused. "I'm trying to find the right way to say this, since you don't actually know him yet. Honestly, lately it feels like I don't know him."

I forced the bite of taco I'd taken down my suddenly too-tight throat. "What do you mean?"

Chase shook his head. "He's been off for a while. He doesn't want to talk to me or his dad. He barely even talks to my mom, and he's usually really open with her." Chase pulled his mouth to the side. "The only person I've even seen him smile at for weeks is the girl we work with. You met her—Ariel?"

I nodded, not trusting my voice to speak.

"He's been into her for months and he was this close to asking her out, and then something happened—I don't know what. He can't get it together. At all. With any of us. And it's not like he's shy or anything. He's got tons of friends, he plays the guitar, he—"

"He plays the guitar?"

"Yeah, and he's not bad."

My heart had wings for a moment, soaring at the thought of Selena and her newfound musical aspirations, the two of them playing together, only to crash again as Chase went on.

"But it's been weeks since I've heard him play."

Weeks since I showed up and he found out about our dad.

"He came to dinner last month and spent the whole meal staring at this picture my mom has up of his mom. He finally got up and took it right off the wall. Wouldn't say why or anything. He went home and hasn't come back since."

With a finger I nudged my plate away. I thought about Brandon's reaction to me the one and only time we'd met. His life was a complete lie and like me, one of his parents wasn't what he'd thought. I couldn't begin to relate to how that would affect him, knowing the one parent who'd undeniably betrayed him was dead. How would that anger morph when it collided with a lifetime of sorrow? My anger at Dad was still molten more often than not, but he was alive, a living person for me to direct all that unadulterated pain and confusion toward. If he were gone, and I had only a memory—less than a memory—I couldn't begin to guess what I'd feel or what I'd do.

I didn't want to cause Brandon more pain than I already had. I would have walked away that day without telling him the truth. I'd have gone back home, curled up on my bed and died a little and maybe a lot, thinking about him and our dad and clueless as to how I could make any of it hurt less. But I wouldn't have dragged him down with me, him or Selena.

Only.

I still would have found that picture, that one that might or might not mean Dad knew, that he'd betrayed Mom not just with his body but with his heart too. And not just her.

And I'd have gone back to Jungle Juice, watched my brother, learned what little I could about him from Chase while discovering another guy I didn't want to hurt, even as he told me I should. And it wouldn't have been enough. It still wasn't.

A small part of me had been holding out hope that Brandon would get past his initial anger and seek me out the way I had him. That his insatiable need to know would be just as strong as mine, despite the consequences and increased pain that knowledge could bring. Because it didn't come alone; it came with a sibling. But I was learning things about him, about my brother, that told me we were very different people. We had shared DNA, but our lives had been drastically different. If Chase was right about his cousin—and he would be—Brandon wasn't going to change his mind; he wasn't going to take the risk I had. Unless, like with Ariel, somebody grabbed him and made him—and that couldn't be me.

All I could do was keep taking that risk, keep looking for the answer that might gain me a brother but cost me a father.

CHAPTER 24

"Ready?"

In answer to Chase's question the following afternoon, I knelt down and grabbed the handle to lift up the door to his garage. Fading sunlight spilled into the space, although *space* was an inaccurate word. There wasn't any actual space, just stuff, more stuff, and stuff that hid behind and underneath yet more stuff.

"Whoa," I said. "You can't even walk in here."

Chase wrapped a hand around my hip and pulled me until I was standing in front of him, my back to his chest. A fire kindled to life, heat spreading through me until I burned all over. The more time we spent together, the more he'd started touching me. Not like he was looking for opportunities to put his hands on me, but like he was growing comfortable enough with me that he could reach out without having to think about it. And even though I still felt a startling burst of warmth every time we made contact, I was growing more comfortable with him too, when the opposite should have been true.

Ahead of me was a sliver of a path to the back of the garage, but it was so narrow that I couldn't imagine Chase fitting through it. *I might not fit.* I could feel him dwarfing me from behind, taller, wider. The hand he still rested on my hip could have spanned my entire side if he moved it up an inch. That thought sent another pulse of heat through my body, and I spun away.

"So when you said your mom was a bit of a hoarder, you meant she was the queen of all hoarders?"

Chase didn't smile.

"Oh, bad joke."

"A little, yeah." He was staring into the open garage. "Inside the house isn't this bad, but it's not that good either."

If it was a fraction of what the garage looked like, it was far from not good.

"She wasn't like this even a year ago, or I would never have moved out, you know?"

I nodded. Chase was finishing his freshman year of college, something that was taking him longer than I knew he would have liked because he was managing Jungle Juice full-time to pay for school.

"My uncle thinks it's empty-nest syndrome, that she's hanging on to everything she can because she knows she won't be able to hold on to me much longer. Plus, once Brandon leaves for college, my uncle is planning on moving out of state, and I know losing them is going to be hard on her."

There I was, listening to him talk about sad stuff with his

mom, and the first thing I asked about was Brandon. I was not a good person.

"When is he going to college?"

"In the fall."

Four months. Panic scratched over my skin at that timeline. What if I didn't know the truth about my dad by then? What if I did? What if Brandon left before we ever got to know him, or he us?

"Hey, you don't have to do this." Before I could respond, Chase was stretching up beside me to pull the handle down. With our height difference, the only safe part of him I could reach were his ribs. I pressed my palm against him and he stopped, glancing down at me and the place where I was touching him, at the warmth zinging from my body to his. Or was it the other way around?

I was much more reserved in initiating physical contact with him. In fact, this might have been the first time. I'd thought about it, but I always killed the impulse before I could act. It was getting harder to pretend that I wasn't lying to him. I lowered my hands.

"I'm still up for this if you are."

Chase didn't say anything about me touching him or how abruptly I'd stopped touching him. It was a stretch to hope he'd think I was being shy, because I hadn't exactly fled from his touch a few minutes before. Whatever he thought, he didn't make an issue of it. I was relieved and a little surprised. Chase was a pretty forthright guy. He didn't back away from uncomfortable topics, even about himself. He didn't pretend one thing when he thought another.

I wished I could be like that.

"Yeah. I need to before my mom changes her mind." Chase released the garage door, pushing it back the few inches he'd pulled down. He brushed the back of my fingers with his, sending invisible little sparks dancing along each one. "Thanks, Dana." It was the smallest of touches, but I felt it everywhere, and I missed it the second there was space between us again. Rather than dwell on my increasing awareness of him, I turned back to the garage.

The garage, it turned out, wasn't as bad as it had first looked. Most things were organized and carefully boxed. I'd been expecting to find chaos and junk mixed together, but Chase's mom had been meticulous in her storage. That wasn't to say there was nothing to throw away. We filled Chase's truck with boxes of old magazines and old toys. There were tattered board games and an entire trunk of self-help books that went too. And Chase's stuff had been scattered throughout, wherever he'd been able to find room when he moved back. We set his stuff aside to bring in later, not wanting to waste what little daylight we had left.

An hour later and I was, if anything, more aware of Chase than ever. I was aware of the way he breathed when lifting a heavy box. I was aware of the way the muscles shifted in his arms when he raised them, and the glimpse of exposed skin below his T-shirt when he reached for anything high. But I was more aware of the way he laughed halfway through the jokes he told, like he'd already reached the punch line in his head and couldn't help himself. I was hyperaware of the way he talked about his whole family with such easy love. He held nothing back. His openness made it easy for me to ask questions and harder to look at him when I did.

It also made the process go the other way. We talked about softball and how I wanted to play in college and maybe even beyond, if I could.

"Why couldn't you?"

I sidestepped a folded treadmill and opened a box marked CDs. "Because there are more girls who want the same thing than there are team spots to go around." I held up a CD. "Please tell me you're the Cher fan."

"My mom's. But back to softball. You don't think you'd make a team? Haven't you been playing your whole life?"

"Do you know how many pro softball teams there are in this country? Six." I let that number sink in. It was a far cry from the NFL. "Each team has a max of 23 players, which means that there are only 138 girls playing at a time. That's it. And to really sweeten the pot, the average player makes between five and six thousand dollars a season. It's not exactly a lucrative career."

"That sucks."

"It does, but there are still way more than 138 girls who want exactly what I want. They've been playing their whole lives too. I'm good, one of the better players on my team, but I'm not the best, not even in my own family. Sometimes I get too caught up in winning and what my dad is thinking—my dad, not my coach—and I don't always play as smart as I need to." I gave Chase a quick smile from over my shoulder so he wouldn't ask any follow-up questions about my dad. "I'm not saying it's impossible, but I need to focus on getting my team to state this year first."

A flicker of resentment hit me when I turned back to the CDs. Selena had had interest from colleges long before she graduated, all wanting her to play for them. Dad hadn't been the only one dumbfounded when she'd turned them all down. He'd been crushed by disappointment—I'd just been mad. She was so good, and she didn't even want to play; it didn't mean anything to her. I supposed she'd already been flirting with the idea of singing, even then, but I still had moments when I couldn't help hating her a little—sometimes a lot— for caring so little about something I'd kill to be as good at.

"Hey, I've seen you hit," Chase said. "I think you're better than good."

"Yeah, well, you should see my sister. She's insane. She could've played anywhere and been one of the best, if not *the* best, players in the country."

"Yeah?"

"Which is why it kills me that she wants to sing. It's like…" I turned again and rested my forearms on the box of CDs I'd reclosed. "Remember when Michael Jordan decided he wanted to play baseball instead of basketball? He could have been a decent baseball player, but he was never going to be anything close to what he was on a basketball court."

"So she's the Michael Jordan of softball?"

"See, that's just it—she could have been the Selena Fields of softball, and she didn't want it. It pisses me off so much sometimes."

"I can see that." Chase shifted another box in front of him. "Have you heard her sing?"

"Not really. She's sung in church before, but always with

other people. If she's really awful, the softball thing will just kill me all over again."

"And if she's good?"

I moved next to Chase, who was sorting through a box of fake flowers. "It'll still kill me." I smiled to let him know I wasn't overly morose about the subject.

"Remind me again when you need to leave for your game?"

Without looking up from the newspaper-wrapped china I was going through, I said, "I have a few minutes."

Chase laughed. "Home or away?"

"Home."

"Cutting it pretty close, aren't you?"

I was. More than close. But despite the speech I'd just given Chase about wanting to play softball, I felt only a little of the urgency that usually flooded me before a game. "I'll make it." And I would. I'd be there on time and not a second sooner. My *coach* could worry all he wanted.

CHAPTER 25

Having a roommate again for the first time since I was four-teen wasn't as bad as I remembered. Selena didn't leave her stuff everywhere or hog the covers, and thanks to her new job at Lava Java, my room perpetually smelled like coffee, which had its perks. It also helped that she was working most evenings or prepping for her next "gig." That was the actual word she used.

"Why can't you just say open mic at the coffee shop?" I asked as we were trying to make two people's worth of cloth-ing fit into my one-person-sized closet.

"Because I'm in denial. So are you coming to the next one or not?"

"Of course I'm coming."

"You're not going to show up at the last possible second?"

I ignored her dig about my last game. She'd already told me exactly what she thought of my "abominably disrespectful at-titude and shameful disregard for my teammates and coach."

The teammate remark had stung, because they'd all been a little to a lot annoyed with me. Jessalyn and I were pretty much back to our pre-not-fight-but-still-mostly-a-fight dynamic after that day at her house, but even she'd been a little frosty for the first couple innings. If we'd lost, she'd have really laid into me.

"I said I'll be there. On time. When is it?"

"Next week."

"And will you be signing autographs afterward or do I have to stalk you in the parking lot?" I braced my back against a mass of hanging T-shirts, propped my foot on the opposite wall of the closet and pushed. Selena squeezed half a dozen more hangers into the newly revealed space.

"Don't."

"What? Push from the other side and you can fit a few more. We won't be able to get anything out, but that's a problem for future us."

Selena's arms stayed at her side. "Don't make jokes. I'm trying to do something here. It's important to me."

"So you can make jokes about me but I can't about you?"

"Just don't. Not about this."

"Okaaaayyy."

"I'm nervous."

"Me too." I eyed the closet, half expecting the whole thing to explode the second I extricated myself from inside. I did it in a dash. The clothing swelled back together and the hanging rod bowed a little but held. Fears abated, I grinned at Selena, but she wasn't even looking at the closet. "Wait, you're nervous because of me?"

"Yeah."

"That's stupid." I grabbed another armful of clothes from her open suitcase, took one look at the near-bursting closet and headed for the dresser instead. "I know you'll be great."

"My feelings aren't stupid."

"Thank you, Dr. Phil. You know what I mean. When have we ever not supported each other? You come to almost all my softball games, and I've been to every one of yours. This'll just be the same minus the giant foam fingers and face paint."

She smiled.

"I'll start cheering when you walk up to the mic." Laying the clothes atop my dresser, I cupped my hands around my mouth. "Come on, Selena! You got this, you got this. Just keep your eye on the—" I lowered my hands, unsure of the singing-related equivalent to *ball* in this case "—crowd?"

"Gavin says it's good to pick one person and focus on singing just to them."

"Okay." I brought my hands back to my mouth. "Keep your eye on the randomly selected person. Wooo!"

The tightness around her mouth eased. "Now I'm nervous you're actually going to do that." She still did look uneasy, so I dropped the teasing altogether.

"I can slip in the back if you want. You won't even have to see me until you're done."

"No, I want you there."

"Then I'll be there."

"Thanks," she said as I knelt and started emptying my bottom dresser drawer for her. "But not Mom and Dad. I'm not ready for them yet."

"Just me and a coffee shop full of strangers." I glanced at her over my shoulder. "And Gavin?"

"He'll be there, but you'll meet him before then. He's coming to your next game."

"Now *I'm* nervous."

"You'll like him. Trust me."

"I can still be nervous. I usually hate your boyfriends, and you basically told me he's going to be my brother-in-law."

Selena's cheeks flushed in a smile. "I kind of did, didn't I?"

I sat on my heels, immobilized by the sheer joy in her expression. "You're not nervous about that at all, are you?"

"Gavin? No. I'm more sure of him than I've ever been of anything. These two weeks he's been home visiting his family have been the longest of my life."

She looked so radiant, talking about him and the future she saw unfolding for them. It was hard not to get caught up along with her.

"I'm happy for you, Sel."

"I'm happy too." She joined me on the floor. "I'm a college dropout, sharing a room at home with my baby sister, working a minimum-wage job. My parents think I'm throwing away my future, and I've literally never been happier."

"You're living the dream."

She grinned. "What about you? Anything new with Nick?"

I hung my head, wishing she hadn't asked. "I kind of broke him."

"Oh no, really? When?"

"About a week ago. It was awful. I'm a terrible person, and he's way too sweet for me." I'd seen Nick at school, and while he wasn't hiding from me anymore, the quick looks away when our eyes met and awkward shared Biology classes made it feel like he was.

"That sucks," Selena said. "I am sorry, but I could kind of tell you weren't super into him."

"I wanted to be."

"I've been there." She rubbed a circle on my back. "I can only tell you that trying to like a guy you don't have the right kind of feelings for will only make you both miserable in the end."

"You also end up miserable when you tell him the truth and he barely talks to you anymore."

"Eek." Her hand fell away. "But then, who have you been going out with so much recently—and don't say Jessalyn, because you did not use up half my favorite lip gloss to look pretty for her."

"That lip gloss looks way better on me."

She gave me a look. "So who's the guy?"

I inwardly winced. Bringing up Chase could be tricky. "Just someone I met. It's not serious."

"Does Mr. Not Serious have a name?"

My brain told me to shut up but my mouth said, "Chase." I got to my feet and grabbed more of Selena's clothes, but she followed me.

"You're not getting out of telling me about him. Spill."

"I kind of don't...want to."

"Oh, then in that case." She shrugged in a way that made her look exactly like our mom before pinning me with a stare. "You still have to spill."

I dropped onto the bed. If I was careful, I could tell her a little. I wanted to tell a little. Apart from everything with Dad and Brandon, thinking about Chase was becoming too easy.

"He's a guy. I don't know. I like him, but..."

"But what?"

"There's just stuff." I clasped my hands between my knees. "I don't know if it'll work out."

Selena rose to her feet and resumed putting her clothes away. "But it might?" She was trying to offer casual encouragement without all the pesky facts getting in the way. It was a nice attempt, but that's all it could be.

I gave her a bright smile. "Sure. Anyway, we're just hanging out for now." I didn't want to field more questions about Chase. The few she'd already asked were way too depressing. "But hey, if it doesn't work out, maybe Gavin has a younger friend he could set me up with?"

Selena pounced on that suggestion and immediately dropped the subject of Chase in favor of Gavin's plethora of awesome single friends. I only half listened, hoping that somehow, in ways I couldn't yet figure out, maybe Chase and I *could* work out.

CHAPTER 26

I closed my door harder than I needed to, wanting to draw Chase's attention when I got out of my car. His back was toward me, muscles straining as he lifted down a cracked fish tank full of random tchotchkes that must have been as heavy as it was immense. He turned and smiled, and I felt a frisson of happiness skip across my sternum as I jogged up his driveway to help him.

My fingers abutted his as I took some of the weight from him—not a lot, since the discrepancy in our size and strength was pretty vast, but enough that he was able to lower the tank without the whole thing shattering.

The thing was huge, barely smaller than a bathtub.

"What did you keep in there, a shark?"

"An iguana."

"Seriously?" It was hard to picture Chase as a little kid with a reptile obsession. He looked more the kind who went straight from walking to weight lifting, bypassing all the semi-nerdy stuff that thrilled the rest of us mere mortals.

"Lizard guys don't do it for you, huh?" Chase asked, starting to unload the tank. I joined him.

"You say *lizard guy* and I immediately think of something like this." I lifted an old comic book featuring a crocodile/human hybrid thing.

"I didn't wear a lab coat." He took the comic book from me, smiling openly as he flipped through it.

"Keep pile? Donate pile?"

He sighed. "I don't need it, so donate."

From the corner of my eye, I saw him glance back at the comic a few more times as we worked, so when his back was turned later, I snuck it into the keep pile. We didn't always need the things we wanted, but some things were worth holding on to anyway.

I moved to another box that looked small enough for me to handle on my own, but when I lifted it, my knees nearly buckled. Hearing my grunt, Chase turned and grabbed the other side, and together we moved it to the space he'd cleared on the shelf.

The box shook the entire metal shelving unit when he slid his fingers out from beneath it.

"What's in there?" My fingers pulsed hot from the brief pressure of holding the box.

Stepping aside, Chase let me read what was written in thick black marker on the box.

"Oh," I said, letting sympathy draw the laughing word out. "You must have been the cutest little nerd."

"A lot of kids collected rocks."

"Sure they did. And I bet all of them still live with their moms too."

I saw a glint in his eye as his mouth curled up. I tried to dart away when he lunged for me, but there was nowhere to go. His fingers dug into my rib cage, forcing an involuntary peal of laughter to burst from my lungs as he started tickling me. I twisted, but he caught me up against his chest. His fingers stilled, and he stopped the retaliatory tickle attack, but he kept his hands splayed on either side of my rib cage, where my heart was beating way too fast. We were both grinning, until we weren't. And when he shifted his gaze from my eyes to my mouth, I stepped back, breaking his hold on me. Our eyes were locked together.

"What did you collect?"

I hadn't really collected anything, except... "Baseball cards."

"So when I was chasing lizards and polishing rocks—"

"Wait, polishing?"

"—you were collecting baseball cards?"

"Go back to polishing rocks. That's like a whole other level of nerd-dom."

Chase grinned. "You were the girl who ran around with perpetually scraped knees and always had a ball cap on." Chase ran his finger over the bill of the one I wore.

I was, until puberty. Then I traded my scraped knees for lip gloss—usually Selena's—but I still felt the most like myself with a baseball cap on.

"Yep, and you," I said, smiling, "were...the boy who had his own rock polisher?"

He inclined his head, conceding without embarrassment.

I grinned. "Okay, I would have had to retaliate a tickle attack, but I'm guessing you had a rough go as a kid, so I'll give you a pass this time."

Chase lifted his arms from his sides. "Go ahead. I'm not ticklish."

I raised an eyebrow, but he didn't lower his arms even when I drew nearer. I was half expecting some sort of trick the second I touched him, and I wasn't exactly put off by the idea. With one last glance at his face, I poked his ribs.

Nothing.

I poked again. Added a few wriggling fingers.

More nothing.

"Oh, come on!" I said, bringing my other hand into the mix and tickling him in a way that would have had me squealing like a pig. Chase barely moved. "Nothing?" I shifted my attack all over his torso.

"Nothing that makes me want to laugh, but keep trying, maybe—"

I pulled my hands back, feeling my cheeks flush. "You're not ticklish anywhere? Not even the back of your knees?"

He eyed my legs. "Are *you* ticklish on the back of your knees?"

I stepped behind a box, hiding that part of my body from view. "I'm ticklish everywhere. When we were little, my sister used to sit on me and pin my arms down and then tickle me until I cried. Hey, that's not funny!" But Chase was already laughing.

"And what did you do in response?"

"I used to pour warm water on her bed while she slept. She still thinks she was a bed wetter up through seventh grade."

He laughed harder, supporting his weight on a box that was labeled Chase and Brandon's Video Games. My laughter tapered off at the reminder of my brother. These were his things too. All around me were pieces of his childhood, memories only Chase could tell me about if I could ignore the wave of guilt that crested inside me each time I used him that way.

"You said you and Brandon grew up more like brothers than cousins. Didn't you torment each other as kids?"

"I would put hot sauce in his pop, or there was this one time he wrote a note on the back of my math homework declaring my love for my fifty-five-year-old teacher."

"He did?" I couldn't help smiling at the small glimpse into my brother's younger years.

"Yeah, but he ended up confessing to me on the way to school and helped me black the whole thing out with magic marker before I turned it in."

My smile grew. He was tenderhearted. I liked knowing that about Brandon.

"But we never inflicted long-running psychological damage on each other. You never told your sister?"

"About the bed-wetting? I'm waiting for the night before she gets married."

"Girls are evil."

"Yeah, well, remember that next time you think about tickling me."

Chase ran a hand over his closely cropped hair. "Not much of a threat. But you can tell me not to tickle you again and I won't."

So fast, I said, "Don't tickle me again."

He half inclined his head. "Done."

I edged out from behind the box, overly hesitating in my movement toward him, even though I believed him. "And you could apologize for the first time."

He considered me. "You had it coming."

"Mom jokes are not the same as tickle torturing. Not that it was a mom joke so much as a *you* joke."

"I wouldn't call what I did to you torture."

I wasn't behind the box at all anymore. "No? Then what would you call it?"

"An excuse to put my arms around you."

Heat rushed my face the way it always did when Chase said something so direct. Another guy might have tickled me for the same reason, but he'd never have come right out and admitted it. He'd have equivocated or lied. *I'd* have equivocated or lied. I still wasn't used to how forthright Chase was, or how much I liked it.

"And what excuse do you need to put your arms around this box of snow globes so I can get to the one below it?"

Apparently, my asking was all he needed.

The day yielded to night as we worked. Before I knew it, it was full dark and Chase and I had made a decent dent in the garage on one side. I was more careful reaching for higher boxes after the rock collection, testing the weight before pulling anything down. Even still, I underestimated one and took a few steps backward before I could steady the weight. Bent over his own box several feet away, Chase might have missed my hurried steps, but not the burst of sour notes that emanated from whatever I'd backed into.

Chase's head turned in my direction.

"I swear I'm not this much of a wuss." I worked out hard almost every day, and my arms had well-earned definition to them. But I kept expecting the boxes to be lighter than they were. I was being impatient, and my reward was that I got to look weak in front of Chase. I hated that. He tried to take the box from me, but I held on to it. "No, I'm fine. I got it." I noticed then that the box had Cast Iron Skillets written on it. Yeah.

I added it to the pile of kitchen stuff for later sorting and turned back in time to see Chase whip a drop cloth off the upright piano I'd awakened. "It's beautiful," I said, admiring the rich mahogany wood.

"Yeah." He was looking at the piano like he'd never seen one before. Or like he'd never wanted to see one again.

"You play?"

He shook his head.

"Your mom?"

Another head shake.

"So your tool of a father, then?"

Chase laughed once. "Yeah, it was his." He finally broke his gaze away from the piano. "Can you play?"

I pulled out the bench that was nestled underneath, sat and flexed my fingers. "Six whole months of lessons when I was eight. Here." I scooted to make room for Chase and tugged him down next to me. "Gimme your hand." I spread his fingers out over the keys and covered them with my own. I pressed down on my thumb, then my index finger and then my pinkie, moving his with my own. Not easy since his hands were almost twice as big as mine, but we got it. I repeated those three notes a few times until Chase no longer needed my hand to guide him. "Keep doing that." I moved my hands down and started playing without any kind of finesse, but Selena and I had played "Heart and Soul" so many times that it came pretty easily.

"Okay, this time, hit each key twice." We played through the duet again and then again until I'd added every little flourish that I could remember and a few that I did not. It was stupid and fun and I was so glad to see that distant look gone from Chase's face when we finished. "So what if the piano was his," I said, sliding my hands from the black and white keys. "It's not anymore. Make it yours if you want it."

"Just like that?"

"Just like that." I stood up and Chase followed, his gaze never leaving me, but when I checked the bench for music, it was empty. I probably couldn't have played anything anyway, but I would have tried just to show him he could too. Still, where there was a piano, there was sheet music. I started to turn and scan the nearby boxes, but Chase caught me with a hand, tugging me toward him until I had to tilt my head back to see his face. He didn't bother with an excuse like when he'd tickled me. He wanted to put his arms around me, so he did. And when I stupidly didn't move away, he urged me that half step closer that brought our bodies fully flush together. My pulse picked up, both from how close we were and from the unabashedly intense way he was looking at me.

"I hate this." He gestured with his chin, taking in the whole garage. "Seeing how much she's held on to is bad enough, but seeing his stuff…I almost want to break out your bats again, you know?"

I could feel each breath he made and knew he could feel

mine. That warning voice I'd been steadily ignoring since we met had grown so dim by then, and it was nothing compared to the thunderous beating of my heart. "Play it or smash it. I'll help you either way."

He didn't do that half-move guy thing where they start to lean in, hesitate, waiting for a go-ahead, before fully committing. Chase went right for it, barely giving me enough time for my stomach to rocket into my throat only to explode the second he brought his lips to mine. And then he pulled back almost before I could register—and revel—in the sensation. That same half smile lifted his mouth as he drew back, leaving his hand on the underside of my jaw a second longer before kissing me again.

CHAPTER 27

I slipped inside and upstairs with only seconds to spare on my curfew. I could have been home sooner, but I'd driven around after leaving Chase, vacillating between euphoric smiles and self-loathing scowls. Kissing him had been so wrong and wonderful and wrong again. By the time I gave my parents' bedroom door the obligatory soft knock and "I'm home" that I was supposed to, my insides were tied up in so many knots that breathing was painful. I was hoping to make it to my room without either of them catching me in the hall, but I wasn't quick enough. Dad pulled their door open before I was halfway to my room. He kept his voice low. Mom must have already been asleep.

"Hey, it's late."

Just hearing his voice made the knots constrict. "It's before curfew."

"You missed dinner again."

"I texted Mom. She said it was fine."

"I know. We just haven't seen you much."

I'd been trying to be home as little as possible, either from games or claiming that I was studying when I was actually with Chase. When I absolutely had to be home, I avoided all but the briefest contact with Dad. And he'd noticed.

"Yeah, well, Selena's here, so it's the same amount of people at the table." I turned my back on him without so much as a good-night.

"Dana."

I glanced back.

"I feel like I've done something wrong here."

His words, the concern I could hear wrapped around each one, made me want to snarl and cry at the same time. *Yes, you've done something wrong*, I wanted to say. *You did it nearly twenty years ago and I don't know how to look at you if you knew about your son and kept him from us, if I had a brother all this time who could have played the guitar with Selena or baseball with me, if it's him you think about, him when you're with me, and that's why I never feel like I can catch you.*

"I'm just tired," I said, hoping he didn't notice the tremor in my voice or the nails I was digging into my palms. "Can I go to bed now?"

"All right." He gestured a hand for me to go but stopped me with his words. "Tomorrow let's runs some drills, okay?"

"Can't." I was facing my door, so he didn't see the tears that stung my eyes. "I'm still studying for that Biology test. If you want to throw the ball with someone, ask Selena." I took the last few steps to my room and shut the door behind me, blinking my eyes dry.

Selena was perched on the edge of the bed, and she stood

as soon as I entered the room. She'd clearly overheard my exchange with Dad. "What's with you lately?"

I ducked into the closet, rubbing away the rest of my unshed tears with my palms and noticing that my nails had broken the skin in a few places. "Nothing."

"You're being such a brat, especially with Dad."

For a second my chin quivered again. *Stop it!* I told myself.
"I'm not being anything other than tired. School, that thing
you dropped out of, has been kicking my butt." To support
my claim, I shrugged off the schoolbag of books I'd brought
with me to Chase's, letting the heavy weight hit the ground
with a thud.

"Yeah, that's the other thing. When did you start lying
straight to Mom and Dad's face—and mine apparently—about
where you go every day after practice?"

I turned and widened my eyes, both for show and because
I thought I'd been doing a pretty good job with my cover
stories. Apparently, I was wrong. "I don't—"

"Yeah, you do. Are you honestly trying to tell me you've
spent every free night this week with your Biology partner—
the same guy you told me you broke—and you're both so
eager to see each other again—"

"It's not about eager." I launched myself into a righteous-
indignation act, because the alternative was right there waiting to pour down my face if I let it. "You never had Mr.
Rodriguez. His class is insane." I moved around her to sit on
the bed. "Why else would I willingly spend so much time
with Nick?"

"There, right there!" She sat right in front of me, her finger pointing at my face. "That's the other thing you've been

doing. Nothing you just said is a lie. I've heard about Mr. Rodriguez's class, so I believe you that it's hard, and hanging out with a guy who probably can't stand to be around you right now *would* be hard too, *if* you were actually spending all this time with him, but you're not, are you?" She folded her legs so she could lean closer to me. "Ever since I moved back, you've been lying or saying things in a way that lets you tell the truth but still supports whatever lie you've already got going. Cut it out and find thirty minutes to play catch with Dad."

I bit my lip and looked up so she couldn't see how close I was to breaking. "Since when is catch with Dad thirty minutes? Maybe I'm like you. Maybe I'm starting to realize I don't want softball to be my whole life either."

"You've always liked softball more than me, so try again."

"Fine, then how about the fact that it's not catch with my dad, it's drills with my coach!" I started to stand up when my voice cracked, but Selena pressed down on my knee.

"Dana…what?" Her tone had softened and I couldn't hold it back anymore.

No one knew me better than my sister, not Nick, not even Jessalyn, no one. I'd been able to lie to Mom and Dad partially because I felt like I had no choice. I couldn't confront him, possibly destroy him along with Mom—and finding out he had a son he never knew about *would* destroy him—without a shred of proof. Not even the website would back up my claims, since Brandon had deleted his account. But it was different with Selena. I couldn't lie to her even when I tried.

I pulled away from her, wrapping my arm around myself as I walked toward the closet again. It was right there, right on the tip of my tongue to say it. *Do you remember the DNA test I submitted for Dad? The one I told you came back a bust?*

I heard the bed squeak as she stood and then her feet shuffling across the carpet as she came up behind me.

It wasn't a bust. I found someone, Sel.

Her hand touched my shoulder. "What is it?"

In my head, I saw myself saying the words, letting them gush out of me. *Dad has a son.* Only it wouldn't end there. Not my pain and not hers; hers would only be starting. She'd have to start walking past the family photos in the hallway and grow sicker each time, knowing someone was missing. She'd have to start watching our brother from a parked car thirty feet away and know she might never get any closer. She'd have to start looking at the father she'd always loved and wonder if he'd ever truly felt the same way about her.

She'd have to start feeling as wrecked as I felt every second of every day and know it might not get any better, that it might get so much worse.

And I could not do it.

I made myself groan as I stepped away from her touch, scrubbing my face as though in annoyance. "Nothing. I can't be tired? You and Dad. Seriously, give me a break…"

"Tired?" she said, still a little soft, but weary too. "That's all you are?"

I'd turned around to face her again, to show my sister what her ears alone wouldn't believe. I locked my jaw tight and pressed my back into the closet doorknob, hard. I focused on the metal digging into my flesh and willed every inch of my face into a blank stare.

She looked at me, her eyes darting between mine so many

times that I welcomed the dizziness they created. At last she stopped, her shoulders slumping as she made a sound of disgust. "I can't even tell when you're lying anymore, Dana."

"I'm telling you the truth." I moved back to the bed, sitting so that I was no longer facing her head-on. "And okay, fine, I've been hanging out with that guy I told you about. It's the same thing you did with Gavin and singing. You kept part of your life from me and Mom and Dad. Are you telling me you never lied about what you were doing? Mom invited you home all the time, and you had excuses for her plenty of times."

"But I was still here. I came to your games. I didn't blow Dad off when he wanted to spend a measly half hour with me. You almost act like you're punishing him for something."

I went cold inside. "What could I punish Dad for?"

"I don't know." She tossed one hand to the side. "Is he not paying enough attention to you? Are you mad about a call at a recent game? Are you upset because you have to share him again now that I'm here?"

I don't know if I want him at all anymore. "Don't be stupid."

"Well, then I don't know what your deal is, but enough already." Her phone buzzed on my dresser and she twisted around to glance at the screen. "And stop lying all the time. You're getting to be pathological, and I have no idea where you got the idea that lying to your family is okay."

"Because everyone else in this family is a beacon of truth?" The words scraped my throat.

"Compared to you, yeah. So cut it out. I'm not going to tell Mom and Dad about your guy, but you have to be around more." She got up to check the message and smiled at whatever she saw. "And you can start tomorrow after the game when you meet Gavin."

CHAPTER 28

I leaped onto Sadie's back as Ivy and Jessalyn collided into her from the front. We were a tangle of arms and I had no idea how we stayed standing.

"No-hitter!" I yelled. "Sadie!"

She couldn't help laughing, even under the onslaught of so many of her teammates surging to congratulate her. "I did it!"

I laughed at the surprise in her voice. "Yeah, you did." I shook her shoulders, hugged her again from behind. We'd won our game, and not just any game, our first sectional. There were only two more until the state finals. Two more games that we had a solid shot at winning. We'd all played well, but Sadie had been unstoppable. Strike after strike after strike. It had almost been like watching Selena again. If Sadie continued to pitch half as well and the rest of us held our own, we weren't just going to the finals—we would take the whole damn thing.

Jessalyn caught my eye, sending that live wire of elation

sparking inside us. I grinned back—for the moment, nothing else mattered.

"You were amazing," Ivy said. "I thought about just sitting down that last inning."

"It was Coach," Sadie said, deflecting praise the way she always did. "He and Selena practiced with me all last week." She laughed. "I think my shoulder is going to fall off, but I don't even care."

I frowned, looking first at our coach, who was beaming at Sadie, and then to where Selena had been cheering in the stands. Selena had never said she and Dad were helping Sadie. I was glad for Sadie and our team—who better to finesse her pitching than the greatest pitcher our school had ever seen—but the sparking inside me dimmed.

Someone knocked hard into my shoulder, and a deafening scream passed my ear as Selena charged into the knot of girls to get to Sadie.

"No one has pitched like that since—"

"You!" Sadie said, hugging my sister.

"Okay, fine, but I wouldn't want to have to hit your curveball. I thought Amanda's catcher's mitt was going to catch fire! Amazing." Selena hugged Sadie again and whispered something in her ear that made our pitcher flush with delight.

"I will. And thank you!"

Selena joined me when I headed back to the dugout. "How about that?" She grinned in Sadie's direction.

"Yeah. Awesome night for her."

"For all of you." Selena sat next to me as I unlaced my cleats.

"I didn't know you were working with her."

"I wasn't hiding it."

"You could have said something."

"Are you seriously mad that I just helped your pitcher win you guys the game?"

"No," I said, keeping my head down as I drew my other knee up to the bench to untie my other cleat. "But it would have been nice to know what my sister and my dad were doing."

"*Now* he's your dad? Last night when I was practically begging you to play catch with him, he was your coach." She sighed when I failed to respond. "Sadie asked for help, and we gave it to her. If you want help, say the word and Dad and I will do the same for you."

I didn't want help, but I couldn't shake the image of the three of them practicing together, Selena showing Sadie exactly how to grip the ball and Dad doling out rare compliments that I had to practically pull from him.

"Look," Selena said. "The point is that you guys won. Don't let petty jealousy over something you've made no secret of not wanting ruin that." She nodded at the girls still congratulating Sadie. "Be happy for her if nothing else."

I *was* happy for Sadie. She needed the emotional pick-me-up after Ryan the turd, plus she'd played phenomenally well. I'd been the first to charge the mound after her last strikeout. Looking at her out there, still grinning as the last of our teammates hugged her, I couldn't help smiling too. It was only when I glanced at Dad that I felt like I was choking on something. And Selena calling me on it only made it that much harder to swallow, because it wasn't that I didn't want it—I didn't know if I should.

Muttering something under her breath, Selena left the dugout. When I followed a few minutes later—after another genuine hug for Sadie—I found her and Mom standing with a
guy that could only be Gavin.

The women on Mom's side of the family were all vertically
challenged. Selena was the tallest of any of us, and she capped
out at a whopping five-four. Gavin was just barely taller than
her, and that might have just been his hair, which was shorn
on the sides and swooped across the top in an undercut.

They were laughing together when I joined them.

"Here she is! Gavin, meet my baby sister, Dana." Selena
had to loosen her grip on Gavin's arm so he could shake my
hand, but she reclaimed it as soon as possible.

"Great game. It's nice to finally meet you, Dana. Selena
talks about you all the time."

I almost said *She only told us about you a week ago*, but it was
painfully obvious that Selena wanted this first meeting to go
well. "Thanks. She's told me a lot about you too."

"Oh, you've got a—" Selena plucked a tiny mesquite pod
that had blown into Gavin's hair.

"Thanks, Lena."

"Lena?" I said, glancing at my sister. "I thought you hated
that nickname?"

"No, I don't," was her immediate answer.

Um, yeah, she did. I distinctly remembered her calling me
Na in retaliation when I'd tried out the nickname years ago.

Gavin ducked his head, but not before I saw a smile play
at his lips. Reluctantly, Selena's joined his.

"Okay, fine," she said to him. "Maybe you were right."
She looked at Mom and me. "I wanted to try it out because

the name Selena is a little crowded in the music industry. I don't want to be eclipsed by these other huge singers before I even open my mouth."

"Trust me," Gavin said, and I noticed his thumb sweep across the back of her hand. "It's not possible."

Selena glanced at their joined hands, smiling.

"Besides, it was your grandmother's name. You should keep it."

I didn't have to see Mom's face to know Gavin had just won major Brownie points with her.

"Tell us how you met, Gavin," Mom said. She was a romantic, but anyone who wanted to take her firstborn child across the country was getting grilled, especially since Dad wasn't there yet.

"Oh, well—" he smiled at Selena "—I happened to be in this coffee shop right by campus."

"And he doesn't even drink coffee," Selena said, grinning back at Gavin.

"I don't, but for some reason, I had this overwhelming urge for—"

"—cappuccino," they said together.

"And while I was waiting, I heard the most beautiful voice singing, and I turned and there she was." The smile slipped away, replaced by a look of awe. "I was gone from that very moment. I never even got my cappuccino."

"He's exaggerating," Selena said, though the color rising in her cheeks said she loved hearing it anyway.

"And whose idea was it to drop out of school and move to Nashville?" Mom asked, visibly charmed by the smitten couple, but not so much that she forgot the important questions.

"Mine," Selena said, her chin lifting.

"Hmm. And what did you think about that, Gavin?"

"I know it was a hard decision for her, but you've heard her," Gavin said. "She was made to sing. I'm only glad I heard her first."

"We haven't, though." Mom addressed Selena, who looked away.

"Well, when you do hear her," Gavin said, "you won't have a single doubt. I don't."

Mom's expression said otherwise, but Dad showed up then, and the introductions started again. I had to give it to Gavin, he had all the right answers, and he was pretty good at minimizing the bad ones too. Even I wasn't wholly convinced that Selena dropping out of college was a horrible idea by the time he was done.

Mom and Dad continued to throw questions at him once we got back to the house. But by the time I went up to bed, I knew that Gavin was head over heels for my sister, and that there was no talking either of them out of Nashville. I wouldn't be surprised if he proposed before they left.

I pulled the covers up high to my chin despite the May heat rolling in and pretended to be asleep when the bed dipped sometime later and Selena slid in beside me. The timeline she had talked about was much faster than I'd been expecting. Selena was going to take every shift she could at Lava Java and hopefully have enough saved up to leave before the end of summer. That was barely three months away. Chase had said Brandon would be leaving for college around then too.

My breathing sped up. I had so little time. They were both leaving. I'd come so close to telling Selena about Brandon the

other night, but I'd stopped because I didn't want the gnawing, gaping hole in my heart to spread to hers. What good
would it do to tell her about a brother she couldn't have if
it came with questioning everything she thought she knew
about our dad?

Nothing. Worse than nothing.

I didn't want to lose Chase either, but I had to find out if
Dad knew about his son. Everything depended on that. Everything.

CHAPTER 29

When I showed up at Chase's the following afternoon, he greeted me the same way we'd parted the other night. The kiss was still shocking—the heat of him, the taste—but I was more undone by how easy it was to rise up and press into his kiss, and how hard it was to pull away.

"So, you did a lot yesterday," I said, grabbing for the closest box in an effort to distract myself from wanting to kiss him again.

He rubbed the back of his neck and smiled at me. "Yeah, my mom is growing more anxious the longer it takes." He moved closer to me. "So how come I feel like I could do this forever?"

My heart felt like it was pressing up against my rib cage, urging me to step closer too so that I could say the exact same thing. But I ignored it. I had to. Because I could think about either Chase or my brother, and after witnessing Selena and Gavin the night before, I knew I couldn't afford to drag things out anymore. I needed to find pictures that either implicated my dad or else helped exonerate him, and I needed to do it before my siblings ended up in different states.

"You want to start on the left side and I'll take the right?"

Before Chase could respond, a car pulled up to the curb behind us. I turned, my stomach lurching in the opposite direction, thinking it might be Brandon deciding to help after all. It wasn't, but my stomach stayed poised to revolt again when I saw the woman who got out of the driver's seat. There was only one person she could be.

"Mom, hey." Chase went to greet her and kiss her cheek. She looked young, late thirties, and pretty in an effortless way. "You're early. I would have had this all cleaned up before you got home."

Her eyes darted to the mess of boxes and items spilling out onto the driveway and snagged on the near-bursting garbage bags. I saw her swallow.

"You okay?"

"Uh-huh." She smiled at him, but her gaze returned to the garbage bags.

"Okay enough to meet my girl?"

His girl. There went my stomach, launching from side to side like a trapped animal. That was wrong on top of wrong. And so many layers that I couldn't see where they began. Chase jogged up to me and took my hand. It was like I was outside my body watching but unable to do anything to stop the scene as he led me to his mom. I wasn't supposed to meet her or any other members of his family. I wasn't supposed to kiss him or hold his hand or any of this. I wasn't supposed to want to.

"Hi—" I didn't know what to call her. Mrs. Anything seemed like a wrong move. "I'm D—"

"Dana. It's so nice to meet you. Please call me Sandy." She kept talking. Each little thing she said sped up the havoc in my gut. He'd told his mom about me. Said lots of nice things about me. Called me his girl right in front of her. He was still holding my hand in front of her. It was too similar to the way Selena had introduced Gavin to our family—Gavin, whom she was planning her entire future with.

I pulled my hand free, earning a puzzled look from Chase that I pretended not to notice.

"It's nice to meet you too, Sandy. You, um, have great taste in music. Chase said the signed Aerosmith T-shirt we found was yours. That must have—"

"Where?" Her neck stretched to peer past me. "Where's the box?"

"Mom, we didn't throw it away. I promised you I wouldn't get rid of anything important."

She pushed past both of us, pulling open the first box she saw, scanning its contents, then moving to the next. I glanced at Chase for direction, but he was staring at her with an expression I felt guilty for seeing. His jaw was locked and his eyebrows were drawn together and lifted, not in embarrassment or anger, but something much more sorrowful. Without a word, he came alongside her and started opening boxes we'd already sealed.

"Dana? Can you?" He gestured to his mom's other side. Wordlessly, I went. It took twenty minutes to find the T-shirt, but by then it was too late. She was pulling items out of the garbage bags, growing more dismayed by the moment.

"Chase, these are good. Why would you get rid of them?" She was holding up a pair of boys' hockey skates from the bag marked Donate.

"They're from when I was seven."

She wrapped her arms around them. "I can picture you with your missing front teeth when I see them. These are staying." She gasped as she drew another item from the bag, and another and another until the bags were empty. All of them.

"Mom. We can't keep all this stuff. You said it yourself just last week." He waded close to her. "We can barely walk through here, and the bedroom is worse. I can't keep sleeping on the couch. When I moved home, you agreed."

Her eyes squeezed shut.

"You needed me home—here I am. You want me to stay, you have to let some of this go." She let him take the bike pump from her hands.

"We should keep that, though."

From where I stood in the corner, I saw the tendon in Chase's neck jump as he pulled his arm back from the donate pile and instead added the pump to the keep pile.

"And this," she said, picking up a child-sized pup tent.

I watched him watch her, the neck tendon jumping each time she retrieved another item. He was so focused on her that he started when I slipped my hand back in his. "Want to get out of here for a little while?"

His hand tightened around mine.

CHAPTER 30

Chase pressed his keys into my hand without a word and sat just as silently beside me as I turned his truck toward Papago Park. Eventually, the neighborhoods gave way to flat desert, barren of all but the heartiest shrubs. Ahead, the normally reddish sandstone buttes glowed golden in the setting sun. I turned off at the first barely there dirt road once we left all trace of civilization behind us and killed the engine as soon as the main road vanished in my rearview mirror.

I glanced at Chase, at the small frown that had remained between his brows since we'd left his mom emptying boxes in front of his house. "Come on," I said, brushing his arm when the sound of my opening door failed to turn his head. He followed me out of the truck and down the path I picked out. There wasn't an actual trail, just rocks and dust separated by ground-hugging brush.

"What are we looking for?"

I slowed and stopped by a small cluster of flat rocks, barely wide enough for the two of us. I sat and took a deep breath, looking out over the empty miles of land stretching to the hills. "I don't know, space? It's open and not..."

"Open's good right now."

I felt his gaze as he lowered himself next to me, but I didn't know how to meet it. We sat, side by side, the sunset painting our shadows long and dark behind us. "This is when I steal your line and say I didn't think this out. There's not really anything to break out here and I didn't bring my bats." When Chase's quick smile at my quip faded, I turned back toward the truck and stood. "Actually, I've got a baseball in my bag. We could play catch or—"

"Dana."

"Yeah?" I turned, my voice and expression light, trying to contrast the scene we'd left at his house.

"Sit with me?"

I returned to the rocks, not sure what Chase needed from me in that moment. When I'd offered him the chance to get away from his house, he'd taken it. I'd thought that's what we were doing out in the desert too, getting away, forgetting. I should have known better with Chase.

He said my name, and when I met his eye, he slid his hand around the base of my skull, bringing me in for a kiss—the softest, sweetest kiss that somehow made me want to cry. When he pulled back, leaving our foreheads tilted together, my eyes felt watery.

"I don't know what to do anymore," he said, letting his hand fall away from me, but not his gaze. "I know she doesn't want to be like this, and she was trying, she was. Letting me go through the garage was huge for her. I mean, a year ago she couldn't have done it."

Before he moved out, he meant.

"Am I helping her, hurting her?" He straightened and shook his head. "Do I push her, do I not? And I love her—" he gestured at his chest "—so much, but I can't live at home indefinitely. I want to do things and go places. I think she knows that. Maybe that's why..." His head dropped.

"I'm really sorry. I don't know what to say." I was falling into a greater intimacy with Chase and his family than I'd ever planned, one that made my ongoing selfishness all the more glaring. It wasn't a nice thing I was doing to him, lying by omission, and glimpsing some of the issues going on in his life made it so much harder to rationalize my behavior.

"What would you do?" Chase asked, his fingers brushing against my knee. I should have moved away, both from his touch and the fragile intimacy surrounding us. I had no right to either, but I stayed exactly where I was, hating myself a little more with each passing minute.

"I don't know. I understand why she's trying to hold on, but...you have to be more important."

The fingers against my knee shifted to my hand. It was so easy to touch him, to be touched by him, that I didn't know who had reached for whom as I held his hand.

"I'm okay staying at home for now, finishing my undergrad degree, giving her time to get used to the idea, but not living on the couch." His hand flexed in mine. "And I want us both to be able to park in the garage so we don't risk third-degree burns trying to open a car door in the summer."

I laughed a little. "Doesn't sound like you're asking for too much."

He didn't laugh. "But I am. Brandon will be going away to college in the fall, and Uncle Bran will sell his house. She knows everyone is leaving. I don't want to leave her too."

For once I didn't pounce on the mention of Brandon's name and twist the conversation for my own gain. I didn't want to hear about my brother in that moment, I wanted to help my boyfri— I wanted to help Chase. This selfless and funny and honest and brave and really beautiful guy. This unbelievably amazing guy.

"Where do you want to go?" I asked.

Turning our linked hands over, he said, "Right now? No-where, but I need to know I can. That I won't be destroying her when I do."

His skin was warm against mine, rough from working but still soft when I traced his palm with my thumb. "Maybe she needs you to do exactly what you're doing—helping her let go of a little now so it won't hurt as much when she has to let go of a lot later."

He nodded. His gaze was on our hands, but he was clearly somewhere else in his head. I wondered if he was thinking about his dad walking out on him and his mom, making a comparison that no one else would have.

"You'll always come back to her, won't you? Whatever you do and wherever you go—"

"She's my home."

I lifted my hands on either side of his face and kissed him. Not because it would get me anything but because I wanted him to know what I felt and could never say.

I pulled away just as his hands settled on my rib cage. "Tell her all that. What you want and what you're willing to do. Tell her why. All of it." I stood and held out my hand to him. "And when she's reminded how unbelievably amazing and selfless her son is—because she loves you and she already knows—you'll be able to help her let go."

Once we got back to his house, I didn't hang around to watch the conversation between Chase and his mom, but I did watch the way he walked up to her, squatted down beside her and smiled.

I made it all the way home before that same expression crumbled from my face.

CHAPTER 31

Pushing aside the sick guilt sloshing in my stomach, I returned to Chase's house on Monday.

He smiled at me, and my heart twisted. He kissed me and unshed tears burned behind my eyes. They nearly spilled down my cheeks when he hugged me too close while telling me about the conversation with his mom, the fruit of which was the partially refilled garbage and donation bags that had been emptied last time I was there.

A start, he said.

While I knew it had to be an ending. I couldn't do it much longer, lie to him when he was more honest with me than maybe anyone had ever been. If I didn't find what I needed that day, then I never would.

I hit pay dirt a few hours later.

Photo albums.

Boxes and boxes of photo albums. *Thank you, Sandy.*

Dropping onto the dusty floor, while Chase was busy checking paint cans to see which were dried out, I pulled the closest box to me and took out the first album. Lots of pictures of Chase stared back at me. Baby pictures, school pictures, vacations and birthdays. I caught myself lingering over one of him and Brandon clutching a squirming brown puppy mid-face-lick, both of them grinning in that manic I'm-so-happy-I-can't-contain-it way only little kids can. Selena and I had photos like that with our dog, Slammer. An ache tugged at my heart knowing that while we'd done so many of the same things, had so many of the same experiences, we hadn't done them together.

I finished one album and started another, and another. I kept turning pages, smothering a laugh when I found one of Chase unwrapping his rock polisher with way more joy than anyone should have opening a rock polisher. That urge to laugh faded as I opened more albums, watching my brother lose baby teeth and learn to ride a bike, seeing his sullen face the day he got braces and the perfectly straight smile the day they came off. I found shots from his and Chase's brief foray into Little League, and then so many more once he discovered he was meant to be racing through water instead of tearing around a baseball diamond. I dragged a finger over my brother's face and across the silver metal hanging from his neck as he stood poolside after a meet. The ache in my chest swelled even as I smiled. If he'd grown up with Selena and me, he'd be holding a bat in most of these photos rather than a pair of goggles—Dad would have made sure of that.

There was so much more in these pages than what I'd found online. I was seeing Brandon's whole life, all captured and carefully pasted into books. And not just his, Chase's too. Somehow that made the sting sharper, seeing them together, the two people I wasn't allowed to have but couldn't stop myself from wanting.

There was only one album left in the box I'd found, and unlike the others, which mostly had plain black covers, this one was powder blue and had a stork embossed on it just above Brandon's name.

"Hey."

It was like the blood in my veins electrified. It jolted through me and I dropped the album, my trembling hands involuntarily flying to cover it. But it was too late. Chase squatted down next to me.

"I wondered what had you so quiet." He slid the album from my lap, and I had to refrain from grabbing it back. "I didn't realize we still had this." Then, before I could stop him, he opened it.

Every muscle in my body clenched. There he was, all eight pounds two ounces of my brother the day he was born. I hadn't expected it to be the same photo Brandon posted online every Mother's Day, and it wasn't. It was the same hospital room, though, the same woman lying in bed with her newborn son cradled in her arms. This one showed the hand on the railing, but also the arm, the shoulder and the full smiling face of the man looking down at them. My shoulders jerked, then jerked again and again as I tried and failed to muffle the sob that racked my body.

Chase's head turned to mine in an instant. "Dana?"

I couldn't look at him. I couldn't look at anything but that photo, that face. I gasped in a breath and it tore out again, sounding as if every jagged piece of fear long lodged in my heart came with it.

I pushed off the concrete to my feet and rushed into the driveway just as the moon was rising in the purple-pink sky. Open air and open space. I filled my lungs, but the air all came back out too fast.

Chase hurried after me, heedless of the boxes his much larger form knocked down.

"It's not him," I said, looking up at Chase, my body still shaking, me still half crying but smiling now too.

Chase's arms came around me, holding me tight. "Not who? What just happened?"

I just shook my head against his chest, looking back into the garage at the other photo albums piled inside. All of it, Brandon's entire life...our dad wouldn't have missed it. The conviction burned through me, sudden and sure, helping— with Chase—to steady my breathing. He wasn't there. He didn't know. He couldn't have.

It wasn't a secret I had to keep anymore, not when it had never been kept from me.

And that was it, the thing that let my heart beat blood through my body again instead of misery: Brandon wasn't a secret, and he wasn't a lie. He was a brother and a son, which meant...

I'd have to tell them. All of them.

My breath hitched again, and some of that pain I'd let go of trickled back in before I even looked at Chase.

It hurt, finding out about the affair, and I still felt it. It hurt more when I thought about Mom with Selena only a baby herself when Dad was with Brandon's mom. It happened nearly two decades ago, but the wound for me was fresh, and it would be for Mom—Selena too—when she found out. We wouldn't suddenly be wrapped up together in a family hug, anxious and excited to welcome Brandon into the fold.

I didn't know what any of them would do, least of all Brandon. He didn't know a thing about us; he didn't even know he had another sister, one who played the guitar just like him.

I started, a different kind of panic jolting me from Chase's arms. "Selena's singing at Lava Java tonight. What time is it?" I didn't wait for his answer—the fading sky told me all I needed to know. I raised my hands to my head and said a word. Then I said it again, looking at him. "It's the first time she's letting anyone in our family come see her, and I promised her I wouldn't be late. I have to go."

"Right now? Dana, what just happened?"

My stomach clenched as I headed in a half jog to my car. "I should have already left." That was more true than I could let myself admit.

"Wait, or let me drive you." He caught my hand as I reached to open my door. "Talk to me."

"I can't," I said, and even whispering the words hurt. "I have to go. I'm sorry."

He let go of my hand, but his hung in the air between us, and that trickle of pain became a stream. As I drove off, I watched Chase in my rearview mirror until it hurt too much to keep looking at him, wishing my heart could shut out what I didn't want to feel as easily as my eyes could close on what I didn't want to see. I hadn't wanted to leave him like that. I hadn't wanted to leave him at all, but the second

I thought about Selena performing tonight—in less than an hour, according to the clock in my car—I had to go, and I had to at least try to bring someone else to hear her too.

CHAPTER 32

I drove to Jungle Juice without a clear plan in mind, hoping that once I saw Brandon, I'd know what to say.

Chase wasn't there, of course, but I was gambling on Brandon's schedule, even as I pulled the door open and walked inside. Screaming monkeys and the girl my brother had a crush on greeted me.

"Welcome to Jungle Juice," she said, near deadpan. "Do you know what you want?"

Yes, I thought, walking up and clutching the counter with a death grip. *But I don't know if it's even possible.* "I'm actually looking for Brandon. Is he working today?"

She placed both palms on the counter and stared at me without blinking. "What do you want with Brandon?"

I remembered the kiss I'd witnessed between them and wanted to make sure she knew I wasn't trying to undermine whatever they had. Brandon was going to need as many people in his corner as possible in the very near future, and if he wanted Ariel to be one of them, then I wanted her for him.

I was saved from having to answer her by Brandon's entrance from the back room. That same needle of pain from the first time I'd seen him up close punctured my heart. It wasn't as sharp, but it was there. I held the counter tighter, waiting and dreading the moment he'd notice me and feel it too. When he saw Ariel, his smile was almost embarrassingly happy, but when he followed her gaze to me, he looked instantly ready to vomit.

"Apparently, she's here for you," Ariel said to Brandon, in a voice that made us both flinch, before disappearing through the door Brandon had entered.

He wanted to go after her, I could tell by the way his shoulders started to turn when she passed him, but his feet stayed cemented to the floor. If he followed her, he'd have to explain my presence, and he looked like he'd rather stick his fist in a blender.

"What are you doing here?" If Ariel's greeting had been chilly, Brandon's was subzero. "You need to leave. Now."

If I'd thought he might have softened toward me in the weeks since we first met, I was so very wrong. Before, he'd been struck dumb, so overwhelmed by his need for denial that he'd been able to generate only a flicker of true anger. But the animosity he was shooting off at our second meeting was lethal. I hesitated under his glare, but since I knew I was bringing him something good rather than earth-shattering, I couldn't slink away. I wasn't adding to the horrible discovery from last time; I was telling him he had another sister, one who played the guitar like he did and, if he wanted, he could see her play that very night.

And then maybe he'd want to play again too. Maybe we could talk about all of it and he wouldn't have to hurt alone. Maybe I could tell him all the other little things that we shared, the three of us. I could tell him we liked fishing too, that we'd all taken the same photo with Chip and Dale at Disneyland. I could tell him that I loved kung fu movies as much as he did, and if he didn't love baseball, Sel and I could teach him why he should.

"Brandon—"

His eyes flared and he was suddenly right in front of me. He'd moved so fast and so forcefully that I took a step back.

"You don't say my name. You don't come to my work. You don't—"

"And I won't do any of this ever again. I'm not here to talk about—" I abandoned the names I'd been going to say when he tensed as though readying for a blow. My eyes swam with tears. I'd done it all so badly before. I'd ruined his life and just left him without getting to share anything good, and Selena *was* good, just like he was a good thing to me and would be to her. Whatever our respective parents had done decades ago, it didn't change the fact that we were siblings. "I never meant to hurt you, then or now. Please, I just need—"

"What about what *I* need!" The sound he made was in-human, like an animal caught in a snare. It startled me into silence and brought Ariel back up front. Brandon's shoulders hunched, and I knew he was aware that we had an audience. He wasn't going to say a single word in front of her, and he was naked in his pleading for me to remain silent, as well. "I'll just be a second," he said, half turning his head in Ariel's direction but never taking his eyes from me. We walked to the door, and his arm lifted to open it for me before he checked the impulse and dropped his hand. I told myself that his anger wasn't wholly meant for me, but my hands still shook as I pushed open the door.

As soon as the door closed behind us, preventing Ariel from hearing us, Brandon turned on me. "Please," he said, letting a sliver of desperation cut through his hostility. "I don't want to hear any more." His head extended forward. "I can't."

I opened my mouth, then shut it. How could I begin to tell him about Selena in the seconds I had before Ariel came out and took him away from me? Already I could see her through the window, edging around the counter and taking slow steps toward the door.

Brandon turned when my eyes left his, seeing Ariel's approach, as well. Looking back at me, he said, "Please don't do this. You get that you're ruining my life, right? Every second you stand here, you make it harder for me to explain you away."

I winced, but if he saw it, he gave no indication. I didn't want him to explain me away any more than I wanted to explain him away. I wanted to tell him he had another sister, one who wasn't any part of the mistakes I'd made with him. Afterward, if he still didn't want anything to do with us, then at least he'd know what he was walking away from.

"I'll go, but there's a coffee shop called Lava Java, and—"

"Fine. My shift is almost over. If you leave now, I'll meet you there." He looked over his shoulder again. Ariel was now on the other side of the door, arms crossed and staring. "Just go, now."

And he was gone before I could say another word.

CHAPTER 33

I waited outside Lava Java as long as possible, but Brandon had only said his shift was almost over. I had no idea what *almost* meant. Ten minutes? Thirty? An hour? It wasn't cold, but I kept rubbing my arms and gnawing on my bottom lip as I scanned the parking lot for… I didn't even know what kind of car he drove, or if he'd had second thoughts and wasn't going to show at all. Or what if he came late and saw Selena before I had a chance to explain? What if she saw *him* before I had a chance to slip him into the back? The point was for him to see her, and then, when I'd had the chance to tell her everything and she was ready, I could tell her that he'd been there and heard her. Except my stomach was steadily punching its way up my throat as the minutes rushed by and there was still no Brandon.

Inside, people were already performing. Selena was scheduled as one of the last to go on, but the longer I stayed outside, the more nervous she'd get, thinking I wasn't going to show.

"Dana!" Selena burst out of the door at my back. "I've been freaking out for the past twenty minutes. Where were you?"

"I'm sorry, I was just..." My voice trailed off as I took in her appearance. She had on more makeup than usual, and she'd made her hair do this soft wave thing around her face. She looked like Selena, and she didn't. She didn't look like Selena the softball player or Selena the college student. She didn't look like my big sister. I wasn't smiling when she reached me.

"Never mind. I don't want to hear another lie anyway." She pressed her hands over her stomach. "I'm so nervous. Do I look nervous?"

"You look different," I said, unsure why that bothered me so much but knowing that it did. Selena's hands flew to her hair.

"Whitney convinced me to try extensions. You can't tell, can you?"

"Who's Whitney?"

"She's a friend of mine—mine and Gavin's really, since he introduced us. I'll make sure you meet her after. Did I mention I'm nervous?"

"Yeah, you—"

"Come on, there's only a couple tables left." She turned, towing me inside with her. "Gavin's running late and there aren't usually this many people here." Selena's gaze drifted around the room. "He put the word out with some people he knows, and I guess a lot of them came."

I spied an open table in the far corner and started toward it, but Selena tugged me to a stop. "No, I need you up front. If I get nervous..." Her laugh was a little shaky. "*When* I get impossibly more nervous, I can look straight ahead and see you." She nodded at a spot much closer to the makeshift stage, which was really just a stepped-up section of the coffee shop with some lighting and audio equipment.

"What am I saying? I won't have to look for you—you'll probably be booing pretty loud by then."

I pulled free of her grip. "Hey, no one is going to be booing, least of all me. I get that you're nervous, but enough. I'm sorry I'm late, 'cause that guy murdering the theme song to 'Zelda' with I don't even know what kind of flute is clearly a once-in-a-lifetime moment, but I wouldn't have missed this, okay?"

She took a deep breath and then flung her arms around my waist. "I'm sorry. I don't know why I'm so panicky. Gavin's usually here when I sing, and you're usually not. And I just don't want to mess this up, you know?"

I did know. From over her shoulder I stole another glance at the window, and my own panic came skittering back. "You're going to be great."

She let me go. "Tell that to my hands. I mean, I never got this nervous before a game. Feel them." She reached for mine only to frown a second later. "Why are yours shaking?" Her face fell. "I really can sing, Dana. Maybe not as well as—"

"No, I know you can." I pulled my gaze from the window. "I just want you to be happy. I want all of us to be happy."

"Then maybe stop looking like you could cry any second," Selena said. "Because I can't be happy if you're not."

I gave her a smile that didn't reach my eyes, but fortunately, "Zelda" guy was finished and basking in his smattering of applause. Selena turned to clap too. In profile, she looked even less like herself. She did look pretty, beautiful even, but standing across from me, she looked like she was already gone, to Nashville or some other stage and spotlight much bigger than the one at Lava Java. She really was leaving. Not two-hours-away-at-college leaving, where I still saw her multiple times a week, but like I-need-to-take-a-plane-to-get-to-her leaving. That thought made my stomach clench.

"Did I tell you what song I'm doing?"

I shook my head. "Something you wrote?"

"Nooooo. I'm not even close to being ready for that yet. 'Landslide' by Fleetwood Mac."

My mouth lifted. "I love that song."

"Why do you think I picked it?" She grinned at me, and I almost teared up on the spot.

"I love you too, okay? Just don't forget that."

"I have to head up in a minute. Where are you going to be?" The table up front was thankfully occupied by then.

"I'll grab one in the back, but I'll make sure you can see me."

She nodded as we started moving in opposite directions. "And if somebody really awesome goes before me, try to make a scene or something awful for me to follow, okay?"

I didn't want to dwell on how easy that request might be. As soon as I took my seat, deciding with a heavy heart and a little bit of relief that he wasn't coming after all, Brandon slid into the seat next to me.

CHAPTER 34

I could only gape at him. There. Next to me. "You came."

"I didn't have a choice." Brandon's teeth were clenched so tight I was afraid he'd break his jaw.

I swallowed. His hostility was still in full force. It was painful to watch, knowing I'd done my part to make him feel that way. "I'm sorry," I said. "I should never have ambushed you that first day. You didn't know me, and I showed up at your work reeling from things that I'd had no time to process myself, let alone figure out how to tell someone else." And I could have tried harder to stop him from reading the DNA results.

Brandon was staring straight ahead, not looking at me, but I knew he was listening by the way his shoulders began hunching up.

"I don't know how to deal with having a brother," I said, a tear slipping down my cheek. Another singer was bowing, and I watched Selena offstage, sliding her guitar strap over her head, readying to take his place. "And maybe you don't know how to deal with having a sister, but that's just it—you don't have one, you have—"

"I can't have a sister." He forced the words through barely moving lips. "All I have is my dad, and all we have is a memory. She died right after I was born and I have one photo with her—one! And now I can't even look at it anymore. There aren't any pictures of her in my house, and I always thought it was because he missed her too much, but that's not it. There aren't any pictures because he doesn't want any, because it's enough to have to see me and know—" the muscle in his cheek jumped "—know I'm not his." His voice nearly broke, and a part of me broke with it. "She died and he had to raise some other guy's kid, but there wasn't a single day where he made me feel unwanted or unloved. And I will *never* do that to him." His head turned sharply to me. "Which means I can't have a sister or anything else that reminds either of us that I'm not his."

He took in my face, the second tear that had joined the first. His voice lost a fraction of its edge, then a fraction more. "This isn't about you. I don't even know you, and you don't know me. We've lived our entire lives without realizing the other even existed, and we can keep on living those lives, because this—" he dropped a crumpled paper on the table, and my eyes snagged on the DNA Detective logo visible on the side "—is the only thing that connects us. I'm sorry, but I don't want more from you, and I'm asking you not to force more from me."

I lifted my tear-filled eyes to his. I understood what he was doing—protecting one relationship by excluding the possibility of another. I might have done the same thing in his position, only I wasn't in his position, and I couldn't just walk away. From the corner of my eye, I saw Selena moving to the center of the stage. "I don't want to walk away, but if it's what you want, I won't come back to your work, and I won't try to contact you again. But, Brandon..." Pain had taken root deep in my chest, and the shoots were burrowing their way through every part of me as I glanced at the paper between us. "It's not the only thing that connects us. Look." I nodded my head toward Selena.

Brandon's eyes moved even as his body fought the movement.

"Hi, everyone. My name is Selena Fields and I'm going to be singing 'Landslide' by Fleetwood Mac." She angled the mic toward her mouth, finding my face as she did. "I hope you like it."

She started picking out the first notes on her guitar and I felt my heartbeat rise along with them. And then she started to sing. I didn't know who to watch, my brother or my sister.

Selena's voice was lovely. It had this twinge of sadness, but it was so pure that I think I might have wanted to cry listening to her, even without watching my brother see his older sister for the first time. Brandon was caught up in her too, her voice, the lyrics. His shoulders began to lower.

I heard when Selena's voice changed, and looking at her, I saw her eyes weren't focused on me. She was looking at Brandon with a slight frown—a frown that shouldn't have been there, because she shouldn't have been able to see him, not clearly. He was supposed to be in the shadows, but he wasn't. He was too tall, just like our dad, and there was no missing him. Her voice caught once, like she'd forgotten to take a breath, and I stopped breathing completely even as she kept singing. I ached to see inside her head—both their heads. Did she know just from looking at him? Could she see it as clearly as I could, or was she reacting to something she saw in him but couldn't explain?

The same confusion didn't linger on Brandon's face. Even with the lights and makeup, he'd heard her say her name— the same last name I'd given him when we met, the same last name on the DNA test results he'd seen. He knew who was singing on that stage.

The song ended, the last note drifting off into a second or two of silence, no more, before every person in the coffee shop was clapping, save two.

Brandon stood, not hurriedly or with any kind of anger. His chair slid back from the movement, and he walked out. With a glance at Selena, who was still frowning at his retreating form, I followed him outside.

He hadn't gone far, right outside the door really. He'd stopped to lean against the wall, his head hanging forward. If he was breathing, I couldn't see it.

With the door shut behind me, I moved to his side and wiped the tears from my face before placing a hand on his shoulder. Instantly, he jerked away.

"I'm sorry. I'm sorry about all of this, but it's not just you and me. She doesn't know yet, but—"

The door opened again, and Selena was there. None of us said anything. We just stood there, no more than a handful of inches between us.

"Dana, what—" She couldn't finish her own question. She

wouldn't have known what to ask to explain the guy standing next to me. Only he wasn't standing next to me; he was
walking as fast as it was humanly possible to walk without
running.

"Brandon, wait!" But he didn't even glance back before he
was in his car, and with a squeal of tires, he was gone.

Gone. And I knew he'd never come back.

My legs were shaky as I turned away from the now vacant
parking spot. Selena was still standing there, still frowning.

"Who was that?" she asked, bewilderment lifting her voice.

And I couldn't justify lying to her anymore. My heart
cleaved clear in two when I said it.

"Selena...that was Brandon. He's our brother."

CHAPTER 35

"He's what?" Selena pulled a face, somewhere between a sneer and a scrunch. "That's a really unfunny joke, Dana, even for you."

"Sel." I took a step toward her, letting her hear how every word killed me. "I would never joke about this. You saw him. You have to have seen it. I *saw* you see it when you were singing."

Selena's gaze roamed my face and her voice went breathy. "I can't believe this."

"I didn't want to believe it either but—"

"No," she said. "Why do you keep doing this? Are you really this starved for attention that you need to make up something like this? Think about what you're saying."

No, I thought, cold creeping up my insides. *She's supposed to believe me.* "Thinking is all I've been doing since I found out Dad cheated with his mom and—"

"This is about Dad? Oh my gosh, Dana, grow up!" Her

arms snapped to her sides. There wasn't anything soft left in her expression. Her eyes narrowed and her tone went sharp. "What has he done to make you come up with something so despicable?"

"This!" I said, but she wasn't listening.

"You can't go around saying stuff like this. What if someone actually believed you?"

"You're supposed to believe me! Just stop and listen——"

"No, *you* stop it!" I recoiled at the vehemence in her voice. "Ever since I moved home, you've been unbearable. Sniping at Mom and being unconscionably cruel to Dad. And I don't get it. Is it me? Am I taking something from you by being there that's making you act up like this? I mean, you're seventeen, Dana." She shook her head in disgust.

"This isn't about you! Of course, you would think that—"

"Uh-huh," she said, like I was making her point for her.

The instinct to grit my teeth was fleeting. If any part of her believed any part of what I was saying, she'd be dying inside, hurting the same way I had. The thought shattered me. "It was the DNA test, Sel." My voice trembled, and I didn't stop it. "That's when all this started, not when you moved home."

So quickly that I almost missed it, Selena's eyes flew to mine and there was a flicker of something other than annoyance. I took advantage of her momentary silence.

"Brandon McCormick came up as a match with Dad, a nearly 50 percent match, Selena. That means he's either Dad's father or his son. Did he look like a member of AARP?"

"Dana. Stop," she said, in the kind of voice used to talk people down from bridges.

"Why don't you believe me?"

"You told me the results were a bust, no real matches."

"I know, but I was lying then because I didn't want to hurt you."

"And this isn't hurting me?" She huffed, more a sound of exhaustion than anything else. "So the first thing was a lie, but this is the truth? Why shouldn't I believe it's the other way around?"

I stepped toward her, reaching for her hand even as she pulled back. "Because I wouldn't lie about something like this—you know I wouldn't."

"No? You've gotten really good about lying about everything else."

"I don't want to believe this any more than you do, but it's true." I pressed my clenched fist to my stomach and forced her eyes to stay locked with mine. "I have been going insane holding all this inside. I've barely been able to be in the same room with Dad, and looking at Mom makes me want to cry. And then I've been feeling so guilty around you, because I was stealing more time from you knowing your brother on top of the years you already missed. And Chase—" I closed my eyes when I said his name, my throat working before I opened them again. "You just have to believe me. *Please* believe me."

But she didn't. I could see it in her face.

"Why did that guy take off, then?"

"Because it's hard. Every bit of this is hard." I drew out the last word. "Brandon's mom died right after giving birth to him, and he doesn't want to hurt the man who raised him by acknowledging us."

She started blinking too fast at me. Then it was like she

shook it off. "No. How am I supposed to believe any of this? He's lying, and Dad's lying, and you're lying some of the time but not all of the time." She leaned toward me. "And I'm supposed to believe you now because this is one of the nonlying times, right?"

"You're right," I said, and the frown crept back onto her face. She hadn't been expecting me to admit that. "I have been lying about a lot, to you and Mom and Dad. But I'm not lying about this. Look, I'll pull up his picture on my phone and you'll—" My hand slid over the flat back pocket of my jeans, and then I was frowning too.

"I'll what? What do you want me to do here?" Her lips compressed, and I saw the hint of a quiver in her chin. "Just go home, Dana."

"Will you talk to me at home?" The quiver in my chin was much more than a hint, but Selena started shaking her head while I was still talking.

"I'll stay over at Whitney's. I seriously can't even look at you right now." She pushed open the door to Lava Java and was gone.

And that wasn't even the worst part. When I looked away from that shut door, I saw Chase standing not ten feet away, holding the phone I'd forgotten at his house.

CHAPTER 36

I wanted to shrink away at the sight of Chase moving toward me. Not because he looked angry or cold, like the last two faces I'd seen, but because he looked like I'd hurt him when he'd never have done the same to me. Any hope that he hadn't heard us vanished.

He stopped a few paces away and stared at me. He didn't say anything. Selena had yelled and Brandon had seethed, but Chase's silence was somehow worse. I had no altruistic excuse for the pain my actions had caused him. I wasn't introducing him to a sibling; I'd used him, and now he knew it. Brandon had begged me to stay out of his life, and I'd done the complete opposite. I'd dug myself into it as deeply as I could, through Chase and even his mom.

And I knew I'd lost him.

Bruising pain gushed through me. I should have walked away that first day we met. I should have let him leave me crying in the parking lot.

He lowered his eyes when mine started to well up with tears. Looking down at his hand, he slid my phone onto one of the nearby outdoor tables. "You left this. You said your sister was singing here, and I thought you might need it."

His voice was steady, neither harsh nor hopeful. He was just Chase, direct and to the point. After everything he'd overheard, and whether he believed any of it or not, only one thing mattered to him.

"Was it always about him?"

Brandon.

My heart slammed against my chest in denial, beating against my ribs as I stayed silent. I wanted to say no, but the truth was uglier than that. All those little and not-so-little ignored thoughts swelled in my gut, accusing me until my heart could no longer move under the onslaught.

"I'm sorry."

Chase tucked both lips into his mouth and nodded more to himself than me.

And I couldn't stop him when he left.

I sat in my car for hours after Lava Java closed and the parking lot emptied, feeling as crushed as the printed DNA results I'd finally remembered to retrieve. I smoothed open the paper on my lap, noticing deep crease lines in several places. How many times had Brandon folded and unfolded this paper? And yet he'd kept it. A tear hit the top corner, blurring a little of the ink as it spread. Would it even have mattered if I'd shown it to Selena? Or would she have accused me of printing a fake result like I had supposedly tried to produce a fake brother?

I hadn't meant to tell her like this. It was just supposed to be

Brandon seeing her and then taking time—however long—to decide what he wanted without pressure. Then, when it was just the two of us, after I had every word planned out, I'd tell my sister about our brother. But not like this. Another tear hit the paper I held. Not when she'd just sung in front of me for the first time and was half expecting me to tell her she wasn't good enough.

She was. I hadn't even gotten to tell her how beautiful she was on that stage, how every eye in the coffee shop was focused on her as she sang, and how I hadn't wanted her to stop.

I put the paper away, following the deep folds Brandon had created, and my fingers stopped on a section that might have been a dried tear. I squeezed my eyes shut so that I wouldn't add to it. I'd had one chance with Brandon to offer him something good, something to show him he didn't have to cry alone, but that chance was gone, and I had nothing more to offer him. And the one ally I'd hoped to have now found my presence so abhorrent that she couldn't even share a house with me, much less a room.

I hadn't stopped at just losing my brother and my sister either. I'd lost Chase too.

I sat in my car, feeling like the wind had been knocked out of me, gasping for air that wouldn't come and knowing I had no one to blame but myself.

CHAPTER 37

The next night was our last game before the finals, and I nearly missed it. I'd thought things would at least be easier around my parents, but I was wrong. I still felt sick over the inevitable fallout that would come when they learned about Brandon, because there would still be fallout. Discovering Dad didn't know he had a son just meant there'd be a lot less anger to temper the pain.

That whole following day after Lava Java, I slunk around my house, hiding from my parents as best I could, claiming, for instance, that I needed to steal a few extra minutes for homework just so I wouldn't have to ride with them to the game.

My team nearly paid the price for my cowardice when I continued to drag about my house after they left, only truly moving when a glance at the clock sent me crashing down the stairs and out the door.

At red lights, I pulled off my shirt and shorts and wriggled into my uniform, not even caring that anyone next to me might see. Once I got to the field, I flung my door open and sprinted toward the lights, my heart sinking as I skidded into the empty dugout. I was the last girl to arrive, but they all turned toward me from the field, where warm-ups were already under way.

Yeah, I'd made it, but it was close enough that no one was particularly thrilled with me.

I didn't offer an excuse—not only because I didn't have one, but because none would have been acceptable—as I joined them on the field, muttering an apology to each of my teammates and finally Dad.

"I'm sorry."

He didn't look at me, but I looked at him. For the first time in more than a month I looked at him without wanting to crawl outside my own skin. I looked at him, and I wanted to cry. Not because he'd hurt me—though he had—but because I knew that soon I'd have to devastate him.

"I nearly scratched you from the lineup card."

I nodded and listened with growing shame to the passing remarks from several of my teammates.

"What the hell, Dana?"

"Where were you?"

"What's more important than this?"

Used to be I would have said *Nothing*, and I would have meant it. Nothing was more important than getting my team to state. But that was before I'd found Brandon, before I had to spend weeks living with the sick dread that Dad had known, before I lost my brother, my sister and the guy I'd fallen for all in one night. It was before I had to look at myself and question the drive to win I'd always thought was for the game itself.

It didn't matter that our team won the game—narrowly. I hadn't pulled my weight, and it was obvious to everyone. The only one who didn't rag on me was Jessalyn, though if we'd lost, even she would have had a hard time not blaming me. When we were finally alone in the dugout, without fear of being overheard, she laid it out.

"I know you are dealing with unbelievably hard stuff right now, and it kills me that I can't help you, but, Dana, you can't keep doing this. We need you here, all of us. We're a team and when you're late like this, it looks like you don't care." She sat next to me, close enough that her shoulder leaned into mine, and the contact helped to soften the sting of her words. "I know you care about every player on this team. I just don't want them to doubt that, okay?"

I nodded, but I couldn't do more than that. Jessalyn wasn't trying to kick me when I was down, but I was so low at that point it felt like it anyway.

I left her gathering her stuff in the dugout and ran smack into...

"Nick."

He'd been MIA at my games since we'd talked. I understood, but that didn't mean I'd missed seeing his face any less. Things between us at school were still strained, but according to Jessalyn, he was fine at work and, though she didn't say it, basically anywhere I wasn't. I wasn't going to assume he'd come to the game just for me, but the fact that he had come despite knowing he'd see me meant I could hope our friendship wasn't done for good. I could use a little hope right then.

"I'm really glad you came."

Nick swallowed three times in rapid succession. "Yeah, I um... Dana, I'm not— I mean, yeah, but—"

I smiled at him. He really was a great guy, even flustered and so nervous that he couldn't meet my eye. I heard someone coming up behind me and I turned back to see Jessalyn emerging from the dugout. She slowed when she saw me with Nick, but I waved her closer. Nick would probably be more comfortable if it wasn't just the two of us. My smile fell as I turned back to Nick, who wasn't having any trouble looking at her. In fact, his expression was almost pleading when she reached my side.

I started as if someone had fired a gunshot. How had I been so stupid? "You like him," I said to her. I would have picked up on it if I hadn't been so distracted by everything with my family.

Jessalyn met Nick's gaze before answering, though the look alone was confirmation enough. "I've liked him all year." She said it almost like a confession. Maybe to him it was.

Guys were kind of a gray territory once they'd dated another teammate. Nick and I had never been officially anything, but it was close enough that Jessalyn wasn't bounding with excitement waiting for my reaction.

"All year?" I asked, my voice registering how stunned I was. "Are you kidding me right now?"

She slowly drew closer but said nothing.

"Jess—" I had no idea what to say to her. I turned to Nick. "And you came tonight for her."

He tried to make his head disappear into his shoulders.

I could suddenly see how it must have happened. All the

shifts they were working together, and they were probably talking at night. Another piece fell into place. "That night I came over and you were weirdly secretive about your laptop, was that because you guys were messaging?"

"Nothing was remotely going on then. I just wasn't sure how you'd feel, knowing I liked him with everything else going on. Are you mad?" Jessalyn asked.

I felt disoriented and hurt, like I'd taken a ball to the head. "No, I'm not mad, but then why did you keep pushing me to…" I'd been going to say she'd been pushing me to go out with him, but she hadn't. She'd been pushing me to decide how I felt without making me take her feelings into consideration. It had never even occurred to me, because Nick was so shy and Jess was so not-shy. But even if I never would've thought of the two of them, I'd have expected her to tell me—and Nick—straight off if she liked him. "Why didn't you tell me?"

"Tell you what? That I was falling for the guy who practically levitated every time he saw you? You kind of did," she added to Nick when he and I both made a strangled noise of protest. "What good would it have done?"

"Dana!" Mom was shouting at me from the parking lot. "I need your keys."

My eyes shut. Dad would want to drive home alone with me so it would be nice and private when he chewed me out for nearly being late again. "I don't know what to say right now, but I have to go."

Jessalyn's face fell. "But we'll talk, right?"

"Dana!" That time it was Dad calling me.

"Yes, we'll talk. I promise." I hurried to the parking lot,

registering the sympathetic look from Mom when I handed her my keys and watched her drive off.

"You've never been late to a game before," Dad said. He didn't get in the car right away. Neither did I. "And now you've been almost late twice in a month." He rested his arms on the hood, his head shaking as he spoke. "You almost didn't play tonight, and college isn't that far away. I've been talking to the coach at ASU about you—other schools too. Is that what you want them to see? You warming the bench the entire game? Because that's what'll happen if you pull this again."

"I don't want that," I said, my gaze on the asphalt.

"You made a commitment to this team, to me. That's supposed to mean something."

The muscle behind my eye started throbbing. I didn't want to think about how little he'd once cared about commitment. I just wanted to feel one emotion at a time. I wanted to be only angry with him or only feel sorry for him, not this stomach-churning mix that kept me from even looking at him.

"I won't be late again. I promise."

I got into the car then, and after a moment, he took his own seat and we drove home, both of us angry and confused, when I was the only one with a right to either of those emotions.

I was lying on my stomach alone on my bed later when Mom knocked and poked her head in. I sat up as she came in and slid around behind me. Without a word, she combed my hair with her fingers before beginning to braid it.

"So, fun ride home?"

I leaned back against her and closed my eyes. "I didn't mean to show up at the last minute, I really didn't."

"If you don't mean to do something, you have to try harder not to." She tied off my hair and rested her hands on my shoulders. "I know it's hard being seventeen, but it's hard being forty-one too. Lay off your dad." And in the same sweet voice she added, "Otherwise, I'll have to strangle you in your sleep."

I laughed a little the way I was supposed to. "You love him a lot, don't you?"

"More than all the Kisses in the world." She leaned in and brushed her mouth against my forehead. "Look at the beautiful girls he gave me."

I caught her wrists when she started to stand. "Always?"

She frowned a little.

"Will you always love him more than all the Kisses in the world? Even when he messes up, when he does unlovable things?"

"Is this about the boy you've been disappearing with, hmm? Not tonight, but we're going to talk about that."

I wasn't even mad that Selena had told Mom. I'd known she would. They were both too alike to keep secrets.

"No, that's...over." I ducked my head, hiding my slight chin quiver. "I'm asking about Dad because—" I met her gaze again "—I need to know you'll still love him even when it's hard."

She pulled her head back, the teasing smile leaving her lips. "Of course I will."

I closed my eyes and started to stand. I wanted so much more than the automatic answer from her.

"Hey." She drew my attention back to her. "Love isn't always easy, not the good kind. The kind that may start here—" she tapped two fingers against her chest "—but finds its way here too." She lifted her hand to her head. "That kind of love is more than a feeling or a word. That kind of love is an action, a promise, and it's not dependent on perfection or ideals. It's real and lasting and it's worth everything. It's worth fighting for. And we're fighters, yes?" She waited for my nod before filling her lungs with air and smiling. "So I fight for the people I love. Always."

She kissed me one last time before closing my door softly when she left. I waited less than a minute before following her. I stopped at the top of the stairs and listened to her slide in next to Dad on the couch. After a moment, her voice drifted up to me.

"I think you should go up and talk to her."

"I already talked to her." And by the sound of his voice, he'd had enough. I drew back farther from the edge of the wall hiding me from view.

"You yelled at her. There's a difference." There was a pause. "She's always trying so hard to make you see her. Maybe she's trying a new way."

"How do I not see her? Practices, games, I was spending hours with her in the backyard until—"

"See her apart from softball."

I leaned into the wall at my side, pressing closer so I'd be sure to hear his response.

"I see her," was all he said, but softer.

There was a sound that might have been a kiss. "I know, *mi alma*, but sometimes it can be hard to feel it. And Dana needs to feel it. If you can't say it, then you have to find a way to show it."

Back in my room I leaned against my door, half wanting to bolt downstairs and...stand there openmouthed, because it wasn't just Dad who didn't know how to say things. I did want him to see me, to fight for me. I'd always wanted that; even now I wanted it. Especially now. I slid to the floor and drew my knees up, hugging them.

I just wanted to skip past all this next part. I wanted to jump ahead to after I told my parents, to after all the pain, to where it was okay again. To where it was just softball and stupid problems with my friends at school. I let my head bang against my door. All year Jessalyn had liked Nick. *All year.* It must have killed her watching me waver back and forth with him. If she'd just told me she liked Nick, that would have made it so easy for me to realize I didn't. Clearly Nick was open to the idea—more than open. It would have been perfect, and no one would have gotten hurt. I banged my head again. And again. Because I couldn't skip ahead. I had to deal with the now. I glanced at Selena's guitar case, which was leaning against her side of the bed, and I knew my brother's was probably in a similar position in his room.

Actually, for all I knew, he'd thrown it away. I hugged my knees tighter, gripping my elbows until the skin turned white.

CHAPTER 38

Selena decided to extend her stay with Whitney indefinitely. Mom thought Selena's ongoing absence was due to lack of support from her and Dad with Gavin and Nashville, an assumption I was in no position to disabuse her of.

"I think my room was just getting a little crowded," I told her on Tuesday while school was canceled due to a power outage. We were grocery shopping, a task that she positively loathed and always needed company to complete. "She doesn't have to share a bed at Whitney's."

Mom was scowling as she turned down the cereal aisle, her flip-flops slapping on the worn linoleum behind her. "She doesn't come to the game, and she's suddenly working double shifts and can't come to dinner." Mom shook her head. "This is about more than a bed."

I added a box of my favorite cereal to the cart, tugging the front of it along behind me until Mom's resistance on the other end stopped me. I looked back.

"Forget something?"

I stared blankly at her.

"Your dad's Raisin Bran?"

With half a nod, I knocked another box in the cart.

"Well, you've talked to her. What did she say?"

I shrugged, randomly adding nonlist items to our cart. I wasn't paying attention to which aisles we turned down, grabbing whatever Mom directed and continuing to make noncommittal responses to her questions, until the cart not-so-gently hit my back and pitched me forward a few jerky steps.

"Mom!"

"Oh, are you alive? You've been shuffling along like a zombie since the canned-goods aisle. You're supposed to make grocery shopping less soul sucking, not more. Between your moping and Selena's absence, I'm starting to question my mothering skills."

"Me too. Maybe don't ram your kids with grocery carts." I rubbed the small of my back for emphasis.

"This is the most alive you've been in days, weeks. Dana, is something wrong? You know you can tell me anything." She shifted from the somewhat playful tone to something more earnest. "Even if you think I'll be upset, I want you to know you can come to me."

I found myself wanting to believe she meant even something as horrible as Dad cheating and fathering a child. That I could talk to her about Brandon the way I'd always been able to talk to her about anything. That she could fight her way through all that and somehow still love him enough to grieve over the son he never knew. And maybe she could, but not without me and Sel there with her.

"I'm sorry, Mom. School and softball have been a lot lately." When she didn't nod at my feeble excuse, I gave her something a little closer to the truth. "And Selena and I got into this fight. That's the real reason she's staying over at Whitney's."

Mom shot a hand toward me. "And were either of you going to tell me this? You know you could have said something." The cart started moving again, and I relaxed, knowing she was accepting my half-truth. "Do I want to know what the fight was about?"

"No," I said, turning away from her. "You really don't."

Mom sighed. "And as long as you work it out before tomorrow night, I won't say another word." She picked up two boxes of cake mix from the shelf.

"What's tomorrow night?"

"I'm going to pretend you didn't say that. Now help me pick." She turned the boxes toward me. "Chocolate or yellow? He changes his mind every year."

Sweat prickled at my neck as I looked at them.

She tossed them both in the cart. "We'll do one of those swirl cakes, *mármol*—what is the word in English?"

"Marble." My steps slowed to a halt as she continued down the aisle to grab frosting and birthday candles.

Thursday was Dad's birthday. We always had a family dinner just the four of us. From the moment Nick had told me about his DNA test results, I'd been dreaming of that dinner and the look on his face when I gave him my gift and told him I'd found a family member of his. Finding Brandon had consumed me so entirely that I'd forgotten why I'd gone looking for Dad's relatives in the first place. I'd forgotten about his birthday and the fact that I no longer had a gift for him, but something much more horrible for all of us.

I pulled out my phone and read the last text I'd sent to Selena.

Me: Please talk to me.

That was two days ago and she still hadn't responded.

Mom was right about my being a zombie lately. I'd felt even less alive since that night at Lava Java. I missed Chase. I had no right to miss him, but I did. And I missed him for *him*, not because of what I could learn from him. He was a channel of information that had been cut off, and I wouldn't have cared if I could still see him.

Brandon remained a distant figure. I was no closer to him than I'd ever been, but knowing I'd wasted my one real opportunity to forge a relationship with him was more devastating than I could have imagined. In the span of two months, I'd gone from cursing his existence to mourning his loss. But as often as my thoughts strayed to Chase and Brandon, the absence I felt most acutely was Selena's.

We'd never gone this long without talking. I couldn't remember us going longer than a day without at least texting. This whole thing with Dad and Brandon was the first time I'd kept something important from her, and I'd been so relieved to finally tell her. I'd been so sure that once the shock wore off, she'd come to me and demand to see the DNA test results, probably even insist on testing Dad again. And I'd have let her if she needed more than Brandon himself and what

I'd learned. I didn't. The truth was inescapable. But I would have done it for her; I'd have waited as long as she needed, even if each day pretending with our parents was torturous.

I'd have done that, but I couldn't do this. I needed my sister, mad or happy or any other extreme save absent.

"Dana!"

I lifted my head to see Mom gleefully holding up a novelty candle that spelled out the word *old*.

"He'll hate it, right? I'm getting it." Into the cart it went. I could see her steps get lighter after that, as she was no doubt thinking up more ways to tease Dad. "Oh, and I'll finally get to see what you got him. What did you call it, the gift to end all gifts?"

I heard my answer like it was coming from another room. "Yeah, I think I have to get something else. It didn't work out the way I thought."

She rubbed my arm. "He'll love anything you give him—you know that right?"

"Sure, Mom. I'm just gonna go grab him a movie up front. Then I'll meet you at the register."

CHAPTER 39

"Hey," Jessalyn said when I pulled in next to her car at school the next morning.

"Hey," I said, reaching to grab my bag from the passenger seat and moving wearily since I'd barely slept the night before. Then I said it again, "Hey!" and that time I had guilt invigorating me. "I was going to call you or come by yesterday. I meant to, honest."

"It's okay," she said. "I know you said you weren't mad—"

"I'm not. Not even a little." I closed my door and turned right back to her. "I was just surprised."

She looked down at her hands. "That's fair."

I made a face when we both lapsed into silence. I'd let her spend a whole day thinking I was upset with her, and now she was acting like I needed to forgive her for something, which was so not Jessalyn. I made another face, but one that was solely directed at myself. I was maybe the teensy-tiniest bit more than shocked at seeing them together, but that was only because all my emotions were tainted lately—joy with guilt, anger with grief, love with loneliness. Jessalyn with Nick, there wasn't anything bad about that, and neither of them had anything to feel guilty about.

"Jess, Nick couldn't do any better."

Her eyes lifted first, then her head. "Yeah?"

"I mean, I play way better than you, but he's not really into sports, so—" I broke off when she shoved me, laughing.

"You wish."

"Hey, if Nick's fine with a subpar player for a girlfriend, then that's all that matters."

"Subpar. Subpar?"

I shrugged, biting back a smile. "Mediocre?" Then I snapped my fingers. "Oh, wait, pedestrian!" My hands flew up to block when she came at me, because teasing or not, Jessalyn could knock me on my butt if she wanted to. But she wasn't taking even a playful swipe at me. Both arms slung around my back.

"Dana, I tried to tell you a million times, but I didn't think it mattered, because he didn't like me back."

"You didn't give him a chance to like you back. Clearly he got on board pretty quickly." I felt her stiffen a little. "No, that's a good thing." I let her go. "It's a great thing."

Jessalyn bit her lip to hide a smile. "I do like him."

"A lot."

"A lot," she agreed. "But I didn't want you thinking I'd gone around behind your back or something."

"What back? There was never anything between me and Nick, and if we'd both been honest with each other from the beginning, you and him would have happened a lot sooner."

"You're making me stupid happy right now," she said.

"Just so long as he is too."

Her smile went a little dopey, and I smothered a laugh.

"I'm getting something out of this too. If the two of you are together—you are, right?"

"Oh, you know I locked that down."

"Then that means I get both my friends back, and it's not even my birthday!" My grin didn't even make it all the way onto my face before it died.

Jessalyn understood why without a word. She settled beside me so we were both leaning against the side of my car.

"It's Coach's birthday—I mean your dad's—today. So you still don't know if he knew?"

"No, I know. At least, I think I know." I told her about that last day in Chase's garage. "I just can't see him missing every moment of his son's life and being able to live with himself. I mean, I know he cheated and that's bad enough, but when I saw that picture from the day Brandon was born, I just knew."

"It still sucks, though. Are you going to tell him?"

"I have to, don't I?" I turned my head to her. "I'm certainly not going to do it on his birthday. Selena would never forgive me and I can't do that to my mom. Not like that."

"So, then…when?"

I didn't have an answer for her.

Mom's marble cake idea turned out solid light brown, which annoyed her to no end.

"I watched three hours of YouTube videos. It should have worked," she said.

I felt another pang of guilt watching her slather icing on

Dad's birthday cake. She hated baking even more than she hated cooking. Dad had never had a homemade cake growing up, so every year since they'd gotten married—including the year Brandon was conceived—she made him one. She poured every bit of love she had for him into those cakes. She never held anything back from him, and if I could believe what she told me the other night, she never would.

I heard the front door open and close, then Selena's voice. One of the candles I was unboxing snapped in my hand. I took a step toward the back door even as I craned my neck to glimpse my sister for the first time in days.

"We're in the kitchen," Mom called. She lowered her spatula when Selena appeared in the doorway. "Look," Mom said as an aside to me, halting my quasi retreat. "She's gotten taller. Doesn't she look taller?"

Not taller, but her expression when it met mine was wary and the corners of her mouth were taut before she shifted her gaze to Mom and smiled.

"It hasn't been that long, Mom."

"I haven't seen you in days." Mom pointed the spatula at her. "Try that again and I'll paddle your cute little butt off. Now come here."

Selena obeyed and Mom peppered kisses on her face. "I missed you." And that time her voice held a note of reproof.

"I'm sorry, Mom." Selena's eyes flicked to me, and I took her meaning perfectly. It was my fault she'd had to stay away. I took another step toward the door. "I have an entire guest room to myself at Whitney's, but I promise to come by more."

"Good." Mom swatted Selena. "Go hug your sister. She missed you too."

Neither of us moved. We hadn't been forced to hug and make up since we were little. A lot of that had to do with the fact that we almost never really fought, and when we did, we were terrible at holding a grudge. But we did as we were told, stiffly putting our arms around each other and releasing as quickly as we could get away with under Mom's scrutiny.

Mom sighed but went back to icing the cake and put us to work finishing dinner. I chopped by rote, eyeing Selena and looking for...I didn't know, anything to indicate that she was willing to talk to me again.

She said nothing.

"Gavin coming?" Mom asked.

"No, he had to work," Selena said. "But I have our gift." She nodded at a small wrapped cube on the table next to Mom's present and the movie I'd picked out at the grocery store.

My gift—the original one, anyway—was upstairs in my room in a sealed envelope on my desk. And it would stay there until...until I could bear to give it to him.

Mom tossed me a lime after the vegetables were finished and I flinched catching it. She gave me a funny look but made no comment before returning to her own task. I couldn't focus on what I was supposed to be making for dinner. I couldn't focus on anything until I sliced my finger while chopping fresh coriander. I hissed as a drop of blood fell on the wooden cutting board. It wasn't a deep cut, but Mom had my finger under cold water the second after I'd made a noise.

"Mom, it's fine." I looked away as quickly as I dared. I couldn't let her see me cry, which I felt perilously close to doing with my sister as far away from me as our kitchen would allow.

"Let me get you a bandage," Mom said, heading out of the kitchen. "Keep it under the water."

As soon as she left, I looked at Selena, who was studiously not looking at me.

"I can't stand you not talking to me, not right now."

She slapped a hand towel down on the counter. "What do you want from me?"

I could only shake my head. "You don't believe me, fine, but at least believe that I believe this."

But she turned her back on me again, and my sliced finger wasn't a blip on the pain scale compared to the rest of me.

I was still staring at her when Mom came back. Couldn't Selena see that I wanted to be lying? That I'd give anything for her to be right about me being a jealous attention monger? I'd rather almost anything be true than Dad having had an affair and son.

"Smells good," Dad said, coming in and dropping a kiss on the back of Mom's neck before she shooed him out to the dining room. My gaze trailed him, staying at the doorway even after he was gone, and in turn, I felt Mom's on me.

"You know what, I think I forgot one little thing upstairs. I'll just be real quick."

Selena didn't so much as glance in my direction while we finished cooking or when Mom returned, squeezing my shoulder with a quick, "Smile, it's going to a happy night," before leading us to the dinner table.

Selena's overly bright and enthusiastic demeanor only high-lighted the contrast between the two of us as we ate. But it was Dad's birthday, so Mom didn't call me out on it. Instead she beamed at Dad, kissed him at least a dozen times throughout the meal, whenever the impulse struck her. I eventually had to stare at my plate to hide the tears that kept springing to my eyes.

At last the cake was brought out, and it was covered in so many candles—way more than the forty-two for Dad's age—and the OLD candle prominently placed in the center. Dad pursed his lips seeing it and Mom howled with laughter in response, almost dropping the cake until Selena and I jumped up to take it from her. Mom kept laughing until Dad pulled her into his lap and kissed her soundly. He kept her in his lap while we sang "Happy Birthday" to him and he blew out the candles. Mom started laughing again because it took him two tries to get them out.

Selena was clapping and I was quietly dying watching them all. Smiling and so damn happy.

"Okay, okay," Mom said when the song ended. "I have to say something. Every year, on this day, I'm the one who gets the gift. I get the best husband, the best father and the best friend I could ever ask for." Her eyes were shining as she gazed at him. She always cried on his birthday. "I don't love you half as well as you love me."

"You love me just right," Dad said, covering the hand she rested against his cheek. "So much more than I deserve."

I couldn't duck my head fast enough that time.

"Dana, *mija*." She reached for my hand across the table.

"I'm sorry," I said, blinking away the moisture in my eyes. "I must be tired or something. Can we just open presents and then maybe I can go to bed early?"

"Yes," Mom said, smiling more than she should have considering I'd been nearly crying a moment ago. "I'll grab them." She scrambled from Dad's lap, returning a moment later with the three presents I'd seen earlier but also a silver wrapped box that I hadn't.

"Who's that one from?" Selena asked.

Mom only smiled at her in response.

Dad opened the Diamondback tickets from Mom first, then a watch from Selena that she'd had engraved. When he reached for my gift, Mom stopped him.

"While I'm sure this is a really great movie, I think this is the gift Dana wants you to have." She slid him the silver wrapped box, the size clothing usually comes in.

I frowned as Dad began untying the ribbon on a gift I had neither bought nor wrapped.

"I saw the envelope on your desk—I didn't open it, I swear," she added when I blanched. My heart fisted its way into my throat.

"I just put it in a nicer box."

Horror froze me to my chair, iced over my limbs and kept me from lunging across the table and tearing it from his hands. Not like this. Not with Mom grinning and half-curled around his side. Not with Dad smiling as the silver wrapping paper floated to the floor.

Dad lifted the lid and opened the plain white envelope. His smile faltered. "Dana, what is DNA Detective?"

"No!" Selena shot to her feet. "It's not— She's not—" And then she looked at me, pure panic widening her eyes.

The mood in the room shifted like a switch had been thrown. Mom was no longer smiling, and she'd gone stiff by

Dad's side. Everyone was looking at me when Selena started to cry.

As though in slow motion, Mom and Dad turned their heads back to the paper as he unfolded it.

"It was supposed to be cousins," I said, choking on the words. "Distant cousins."

Dad had been reading as I spoke. The paper was in his hands, and he kept scanning it. I knew the second his eyes saw the top result. I could see it perfectly in my mind, the logo in the corner, the male and female avatar icons, the information listed beside each one: 4 percent match, 7 percent match, 3 percent match, on and on, up to the one that matched 47 percent with Dad—the "father or son" match.

Tears were streaming down my face when I said it. "His name is Brandon. He's eighteen years old, and he's your son."

CHAPTER 40

No one made a sound. Selena was sobbing silently but not a single word escaped her mouth. Mom was the first to speak.

"That can't be. They obviously made a mistake." There was nothing grasping in her voice. She wasn't trying to deny something her brain had instantly accepted. Her faith in Dad was unimpeachable. And unlike Selena when I'd told her, Mom didn't lash out at me. "Honey, I'm so sorry. Is this why you've been so upset lately?" She came around to wrap her arms around me in my chair. "It's not true, okay? Look at me, Dana." It was impossible to resist the gentle command in her voice. "It's not true."

She blurred in my vision as my eyes continued to well up and spill. "His mother's name was Maggie McCormick and she got pregnant when you and Selena were in Texas."

Mom's arms fell slack, releasing me. She stared straight ahead, not at me or Dad or the paper that slipped from his hands when he stood up only to fall to his knees.

"Dad!" Selena was out of her chair and at his side in a second.

"It can't be," he said, his voice hoarse. Like Mom's, his eyes focused on nothing.

Mom's chin lifted and a wounded sound broke free. Dad was on his feet an instant later.

"Adriana," he said, reaching for her. Mom came to life for an instant, slicing her gaze to him. I'd never seen her look at him that way, not in the throes of their most heated argument. Her look cut me as deeply as it clearly did Dad. Drawing back, he aborted the gesture, but he couldn't break free from her Gaze. It pinned him in place. The flare of anger died out, leaving despair and agony in the ashes. There was no fight in her eyes.

"Mom," I said, my chin quivering. "I'm so sorry."

She looked at me, blinking too fast, the only part of her to move. Then her arms jerked back into motion and she wrapped one around me while pulling Selena up and folding us both in her arms.

Selena sobbed uncontrollably into Mom's embrace, the sounds coming just shy of wailing.

Dad had never looked so small or so broken. I cried for him too. For what he'd lost and was actively losing before my very eyes.

Mom spoke first into my hair, then Selena's. "I love you and I love you." Then she released us and walked out of the room and through the front door. A minute later I heard the car backing down the driveway.

Dad said Mom's name and then he was on his feet and moving through the dining room. He grabbed his keys on the way, and then he was running out the front door. I heard his car as he peeled out, and I ground out the ember of hope that had warmed for the tiniest second inside me at seeing him go after her. I remembered Mom's expression too well for anything but ice and ash to fill me.

Alone with my sister and Dad's untouched birthday cake, I gave in to some long-forgotten childish impulse to reach out for Selena's hand, but the second our fingers touched, she spun away from me. Her face was a blotchy, teary mess.

"*Why?* Why did you have to do this?" It was as if she'd sucked all the energy from the room.

Her words stabbed straight through my heart. I kept my knees locked as she grabbed her purse. "Please," I said, watching her jerky movements. "Stay with me. Be mad, but don't leave."

The front door slammed behind her. I let my knees buckle and I sank to the floor, surrounded by torn silver wrapping paper and nothing else.

CHAPTER 41

I was still sitting on the dining room floor when my cell phone rang two hours later. Recognizing the ringtone Mom had programmed for herself, "Enter Sandman" by Metallica, I dove for it. I held the phone to my ear with both hands. "Mom? Mom, I'm so sorry. I didn't mean—"

"No, no, no," she replied, soft and soothing. "You didn't do anything wrong."

"You left," I said. And there was a long pause before she answered.

"I didn't leave. I'm at Dulce's—just for right now."

"Dad went after you. Did he find you? Did you talk to him? Mom, he didn't know. He—"

"We're going to talk about all of this, okay? I promise." And I heard a sound like a muffled sob, like she'd turned away from the phone. "But not right now. Are you okay?"

I tried to sound okay even as my voice shook. "I'm fine."

"Because I will come get you—"

"Mom, it's okay. I've got school in the morning." Aunt Dulce was the only one of Mom's sisters who lived in Arizona, but her apartment was two hours away, and her guest room consisted of a sofa bed in the middle of the living room. But the real reason I turned down Mom's offer was I didn't think I could handle watching her cry. It was bad enough listening to her try to hide it from me over the phone.

"No, you're right, and it's late. I'm going to stay here tonight, but I'll call you in the morning, okay?"

"Okay."

"I love you," she said. "Always."

I still don't know how I said it back, but I did, and eventually, I stopped crying. I got up off the floor and washed my face and, like a robot, cleaned up the dining room and kitchen. When I came back inside after throwing away the birthday cake no one would ever touch, I made it to the top of the stairs, saw the open and empty bedrooms on either side and sank right back to the floor again. I was still sitting there on the top step hours later when Dad came home.

I jerked to my feet at the top of the stairs, watching him lock the front door, then turn, his movements slow to the point of being painful.

I had never seen him cry before, not once.

He'd caught a fastball to the face at a practice a few years ago, and it had hit him with enough force to leave stitch imprints on his forehead for a week, not to mention the close-to-baseball-sized lump that had formed right between his eyebrows. Mom had cried buckets just looking at him, but Dad's eyes hadn't even watered.

Then there'd been the late-night phone call right after

Selena's high school graduation telling us that she'd been in a car accident. Turned out she'd been only banged up a little, but Dad could have been driving to get a haircut instead of to the hospital for all the emotion he'd shown.

Dad was the one who'd had to drive Slammer to the vet when the doctor told us he'd become more cancer than dog and it was time to put him down. Slammer couldn't even stand then, so Dad had scooped up the once-hulking-but-by-then-skeletal ridgeback and carried him to the car. There hadn't been a single tear even when Slammer, the dog Dad had gotten as a puppy before he'd even met Mom, had tried to lick his cheek.

So seeing his tearstained face when he looked up at me was so horrifying that I couldn't breathe. He stepped forward and rested his hand on the banister, but that was it. Actually ascending the stairs seemed beyond him.

"Mom is—"

"Staying at Aunt Dulce's," I said, unable to blink away from his face even as my eyes welled up. "She called."

Dad's head lifted and his hand slid higher on the banister, tightening as it did. "She called? When?"

I told him, then I inhaled in a half gasp, half sob. "I think I know, but, Dad…" My eyes squeezed shut. He couldn't have faked the devastating shock that had brought him to his knees earlier. But I wanted to hear it. "Please tell me you didn't know about him."

"I would never have left my child," Dad said, ascending the first step. Emotion flickered across his face, pinching his brows and forcing him to swallow. "Does he know? Did she tell him?"

My chin quivered. "He didn't until I found him. She died right after he was born."

Dad's eyes fell shut. "I'm sorry to hear that, but his mother was not— It was never—"

"No, stop." My back bumped against the wall and my eyes squeezed shut. Either way, his answer would be unbearable. Either he regretted losing Brandon's mother, or he'd betrayed Mom for something he didn't even care about. Dad's foot stopped on the second step.

When my eyes reopened, Dad was too close, only a couple steps below me. His eyes were red, and he looked like someone who'd just witnessed a horrible accident but hadn't processed it yet. Looking at him and seeing tears in his eyes for the first time, I felt like I'd been in that accident and was bleeding out before him.

"I was going to tell you about Brandon, but not like this. I didn't want Mom and Sel to leave. Dad, I didn't."

Dad blinked rapidly at the sound of his son's name. "Brandon," he repeated. "And he's here, in Arizona. All this time, he's been here."

I started to tell him about his son, I did, but how could I tell him what little I'd learned when it wouldn't come close to making up for all that he'd missed? The words wouldn't come, but the tears did, mine and his.

CHAPTER 42

Mom continued to stay at her sister's, and Dad was...I didn't know. I couldn't talk to him, though every time I entered or left the house, I knew he wanted to ask questions about Brandon that I wasn't ready to answer. Our conversations consisted of the same sentences repeated each day when I got home and he was no longer in coach mode:

"School okay?" he'd ask.

"Fine," I'd say. "Did you talk to Mom?"

He'd shake his head, and I'd turn right back to the door.

"Where are you going?"

"A friend's." I'd already be shutting the door as I answered. Only I never went to a friend's house. I would have gone to Jessalyn's, but now that things were open with her and Nick, she was more than happy to pick up extra shifts at the café with him. And even though Nick and I had had our first non-excruciatingly-painful Biology class in weeks, he was still a little uncomfortable around me, though from lingering embarrassment rather than unrequited love. It was better, though, and each day I saw more and more of the sweet friend returning. I had gotten the chance to tell both him and Jess what had happened with my family, but they could do even less to help than I could, and that was nothing.

Mom was hours away at her sister's. She called every day, asking me if I was okay and assuring me that she loved me. I couldn't blame her for staying away, but I'd always ask, "When are you coming home?" And her answer was always a variation of the same: "I don't know, Dana."

I presumed she talked to Selena too, but if that door had been shut before, it was bolted and chained now. I even tried calling Gavin, but he said only that he'd tell Selena I'd called and then, in a quieter voice that made me think Selena was nearby, said he was sure that if I just gave her some time, she'd reach out to me on her own.

And Brandon. I'd made my promise to him that he'd never have to see me again, and I had to keep it even if it killed me, even if I thought about him every time I looked at Dad or talked to Mom or my calls went unanswered by Selena. And when I thought about Brandon, I also thought about Chase.

So that's where I was four days after Dad's birthday, parked under a massive mesquite tree at dusk, waiting for a glimpse of the person who had the most reason to detest me. I really did just want to look at him. I'd had no intention of getting out of my car and calling out to him as he was getting into his, or walking right up to him until he was forced to look at me. But that's what I did the second I saw him leave his house.

"Chase?" I didn't call out loudly, but he heard me. His head turned in my direction. The expression on his face should have sent me back to my car, but my legs were intent on bringing me closer until we stood just a few feet away from each other.

"Dana." He half lowered his head, shaking it. "You can't come here anymore." He held my gaze with his, not in anger, but resigned and unmoving. As if he shouldn't have needed to say it. That was the only hint of reproof in his voice.

"I know," I said. Because I did know, I did. "I'm so sorry."

"Okay," he said, but not like he was accepting my apology, just acknowledging that I'd said it and dismissing it as easily. He was so distant, and I was crumbling more and more by the second.

"I just want you to know that I—"

"Hey, Dana?" He cut me off without any vehemence or even needing to raise his voice. Like the rest of him, it was steady and aloof. "You don't have to say anything."

Something fluttered in my chest. "I don't?" I took a step closer, needing to be nearer to him and to let that flutter grow.

"Not to me."

The flutter weakened, slowed and stopped, halting my heart along with it. I didn't need to say anything, because there was nothing I could say. That was what he meant. Not that my words to him were unnecessary, but that they were impotent.

"You should go home or wherever, but don't come here, okay?" He still didn't yell or sneer. Nothing in what he said or how he said it held anger in it, just indifference, and it hurt so much more for the lack. Anger I could meet head-on, but I wasn't even worth his antipathy.

It shouldn't have hurt that much. I shouldn't have had any room left for hurt over him on top of Dad and Brandon,

Mom and Selena. But I did, and the pain was no less sharp for the company.

I'd crossed a line with Chase from the very beginning. Whatever evolving rationale I'd used to keep seeing him felt so flimsy in hindsight. It had never been okay to fall for him, and worse, let him fall even a little for me.

Chase waited for me to say okay or nod or show some sign of acquiescence to his request that I go. I don't know which I gave him, but I must have done something, because he got in his car. He looked at me one last time before driving off. The look was less guarded, less controlled. I'd hurt him, badly, maybe even more than I'd hurt myself. And as I watched him leave, even the shreds of my heart shriveled into dust and blew away.

CHAPTER 43

I had another softball game, our last before a weeklong break and then the state finals—if we won. Mom came. I saw her in the stands, but she looked awful, half-dead inside. I already knew I wouldn't play well, a fact that more than a few of my teammates commented on during warm-ups.

"Dana, you okay?"

"Are you sick?"

"Don't worry, we've got this."

I felt slow and sluggish, like I was playing underwater. I was more aware of my parents, separated by dozens of people and a dugout yet closer than they'd been in days, than I was of anything happening on the field. My coach's comments to me were perfunctory. He was watching Mom too.

"At least she came, right?" Jessalyn nudged me with her shoulder as we made our way back to the dugout before the game started. She'd been awesome since I unloaded my family situation on her; Nick too. Neither one of them let me mope, but they were there, they understood. Whenever I fell silent for too long at school, one of them would shake me out of it. Sometimes literally, in Jessalyn's case.

"Yeah," I said, but my funk lingered throughout the game. I started with a pathetic dribbler to the pitcher and didn't get much better. I wouldn't have been nearly as kind to me as some of my teammates were, Jessalyn especially.

She clapped a hand on my shoulder, saying, "We all suck out sometimes. Shake it off."

Only I couldn't, not until the last inning. We were down by two runs with runners on first and second. Fortunately for our team, I wasn't up; Ivy was.

We all had our fingers curled through the chain-link fence around our dugout, and every one of us had our rally caps on—our hats turned inside out—screaming for all we were worth as Ivy lifted her bat and twisted her toe into the dirt in anticipation. She whiffed on her first swing, but on the second she hit a frozen rope deep in the left-center-field gap. Sadie took off like a bullet from first, rounded second and nearly reached home on top of Ainsley in front of her. They turned as one to catch Ivy tearing around third. We held our breath as she raced down the line and dived headfirst into home, just as the throw hit the catcher's mitt.

Cheers erupted from our dugout when the umpire said, "Safe!"

We clogged the entrance getting onto the field. It was a momentary high, winning the game. We were going to the finals. The first thing I did was look into the stands, searching for Selena's face, forgetting that she hadn't come. My winning high plummeted, dragging my heart down with it.

Hands clapped my shoulders. It was Jessalyn. She shook me until a smile was forced to my lips.

"That's right," she said. "We are going to state!"

It was a good feeling, one I focused on to carry me through rounds of hugs with my teammates and shore me up as I texted my sister, even knowing she wouldn't respond.

Me: We won the game 8 to 7. Mom came. Have you seen her?

Nothing.

I caught a ride home with Jessalyn and Nick, not wanting to further infect Dad's sadness by adding my own to the confines of his car. The drive to the game had been depressing enough.

We piled into Jessalyn's Fiat, and she glanced at me once we left the parking lot. "Should we go out for ice cream or something to celebrate? Ooh, we could go to Mostly Bread and get some of the red velvet cupcakes we have right now." Her eyes rolled rapturously into the back of her head. "They are the second best thing to ever touch my lips."

I turned my head to look at Nick, who'd insisted on cramming himself into the back seat so that I could ride shotgun. "And what's the first?"

Nick turned his version of crimson, but he held Jessalyn's gaze in the rearview mirror and he couldn't hide his smile.

Never having kissed Nick, I thought the cupcakes were the best thing to ever touch my lips, but after another hour with no response from Selena, I had trouble finishing mine.

"I don't get why she's this mad at you." Jessalyn licked the cream cheese frosting from her empty cupcake wrapper. "I mean, yeah, okay, you did lie to her a bunch, and your timing for springing Brandon on her sucked monkey balls, but that was an accident. And your dad's birthday disaster wasn't your fault at all. If it was me, I'd go to her work or wherever and I wouldn't leave until she talked to me."

"Her boyfriend thinks I should give her some time."

"Yeah, but it's been a week, right?"

I glanced at Nick over my half-eaten cupcake. I hadn't expected him to jump to my side, especially since he knew firsthand what it felt like to be lied to by me.

"More than a week since her open mic night."

"I would go find her," Jessalyn said, eyeing my cupcake and then grinning when I slid it toward her.

"Might help," Nick said, looking at me with his old, totally unromantic tenderness. My heart lifted from that sight alone, and it rose even higher when he went on, "She's hurting too, right? I'm sure it's easier for her to be mad at you than to deal with finding out she has a brother, but she still does have a brother, and you're the only one who can tell her anything about him."

CHAPTER 44

After practice the next day I parked in front of Lava Java next to Selena's car, got out and sat cross-legged on her hood, ready to sit and wait for however many hours it took for her to get off work. She saw me, of course, during her shift, but after the first startled glimpse, she ignored me. That was fine. I had nowhere else to go, and she couldn't stay inside forever. At least knowing I was waiting for her would give her time to resign herself to seeing me. And in a public space, she wouldn't scream in my face again.

Her arms were crossed when she finally came out. She didn't try to ignore me, which was good because I had a spare set of keys to her car and was fully prepared to let myself in the passenger side if she tried to take off. The surprise was that she was the first to speak.

"All my coworkers think you're unhinged."

"What did you tell them?"

"That you're unhinged."

Smiling felt like the wrong response but I did it anyway. "Thanks for coming out."

"You're sitting on my car, Dana. What choice do I have?"

I wasn't sure if she'd even looked at my text the night before, so I told her again. "We won. State finals next week."

An unguarded light came to Selena's eyes. "Dana! That's—" the light dimmed "—good."

"Mom came," I said. "Have you been talking to her?"

"Yes." That was it, a single-syllable response.

"And?" I said.

"And what?"

"How is she?"

"You're talking to her too. Ask her yourself."

I scooted forward, sliding off the hood until I was leaning against the front bumper. "I've tried. She's not ready to talk about it."

Selena shook her head, looking down at her feet. "I don't think I'm ready to talk to you either."

That stung, much more in person than my unanswered texts. "Don't do this again. However upset you are with me, I know you don't believe this is all my fault." Or, I thought I knew. At my words, Selena bit both her lips, a telltale sign from when we were kids that she wanted to hit me. I would have backed away if the car hadn't been at my back.

"You were the one who had the brilliant idea to test Dad's DNA. I told you over and over again not to do it, that it wasn't worth finding out something horrible that we would have gone on happily not knowing."

"Happily?" I looked at my sister like I'd never seen her before. "You would have been happy never knowing you had a brother?"

Selena's eye twitched.

"'Cause I can't, and I wouldn't want to. Finding out that we have a brother was horrible, but it was amazing too. I know that it's a mess and it hurts because even though he's Dad's son, he's not Mom's, and I don't understand how that could ever happen to two people who are so stupid in love that they'll sit in the same chair at the dining table when there are six other empty chairs. It'll never make sense, and if I hadn't seen what was undeniably our father's son when I met Brandon, I'd have been where you were, calling me a liar."

She flinched, still biting her lips, but now it looked like she was trying to hold back tears.

"And I'm sorry that I lied to you and that I didn't find the right way to tell you the truth. I'm sorry I left that envelope on my desk for Mom to find. I'm sorry she left and that you're gone. I'm sorry that Dad cheated on Mom when you were a baby, but I'm *not* sorry about Brandon. Take away what Dad did and what I did. Take away everything else but the one fact that we have a brother. You have a *brother*." I dashed away the first tear when it fell, and I smiled. "I don't know how well you got to see him, but he's really tall and still kind of skinny, like the pictures of Dad at his age. He looks a lot like Dad, and a little like us and, I don't know, maybe he has your sense of humor. I do know he taught himself to play the guitar just like you, and when he heard you sing, Sel, his expression was just like yours is right now."

Her eyes were so full of tears that I didn't think she could see me anymore. I could barely see her out of mine. She still hadn't moved closer to me, and I hadn't taken that last step to hug her. And in that moment, we were saved from having to. Our phones chimed simultaneously.

I reached mine in my pocket before Selena pulled hers from her purse. Our eyes met, and we knew we'd each received the same message. It was from Mom.

Mom: Please come home. Your dad and I need to talk to you.

Without a word, we both spun for our cars, our eyes meeting one last time before we climbed into our separate driver's seats.

"It's going to be okay," she said.

"I know," I said. But what I was thinking was that, between the two of us, I was supposed to be the liar.

CHAPTER 45

I drove home in a blind panic, constantly seeking out Selena's car behind me in the rearview mirror. Together we parked in front of our house, noting Mom's car in the driveway alongside Dad's. I slowed as I approached the front door, waiting until Selena was by my side before opening it.

They were sitting next to each other at the dinner table when we walked in. I blinked away the ghostly memory from Dad's birthday. Mom wasn't sitting in Dad's lap, but neither was she at the opposite end of the table either. They were sitting side by side, not too far and not too close. Their proximity to each other told me nothing about the conversation we were about to have. Reluctance to find out slowed my steps, and Selena matched my pace. Dad looked much the same as he had the night Mom left—bereft. Mom, usually so put together even when she had her hair piled up on her head and in a T-shirt, looked like she hadn't slept in days.

There was such a dichotomy between my emotions. I hated

that Dad had cheated on Mom and hurt all of us, but I also wanted to see him and Brandon play catch in our backyard, to join in, and Selena too. I understood Mom leaving the way she had, but I didn't want my parents to split up.

"Come on," Mom said. "Sit down."

We did, but with equal apprehension, noting the glance our parents exchanged. As soon as we were seated, Mom reached out and took my hand and also Selena's.

"I'm sorry I left like I did. I should never have done that to you two, no matter what is going on between me and your dad."

"Mom," I said, trying to tug my hand free, but she only held tighter. She didn't have to apologize to me. In fact, I didn't want her to. As much as Selena and I clashed over blame in this situation, I had been the one to reveal that Dad had a son. I'd brought that pain to her, and I'd always feel guilty over that.

"No, Dana." She forestalled another of my attempts to wriggle free. "This is not your fault." Her eyes drifted to Selena. "It's not."

Beside me, Selena stiffened. She wasn't ready to acquiesce that easily. "She shouldn't have—"

"Selena, I already knew."

My sister and I both went perfectly still. "You—" My eyes shot back and forth between my parents and found the same slightly uncomfortable but determined expression on both their faces. "No," I said. "How could you—"

"No, no," Mom said, her hand once again locking onto mine. "Not about Brandon, about the affair."

Selena's hand jerked free of Mom's, the first real flash of

anger lighting her eyes. "You wouldn't have stayed. I know you wouldn't have."

Our parents exchanged another look.

"This isn't something we ever intended to talk about with you," Dad said, flushing bright red around his neck. "When—"

"Let me," Mom said. She released my hand—I'd stopped trying to free it by then due to sheer shock—and placed it atop Dad's forearm. Even when she began addressing me and Selena, I couldn't look away from her hand on his arm. She knew he cheated, yet she was touching him.

"After you were born, Selena, we had a really hard time. Really, really hard. I was taking time off from school and your dad had blown out his shoulder and was having to work twice as hard while going to school himself after losing his scholarship. We never saw each other, and we had no money. We were living in this tiny apartment hours away from my family, and I was still so young." She looked at Dad. "We both were. I started to think we'd made a mistake, and that it would be better for all of us if we separated, so I took Selena and moved back home for a while. And that's when I started talking to a lawyer."

Mom's hand slid off Dad's arm, and I knew she didn't want to be touching him for what she said next.

"I told your dad that I wanted a divorce. We'd gotten married too young and we weren't ready." Her eyes lifted to Dad's. "I think maybe we were both relieved to hear one of us say it."

Dad's response was immediate. "No, I wasn't. We were young and it was hard, but you know I never wanted out."

"That didn't stop you from wanting someone else." Three

heads turned, not in my direction but Selena's. I'd been thinking something similar, but Selena had been the one to say it out loud.

"I don't have an excuse. I did have an affair. It was very brief, and it nearly cost me my marriage and my family. There is not a day that goes by that I don't regret it." Beside him, Mom's attempt at stoicism was weak at best. "I thought I'd lost everything and I was working with someone who was also in a struggling marriage, and I made the worst decision of my life. I knew it was wrong from the beginning—we both did. And we both wanted desperately to reconcile with our spouses. I quit that job and told your mom everything. That was the last time I saw Maggie—Brandon's mother. She never told me about him. I don't even know if she would have. By then I was too grateful that my wife was willing to give me a second chance to be a better husband and father."

"It wasn't just his second chance—it was mine, ours. No, I didn't have an affair," she said to Selena when her eyes flashed. "But I abandoned my husband." Her voice grew thicker. "I walked out on him when things got tough, and I took his baby girl with me. I don't know that I could have forgiven him that, but he did. I won't lie to you and say that forgiving him was easy any more than it was easy for him to forgive me, but we worked through it."

I couldn't remember a time in my life when my parents weren't the most disgustingly in-love people on the planet, so hearing them talk about how close they'd come to getting a divorce made me feel sick.

"We were still broke most of the time and living in a tiny apartment," Mom went on. "But we found a marriage counselor at a church nearby, and I started taking online courses in computer coding. Things got better—not overnight, but they did. Over the next few years, they got more than better." She looked at Dad, her eyes shiny, nodding a few times before saying, "I did forgive him, but hearing there was a child—" She shut her eyes. Dad lifted his arm as if to wrap it around her but left it hovering just shy of touching her, like he wasn't sure if he could offer comfort over something like this. Mom's eyes opened again. "I can't describe what that was like, learning that he had a son out there, the product of the most painful thing to ever happen to us."

Dad lowered his arm to his side.

"All that hurt came right back to the surface and I had to— I wanted to have some time to deal with it on my own. Knowing that another woman bore my husband's child while we were married…" She paused. The rest of us could only sit there and wait and feel sick over the fact that she had to say something like that. "I forgave him for the affair, and this doesn't change that, since neither of us knew about Brandon before last week, but it doesn't make it hurt any less. And I can't not feel devastated and angry all over again. I am, and I do, just like it happened yesterday." She turned to Dad, laying her hand on his cheek. "And at the same time, I'm grieving with you for missing his whole life." She started to cry, shaking her head like she couldn't understand her own emotions.

Dad didn't hesitate to take her in his arms then, and she went to him.

I struggled, watching them embrace, still feeling emotional pulls in opposite directions. Beside me, Selena's posture went rigid.

"So is that it? Whoops, Dad had a kid, let's all get over it?" Selena wasn't pulling any punches. Our parents let go of each other.

"Selena, no," Mom said, her voice thicker than usual, her accent growing more prominent. "No one is just getting over this. We're all going to have to hurt and grieve in our own way. We'll help each other, and we'll get help together, okay?" Her eyes moved to include me. Before she could say anything else, Dad was talking.

"I'm sorry," he said to me and Selena. "I didn't just hurt my wife—I hurt both of you. I wasn't any kind of man back then, and I want better for you than your mom got in me." His eyes moved slowly to my face. "I'm sorry and I hope someday you'll be able to forgive me."

My eyes stung looking at him. I wanted that too, but it wasn't as easy to feel. I didn't know if I could ever get back there. Mom must have seen some of the conflict I was feeling, because she addressed me and Selena straight on.

"You're not little kids anymore. I can't tell you to hug and make up. You understand what's going on here and we're not going to hide the reality of this situation from you. What we are doing is telling you that your Dad and I are staying together. As much as all this hurts right now, it happened twenty years ago. Dad and I have worked hard at our marriage and loving each other these past decades and we're not—" she stole a quick glance at Dad "—I'm not going to discount that. The truth is, we're neither of us the same selfish and immature people we were when we first got married. Back then, I was too in love with myself to love anyone else the way I should have. I wanted to quit, so I did, and it was the biggest mistake of my life."

"I should have gone after you," Dad said, gazing at her. "I was a coward and a fool, and I will regret every second that we were apart until the day I die."

The regret clawing though Dad's voice brought goose bumps to my skin. And it was more than his words and hers; it was the way they looked at each other when they said them. It was so naked that I had to look away. But the second I did, my gaze fell on Selena and the tears swimming in her eyes. They were for our parents, for the scene before us and the love no one in that room could deny, but I felt them for someone else too.

Whatever equilibrium I'd regained watching my parents recommit themselves to each other and our family lurched away. There was one other big question that hadn't been answered.

"Mom," I said, slowing after that because I needed to pick my words very carefully. "What about Brandon?"

CHAPTER 46

I already knew Dad wanted to know and be known by his son. He didn't even know the name of his own father, and he loathed the idea of denying his son even that same basic knowledge. But Dad didn't yet know how vehemently opposed Brandon was to having any kind of relationship with him. So then what? Have Dad join me for a little parking lot stalking to catch the occasional glimpse of his son? Should we ambush Brandon again and force him into an unwanted role in our family? Or worse, should we all try to go back to our ignorance? Pretend Dad didn't have a son and Selena and I didn't have a brother? Could any of us do that? I'd already shown how incapable I was of walking away from him. I'd sunk pretty low in my desperate attempts to feel connected to my brother. So when I asked my family what about Brandon, I meant it. What could we do?

The answers were not forthcoming, from anyone. We must have all been running though similar questions, and none of us had any good answers. Mom was the one to break the silence.

"You met him?"

I nodded.

"Okay." She breathed deeply, like she was in physical pain but determined to push through it. "Tell us about him."

So I did. I told them everything from the first messages we exchanged to showing up at Jungle Juice. I didn't look at Dad when I relayed how adamant Brandon was that I stay away from him. And I didn't look at anyone when I mentioned spending time with Chase and the secondhand info I'd gathered from him. When I got to the last meeting with Brandon, the one at Selena's work, I pitched the conversation to her and she continued it. It was strange, hearing her side, knowing that beyond that first flicker of recognition while she was singing, she hadn't allowed herself to see Brandon for who he was. Her actions and disbelief that night had been as genuine as her anger toward me. The disbelief was gone, but the anger still simmered, though more in Dad's direction now than mine.

Mom didn't say a single word while we spoke. Occasionally, the whites of her knuckles showed through her tan skin, the only real sign that she was struggling with hearing about her husband's son. Dad asked questions though, a lot of questions. It was as if Mom being there beside him allowed the floodgates to open, and it fell to me to answer. I did the best I could, but the reality was that I didn't know a lot about my brother. I also was far from comfortable talking to Dad about him, especially given the audience we had.

I felt a genuine pang for Dad when I had to tell him that

Brandon had refused all contact with us. I told him we couldn't know what might happen in the future, but I wasn't holding out hope that Brandon would change his mind, at least not without a major intervention, and he'd refused to hear more from me. What did give me hope, however, was watching Mom take Dad's hand in front of me and Selena and seeing the look they shared in the wake of real but forgiven pain.

Knowing Dad hadn't been lying to her for their entire marriage but had confessed and sought her forgiveness did mean something to me. I didn't have to torment myself wondering if every sweet exchange between my parents might have been changed if Mom knew the truth. She did know, and her smiles and kisses were as real as they'd looked. She was still holding his hand even then.

And I felt the balance between my conflicting emotions shift in a direction I wouldn't have thought possible even a week ago.

It was late by the time we finished talking, so Selena didn't protest too much when Mom suggested she stay the night. Mom and Dad didn't get up when Selena and I did. Late or not, they still had a lot to work through together, but the operative word was *together*. I carried that thought with me as Selena and I traipsed up to my room.

All her clothes were at Whitney's, so I loaned her some shorts and a T-shirt to sleep in. Neither of us spoke until we were under the covers and staring up at the faintly glowing star stickers on the ceiling.

"Why haven't you taken these down? We put them up when you were eight."

"I never notice them during the day, and at night—" I shrugged "—I guess I still like them."

Selena exhaled, and it was almost a murmur of agreement. "I put some up in my dorm room."

I turned my head toward her. "You did?"

"I guess I still like them too." She turned her head toward me. "It's a lot, isn't it?"

We weren't talking about glow-in-the-dark stickers anymore. "Yeah."

"I'm sorry."

"Yeah?"

She nodded. "I wasn't fair to you. I honestly have no idea what I would have done if I'd been the first to know." Selena squirmed. "I couldn't reconcile one thing being true at the expense of the other, so I blamed you. I didn't even know I was doing it. Honestly, Dana. I didn't mentally flip a coin or anything. I think I thought I could get past you lying, but Dad having a son? I still can't— I mean, how is—" She stopped herself. "That doesn't matter right now. You're my sister and I should have believed you no matter what."

"I wouldn't have wanted to believe me either, but thanks."

We were lying shoulder to shoulder in the same bed that had been our childhood flying carpet, our *Dawn Treader*, our hidden castle when we'd draped sheets from the ceiling fan. Our days of sharing a room had already ended. Even if we resolved everything between us, it made sense for her to stay at Whitney's. And in a few months she'd be moving to Nashville. After having heard her sing, I knew she had a real shot at making it. Who knew where her voice would take her? We might never again be as close as we were at that moment.

"That night you met Brandon—"

"I'm sorry I didn't believe you."

"I know. I was going to say you sang really beautifully."

"Really?" She shifted on her shoulder to face me.

I nodded. "It makes me hate you a little less for giving up softball."

"There are city leagues I can join in Nashville. I'll still get to play a little."

"I hate that you're moving so far away. What am I supposed to do once you're gone?" My voice cracked.

She tucked her head against my shoulder. "There's still the chance I'll be really crummy and everyone in Nashville will hate me."

I smothered a laugh. "You forget I've already heard you. You'll be amazing, Sel."

"You'll visit, and I'll come home all the time. It'll be like I'm not even gone."

But she would be. So much was changing. I already missed her and she hadn't even left yet. Tomorrow she'd be back at Whitney's, but this night was still ours.

"I just realized what you would have done," I said.

"What?"

"If you'd been the first to know about Brandon instead of me. You know that scene in *A Christmas Story* where Ralphie blames his friend for teaching him the word *fudge*, and then Ralph's mom is on the phone with his friend's mom, and you hear this screaming through the handset, 'What? What! *What!*'" I tried to whisper the shrill screaming. We both suppressed a grin. "We'd have all heard you screaming and we'd have had to have the whole thing out, right then. That's what you'd have done."

"Probably," Selena admitted, and I could hear the smile she still wore. "So you forgive me?"

"Yeah."

"And Dad?"

My lingering smile faded. "I don't know. Do you?"

"I want to. I don't want to feel this way about him, you know?"

I shoved her. Not hard enough to push her off the bed or anything, but enough so she'd feel it. "*I* know. How do you think I've been feeling all this time?"

"Ow! Well, I hate it."

"Me too."

"And I can't even begin to think about *him*."

Brandon.

"Except..." she went on "...I hope he changes his mind. I still want Dad to get to meet his son. Is that wrong?"

I could feel Selena's eyes on me, waiting for my answer. I knew how she felt, that undeniable longing for Dad and Brandon to see each other, even if it was only one time.

CHAPTER 47

Dad's back was to me when I entered the kitchen early the next morning. It was the first time since finding Brandon that I'd willingly sought out my dad. Silently, I pulled the box of Bisquick from the pantry and a mixing bowl from the cabinet next to the sink, then grabbed eggs and milk from the fridge. I sat down at the kitchen island and started mixing the pancake batter while Dad lit two burners on the stove and dropped a pat of butter on the griddle he pulled out. A minute later I was ladling batter, silver dollar–size for me and Selena and larger ones for Dad. Mom only drank coffee in the mornings.

As I watched for the little bubbles to appear and tell me it was time to flip, I remembered a much younger me, still in footie pajamas, lifted in Dad's arms as he showed me the exact right time to flip pancakes. He'd always been my coach, on the field or in the kitchen and everywhere else.

"State is in less than a week," I said, turning the first pancake while Dad began frying up bacon beside me.

"Yep."

"I think we have a real shot. Sadie's pitching is almost better than Selena's at this point."

"She's been working hard," Dad said. "Hard work always pays off."

Maybe that was a dig and maybe it wasn't. But it felt like one, since I obviously hadn't been working as hard as I could have been these past weeks. I paused in the act of flipping the last pancake. "I have worked hard at this for years even though we both know I'll never be as good as Selena, but you know what? She never cared half as much. Maybe your son would have been the perfect blend of talent and determination, but with me and Selena, we only each got one." I whirled away from the stove, taking my plate of pancakes to the island with me. In the silence that followed, all I heard was the sizzling bacon and the occasional pop from the coffeepot. Dad stayed quiet until a pile of bacon joined the pancakes in front of me and he sat on the stool beside me.

"When I was eleven, I lived with the Scudder family. Mom, dad, two kids a little younger then me. They were nice people, not overly affectionate, but they never hurt me."

My ears perked up. Dad almost never talked about his childhood. A lot of it was bad, but I knew there had been some good things too. He was somber enough in that moment that this story could go either way.

"Joe, the dad, worked a lot," Dad went on. "And he wasn't up for much when he'd get home at night, but he liked baseball. His sons didn't, but I didn't know much about it. We watched games together, and one night he brought me home a glove."

"The one you gave Selena?"

Dad nodded. "Joe was the first one to teach me how to catch a ball. Said I had a good arm and that if I practiced, I could have a great arm." He smiled. "After that, the only time that glove ever left my hand was in the shower."

He'd given it to Selena for her twelfth birthday. I remembered, because she'd told me later that she'd wanted a new one but refused to let me have it when I'd asked. I'd been able to tell it meant something to Dad when he gave it to her. He hadn't told us how or when he'd gotten the glove, just that it used to be his and now it was hers.

"You never told us about him."

"I was only there for about eight months."

"What happened?"

"They got pregnant, needed the room I was using."

"Oh." That struck me as unbelievably sad, Dad being shuffled off to another family just as he was connecting. He'd been in a lot of foster homes. I think I remember him saying he lived with more than a dozen families before aging out of the system at eighteen.

"Did the next family have a dad who liked baseball?"

"No." A simple one-word answer that spoke volumes. "But I kept playing when I could, high school, college. It was the only thing I was ever good at. And I wanted to have that great arm. I had good coaches, and they pushed me, but I always pushed harder, right up until I blew out my shoulder."

After talking together the night before, I knew more about that time in his life than I ever wanted to. I nudged my fork at a pancake.

"I've always pushed you hard, both of you. Maybe too hard."

Thinking about all the nights I'd gone to sleep half crying over burning shoulders or bruised shins, I couldn't argue with that statement. Still, I said, "You wanted us to be good."

"I did," Dad said. "But I wanted you to *want* to be good. It wasn't enough to play well—I wanted you to need it. But you don't, either of you—not the way I did."

I frowned, looking up at him. "I don't understand."

"What you tried to do for me, find me family? Dana, it wouldn't have mattered. I don't need people now. I needed them then. If I'd stayed with the Scudders or stayed anywhere, maybe it would have been different." He drew himself up. "But I didn't. The nicest man I ever lived with happened to like baseball and played catch with me a few times. If he'd liked golf, I'd have a house full of clubs right now instead of bats. I doubt he remembers my name, whereas I've spent every game I've ever played looking for his face in the stands."

"Dad." His eyes grew shiny, which made my chin quiver.

"I've made so many mistakes in my life, and I've passed them on to you. You don't have to kill yourself in the backyard at night running drills. You don't have to be the greatest softball player or win a state championship. You don't have to compete with Selena or anyone else. And I'm sorry that I've hurt you so much. I'm sorry that I ever made you think you had to compete with anything or anyone for what you'll always have from me. I see you without any of that. I love you, kid."

The rest of my expression crumbled, and Dad caught me in a hug that didn't erase the hurt from past months and years but came close.

CHAPTER 48

I knew exactly where to park, having done it a dozen times or more the previous week. I wasn't going for stealth anymore, though. I needed Chase to see me, and I prayed he'd be willing to hear me out before shutting me down again.

I drove over the morning after Dad and I had breakfast together, before anyone else was awake. Hopefully, I'd be back before they even knew I'd left. Chase usually opened Jungle Juice during the week, so I knew roughly when he'd need to leave his house, and I made sure to be out front when he did.

It was still dim outside. Day was just beginning to press back the night, a soft hazy purple against the blue-black sky. Mornings were already warm by the end of May, even before the sun fully rose. As I waited, night weakened further. The sky was glowing pale pink and orange when Chase opened his door and stepped outside. He took a few steps before he saw me. As before, he didn't scowl, but even from across the street I could see the slight shake of his head before he crossed to me.

"This isn't cool, okay?"

"I know. And I'm sorry."

He squinted at the ground before slowly angling his head up at me. "What are you doing here, Dana?"

I couldn't help it. Standing that close to him, I remembered the feel of his lips on mine and the warmth of his hands. I remembered being held in his arms, his breath ghosting against my ear. It physically hurt to think I'd never feel any of that again. He was standing there, not walking away or berating me, but he was as gone for me as if he were. And after what I'd done to him and his family, I couldn't begin to give him a reason to come back.

"I'm not here because of us. I wish I were. I wish that there was something I could say to you to make up for my actions, but I know there isn't. And I get it. If the situation were reversed, I wouldn't want to be within a hundred feet of you. So, I promise this is it. I won't show up at your house or anywhere else again."

He hesitated, then nodded.

"It's about Brandon."

Chase's mouth thinned but he didn't say anything.

I swallowed. I wasn't looking forward to telling yet another person this story. "You know he's my half brother. His mom and my dad... Well, apparently, no one ever knew until I submitted a sample of my dad's DNA and it matched with Brandon's."

"I know. He and I talked about everything."

I tried not to flinch as my eyes fell shut. Brandon knew what I'd done, all of it. "I told my parents too. So they all know. My mom, I guess, knew about the affair from back then." My chin quivered and before I could stop myself, my eyes were swimming with tears. "But no one knew about Brandon. I don't know if that matters to him or not, but my dad wouldn't have abandoned his son, no matter what the circumstances. My dad is kind of a mess right now." I tried to laugh but it didn't come out right. "We're all a mess. I thought it'd be better once everyone knew, but it's almost worse. I'm still figuring things out with my dad, but I see him in agony over this person he's never met and might not ever get to see."

"Dana." There was a hint of warning in Chase's voice.

"I know. And I'm not going to force Brandon to see him or anything," I added, needing to be clear because my track record in that department sucked. "I'm glad you guys talked. I didn't want him to feel alone in this, and with you, he doesn't have to." My chin was all over the place. I couldn't stop it. "I'm done pushing this on anyone. My parents and sister all understand that Brandon doesn't want to hurt his family by starting any kind of relationship with us, and we've all agreed to respect that and keep our distance." I had to look away when I said, "And you too." There was no protest from Chase. I hadn't expected one, but I'd wanted it all the same.

"You still haven't told me why you're here."

No, I hadn't. Probably because I had even less hope of a favorable response to my request than I had of Chase forgiving me. But I still had to ask.

"You don't owe me anything," I said. "Or rather, you don't owe me anything good. And I'm going to ask you something huge. You can say no, you can tell me to get off your street and never come back again." My voice broke and I had to blow out a steadying breath before I could speak again. "But I can't leave without trying. And this time it's not for me.

"I still love my dad." And no steadying breath was going to help me that time. Tears spilled onto my cheeks. "He'll never be for Brandon what he's been to me. And from everything you've told me about Brandon's dad, he's already got everything he needs—but maybe it could provide closure for both of them if they met. Not as father and son, but just to see each other and to know. To not carry around a giant question mark for the rest of their lives. I thought if anyone could persuade him, it'd be you. That's why I'm here. Just to ask you to ask him."

Chase still hadn't left. That was a good sign. But he didn't look convinced either.

"You don't have to decide right now. Wednesday is my last softball game. It's the state championship. My family will be there, along with a lot of other people. If you both come, it wouldn't have to be a big production. They could see each other, and if that's all he wants to do, then you guys could just walk away. My dad could see and know that Brandon is okay, safe. And Brandon could see a man who would have loved him as much as he loves me, which is a lot. I think he should get that, they both should. All I'm asking is that you make this one appeal to him." I held out a paper with the information for the game, and wonder of wonders, Chase took it.

"I can't promise he'll agree or that I'll even ask him." Chase looked at the paper. "Either way…Dana, this has to be it. I'm not going to yell at you or try to make you feel bad, but what you did…not just to me…that's it for me. I don't want you coming around." The paper disappeared into his pocket. "I need you not to."

I felt each of his words tighten like a noose around my heart, and tears for him joined the ones for my dad. I nodded the whole time. I had used him—I hadn't meant to, but the outcome was the same. Everything I knew about Brandon had come through Chase. I'd lied and hurt them both, which meant I'd lost the chance to tell him that learning about my brother had been a side effect of falling for him. And I had, utterly and completely. That was the only part of all this I wouldn't take back.

He started to turn but stopped. "He's leaving for college in less than a month, Penn State. He was planning on staying here the whole summer, but he decided to go early. My uncle already put their house up for sale."

"Does that mean...he told his dad?"

Chase shook his head. "No, he's pretty adamant that he'll never do that."

"I'm sorry," I said, a blanket apology that was quickly chased by one much more specific. "Oh, your mom. Chase, I'm really sorry. Is she—" I didn't know how to finish that question. How was it possible to feel any worse? I'd caused so much damage already, and the effects were still rippling. I hadn't been content with my own family's ruin—I'd had to take Chase's along with us. I didn't know what was hidden in Chase's garage, but I wouldn't have been surprised if it was packed full again, with Chase stored along with it.

Chase's eyebrows flickered together before smoothing again. In my chest my heart gave one last strangled lurch.

Not because I hoped he'd forgive me that time, but because I knew he couldn't.

"Take care of yourself, Dana."

CHAPTER 49

The day of my state finals, the game my softball team had worked so hard to get to, came without any of the emotional fanfare I'd been expecting. I wanted to win—I always wanted to win—but it wasn't with the same all-consuming, single-minded determination that I'd thought I would have. It wasn't the chief focus of my mind. I was thinking about my family, old and new, and the possibility of the meeting that might occur. That was the question spinning dizzyingly in my head: not would we win or lose, but would Brandon show or not?

Every at bat, every out, every inning, that's what I thought about. Every time I didn't need to focus on the game, my gaze was on the stands scanning for something that had become much more important. Distracted as I was, I knew the only reason I played as well as I did was because, in the back of my mind, I kept thinking my brother might be watching me for the one and only time in my life.

But it wasn't enough. We lost. Not by a lot, but that didn't

matter. Our team played well, but the other team played better. It was that simple. No one pointed fingers or cast sideways looks at anyone. There wasn't anyone to blame. I might
have played better under different circumstances, but not by
much. Selena's team had handily trounced the opposing team
for their final, but my team couldn't. I couldn't. For once, I
didn't let that bitter truth devour me. I was good but Selena
was great. She was the one who'd gotten the scholarship offers, whereas I already knew not to expect the same interest
when I graduated next year.

Tom Hanks was a liar—there was a lot of crying in softball
when your team lost a state championship, especially from the
seniors. Ainsley was practically inconsolable. Her mom had to
physically walk her off the field. Between all the tears, there
were hugs and empty words that no one heard. It was pretty
damn miserable in that dugout, and there wasn't a thing any
of us could do about it.

I cast a glance at Jessalyn, slumped dejectedly on the bench
beside me. Most of the other girls had left by then.

She looked up, tried to smile but couldn't quite manage it.
"I thought we were going to win, you know?"

"Your boy," I said, using her words for Nick, "looks like
he thinks we did." Nick was waiting by the stands, and when
our eyes met, he gave me a tentative wave that I returned. I
missed what we'd had, but I was grateful for what we were
slowly rebuilding.

Jessalyn glanced at Nick, and there was nothing tentative
about the smile he gave her. He had a booming-loud voice
when he chose to use it and had drowned out every other
person at the game whenever Jessalyn was at bat—and a lit-

tle for me too. Jessalyn smiled back at him. "He knows we lost, right?"

"Yeah, but he won."

She turned her smile on me. "We didn't suck tonight. That has to count for something."

I laughed a little. "I think it might have been your best game of the season," I said. "I know Coach is already talking to colleges about you and Sadie."

"You too," she said.

I wrinkled my nose. "Probably not going to be fielding too many scholarship offers, but I'll still get to play. Honestly, I think that's all I want." Selena was the star player in our family. I didn't have the heat, and she didn't have the heart. No doubt I'd feel torn up about that in the future and have to battle fresh resentment toward my sister, but that day and that game, I didn't. Because as soon as all the trappings that went with a state game were over, I was once again scanning the stands...and this time, I saw them.

My gaze stuck on the figures of Brandon and Chase, standing side by side to the far left of the bleachers. In a trance I walked toward Dad—he was on the field, passing on reassuring words and hugs to a couple of still-crying seniors, so he was still technically in coach mode, but I no longer cared about our rules and separate roles. The season was over, and the biggest moment of our lives was about to happen.

"Dad."

He looked up, forlorn like a coach whose team had just lost the championship game.

"He's here." I didn't say who. He knew I wasn't talking about some long-lost foster father.

Dad turned so slowly. And if I hadn't been right at his side, I'd have missed the way his knees buckled before locking again the moment he laid eyes on his son.

I'd shown Dad pictures online, so there was no question as to which McCormick his gaze rested on. Mine, however, was torn between the two. I let myself look at Chase only briefly, silently thanking him for doing the impossible. Then I made myself look away before the tears I was holding back broke through. Nothing less than my brother meeting our father could have done it.

The majority of the crowd had gone by then. A few tiny clusters remained here and there, but none near where Brandon and Chase stood.

Mom and Selena met Dad and me at the base of the bleachers. Gavin was there too, but after looking at each of our faces, he suddenly got a leg cramp that he said he needed to walk out. By himself. On the opposite end of the field. I'd have to thank him for that later.

We none of us said a word. I didn't know what to do next, and based on the wide eyes of both Brandon and Chase, neither did they. So I moved. I tugged Selena's arm, and the two of us, leaving Mom and Dad behind, crossed the dozen yards that separated us from our brother. A few steps away, we slowed, and Brandon, after a moment of hesitation, moved toward us in slow jerky steps, like he had to force himself to take each one. When we all stopped, no more than an arm's length from each other, I had to blink to keep from tearing up. There we were, me and my sister and my brother, standing together without lies or deception between us. We all knew who we were. It was the genuine counterpart to the moment I'd failed to manufacture before. No one was scowling or yelling, and at least on my lips there was the tentative hint of a watery smile. In a few minutes, we'd turn and walk away and maybe that would be it. But that moment, fresh off the biggest loss of my life, when I should have been lower than I'd ever been, I couldn't not smile.

And it wasn't just me. Selena had come of her own accord, and Brandon too. We all wanted and needed this. Uncertainty flickered in all our eyes, but not regret.

"You came," I said. My eyes were everywhere on his face, taking him in freely the way I hadn't been able to before.

"It's just this once. I'm not   It can't be more than tonight."

Something caught in my throat and I could feel my expression trying to crumble even as I nodded. I'd known that if he came at all, it would be only the one time.

For his part, Brandon looked uncomfortable, but I thought that might have a lot to do with his own inner battle.

"I'm so sorry for—" My words cut off. That list was long, too long for the time we had. I was sorry for ambushing him that first day at Jungle Juice, for exposing him to the most painful truth either of us would likely ever hear. I was sorry for the lies and hurt, not just to him but to Chase. I was sorry it had taken me so long to realize that far from making things better, my actions had caused more trauma. "I'm sorry for everything," I said at last. "Except for you and this right now. And I know you're leaving soon. Penn State." I choked on the words—the distance they represented—and tried to cover it with a smile. I told myself it was better that he be gone and far away than close but still forever out of reach. "That's great, it's really great. I'm sure you'll..." I was tiptoeing toward babbling when I felt Selena's hand in mine. I squeezed back, never looking away from our brother. I wasn't sure of anything, least of all Brandon. He was having a hard time meeting our eyes.

"We're not our parents," Selena whispered, drawing both my and Brandon's attention. She was squeezing my hand so hard that my knuckles were whitening under her grip. "We don't have anything to do with choices that were made twenty years ago. It's a mess, I know, but it's their mess, not ours."

Her words did what mine couldn't. Something shifted, maybe only for that moment in which we stood together. He stopped seeing our parents and just saw us. Brandon met my eye.

"You played really well," he said. And I felt a surge of elation at my brother's praise. "You too," he told Selena. "I didn't get to tell you the other night." He lifted one shoulder. "I play guitar a little too."

A tear slipped down Selena's cheek. "I know. Funny, huh?"

He almost smiled at her.

It was the smile that undid me. It wasn't like Dad's exactly; it was like ours, mine and Selena's.

"Can I—?" I took half a step. "Can I hug you?"

He took a very long time answering, so long that I had to lower the arm I'd lifted when I'd asked. But then he nodded. I hoped he could feel everything in that embrace. It was wonderful and terrible and it was over way too soon.

Selena turned away first, covering her mouth as she hurried back to Mom. I stayed a second longer. Brandon's eyes glistened in the stadium lights as they shifted beyond me. I was looking in his face when he met Dad's gaze. I knew that was my cue. It was so much harder to walk away from him than I thought it would be, but I did it. I retraced my steps to where Selena stood with our parents. When I reached them, I intended to take Mom and Selena aside with me, to give Dad and Brandon the private moment they both needed. Selena came willingly, but Mom, whose eyes had never once left Brandon's face, stopped me.

"Wait," she said. Then she walked purposefully toward Brandon. Brandon had no idea what to expect from the woman whose husband had fathered him. She might have been approaching him to spit in his face for all he knew. But I wasn't surprised when she hesitated for the tiniest second before wrapping him in her arms.

It was a quick hug. Brandon barely had time to respond, either by stepping back or returning the embrace. When she pulled back, she was nodding and at that stage right before someone starts to weep openly. She raised a hand to his head.

"You look just like my girls." Her breath came out in a half sob but she smiled up at him. "I'm saying this because I want you to hear it and believe it. You will always be welcome in my home. Okay? Okay." She nodded as she turned back to Dad, releasing Brandon only to catch his hand and lead him back to Dad. "This is my husband," she told Brandon. And then to Dad, "And this is—" A sob hit her hard. "This is your son." She missed Brandon's flinch at the word *son*, but Dad didn't. She smiled through the tears, or she tried to, glancing between the two, before coming to join me and Selena, gathering us both as tightly as she had Brandon.

My vision was a blur from my own unshed tears as I watched them. There was no embrace or tears. They stared at each other, knowing they weren't afforded the same emotional freedom that Mom and Selena and I were. They were father and son, but that relationship was predicated on events that neither could ever view without remorse on Dad's part and likely some level of animosity on Brandon's. They were bonded by an affair, and that could never be erased. Dad knew it; Mom too. Maybe that was part of the reason she'd hugged him, knowing her husband never could. Though I knew that when she saw Brandon, she didn't see only the results of the affair. She saw a motherless boy who looked so much like her own children that she couldn't stop herself from tearfully embracing him.

They were of a height, Dad and Brandon, and similar build. They had the same eyebrows too—the left one twitched when they were struggling with intense emotions. I think I could have watched them endlessly, but Brandon appeared to be approaching his limit. His shoulders had begun creeping up and his hands were shoved deep in his pockets. Dad took in all those signs too and didn't waste what little time they had with small talk.

"Did you have a good life?"

Brandon's answer was instant and showed none of the tension I saw in his posture. "The best."

"Good, that's good."

They both seemed to realize the captive audience a few feet away, so when Dad asked Brandon if he wanted to walk with him to the dugout in order to retrieve a forgotten ball, Brandon agreed.

I don't know what they said to each other during those few private minutes, but it was clear from the handshake

they shared before walking back that it was something neither would ever forget.

There were only five people left at the field by then. Dad
and Brandon didn't return together. Brandon hung back.
Maybe he couldn't handle passing us again. I understood
the reasoning. I felt so emotionally raw, happy and sad at the
same time. Happy because we had this, all of us together. I
got to see my brother and it wasn't horrible. I got to watch
him meet Dad. Sad because it was already over. I wouldn't
ask him to see us again, and he wouldn't seek us out. He'd
said he wouldn't risk hurting the only man he'd ever call Dad.

Maybe he'd catch Selena on the radio someday. Maybe
he'd watch me play in a real stadium. Maybe we'd get to see
him rocket into space.

Or maybe we'd all be in the same coffee shop someday.
We could sit at the same table and... Maybe.

It felt good to think about a *maybe* somewhere in the future when we couldn't have a *now*.

It also felt good because when Dad reached us, Mom took
his hand in both of hers.

And because when Selena saw me glancing back toward
Chase, she pressed Gavin's car keys into my hand.

"Stay. Talk to him. We'll ride with Mom and Dad."

CHAPTER 50

Walking toward Chase, I knew I wouldn't say the right things to him. I hadn't been able to the two previous times I'd seen him, and with my emotions so heightened from seeing Brandon with Dad, I had no chance. And really, there was no right thing to say. I'd accepted that even while it crushed me. But I'd just had what was likely to be the most bittersweet moment of my life, and Chase was the reason it had happened. I knew he couldn't hear another apology from me, but I was hoping he'd hear a thank-you.

"I'm sorry about your game," he said when I stopped in front of him.

I waved off the comment. Losing was the last thing on my mind in that moment. "Is he waiting for you?" I didn't look in Brandon's direction, but it was clear who I meant.

"He already went to the car. He probably needs a few minutes."

Something like panic crawled up my spine. A few minutes. It wasn't enough, but I let myself look at him for a few seconds, his face and his eyes, storing up for the famine that would come when he left. One last bit of selfishness before I lost him too.

"I don't know if I'll ever be able to tell you what you did for me tonight. Getting Brandon to come, getting to hug my brother and feel him hug me back." I clutched at my uniformed chest, imagining that I could still feel that embrace. "I didn't think I would ever get to do that. So thank you."

Chase started to open his mouth, but I wasn't done. He had to let me say it all.

"My sister got to hug him too and hear him say she sang and played well. You can't know what that means, but thank you. And my mom—" I clamped my mouth shut until I could steady my voice again. "I didn't know what she was going to do if she saw Brandon—I don't know if she knew—but she got to love him. I know it was only for the briefest of moments, but he got to feel that. You did that."

Chase's eyebrows drew together, not in anger, but like he was focusing hard on something. I kept going, knowing once I stopped, I wouldn't be able to get the rest out.

"My dad—my dad got to shake hands with his son, face-to-face. A son he didn't know he had until two weeks ago. And Brandon got to meet his father. I don't know what that means to him, but it has to mean something. He won't have to wonder, about any of us. And if he ever decides to tell his dad about us, we'll be more than names. Chase, I don't know what you said to convince him to come here tonight..." I inhaled a shaky breath as I ran out of words.

"I didn't."

His bald answer caught me up short, but Chase went on before I could say anything.

"I was still figuring out if I was going to say anything to him when he came over to get some stuff to take to college and he saw the garage. It's not empty, but we can park both cars in it again."

"Really?" I said, a smile lifting my voice despite everything else. I'd somehow found room to worry about his mom and what Brandon's early move would mean to her and Chase. I needed every victory I could get, and that was a big one for them, and somehow for me too.

"Really. I told Brandon about us going through it, about you helping me and what you said after my mom started to lose it. She's the only person in my life I have a problem being direct with. You helped me find a way to say what I needed in a way that she could hear. That's why he let me tell him about you, about his sister," Chase said. "So I didn't convince him to show up today. You did."

He wasn't there anymore, but I turned to where I'd last seen Brandon walking across the empty field. Something tight in my chest loosened. There was plenty of bad that Chase could have told Brandon, especially now that he knew how I'd lied to him, but I knew he hadn't. Happy tears stung my eyes hearing that Chase had given my brother something of me to take with him, since I'd been unable to do that myself. It was yet another kindness I didn't deserve.

"It's the best thing anyone has ever done for me, for my family." I faced Chase again. "Thank you."

His response was a sad smile. Just his mouth lifting a little on one side, and his eyes ever on mine.

I should have stopped then. Left it at thank you and walked away. But I couldn't, not when this was my last chance with him too. Even if it changed nothing—especially if it changed nothing—I had to tell him the truth.

"At the coffee shop, you asked me if it was always about Brandon, you and me. At the time, I thought any answer I gave you would be me making excuses for myself, but there aren't any—there's just the truth. The day I met you was the worst day of my life. I had just come face-to-face with proof of my father's infidelity and discovered a brother who couldn't stand to look at me. You weren't supposed to be part of it, but you were. You were nice to me, and without realizing it, you offered me something that I couldn't walk away from: a chance to know my brother. But, Chase, from that very first night, it was more than that—*you* were more than that." My eyes swam looking at him, but I didn't let any tears fall. "I wish I could go back to before."

The muscles in Chase's face kept twitching. "Before what?"

"Before I knew how much losing you would break my heart. Before I knew I'd still rather do that than break any part of yours."

Chase's silent response was profound. He didn't move or sigh or give me any indication that he'd even heard me. Which, I guessed, was the only response I was going to get. I sucked in a shaky breath.

"Everything I felt for you was real. For me, it's still real, but I only meant to say thank you. This, tonight, with Brandon and my family. It was a good thing, and it wouldn't have happened without you." I was going to turn away then, but something stopped me. One last thing I needed to thank him for. "I only got to know him a little, but I know you. Chase, you are the kindest, most selflessly amazing person I've ever known. I'm glad that my brother has you. For the rest of his life, I get to know that." I tilted my head as I raised a shoulder, a light gesture that was completely at odds with how heavy I felt.

I did turn away then. I had to. If I had to look into his eyes for one more second, I'd break. I didn't run to Gavin's car, but I wanted to. I kept my head and my eyes straight ahead as I crossed the parking lot. All of it. All of it. Weeks and weeks of frayed nerves and emotional battering were hitting me hard. I got to meet my brother and see my whole family embrace him. I got to leave him knowing he was returning to a loving family of his own, which was more that I'd ever dreamed possible in this situation. On top of that, my own family was at home waiting for me, together. My parents were still going to be my parents, together. My sister was going to smile when she saw me instead of look away. We were going to shed more tears over this night and the events that preceded it, but we'd do that together. And if I looked into our future, I could see the four of us—five if Gavin stuck around, which might not be the end of the world—together. It was greedy of me to want more, but I did. I wanted the guy I'd walked away from. It was all I could do not to look back and steal one last glimpse of him.

I fumbled with the keys when I reached the door, dropping them before I could fit the key into the lock. And then he was there, stopping the door with his hand before I could open it.

"Wait," Chase said.

With one word, my heart went from a sluggish beating

to a thunderous pounding. His breathing was uneven—he'd run after me.

I turned to look up at him. "Wait?"

He didn't answer, just kept breathing more rapidly than his sprint across the parking lot warranted. He was right in front of me, his chest rising and falling as fast as mine. "All he wanted to do was protect his dad, and leaving is the only way he thinks he can do it. I don't agree with him, but it's his choice. You can't ever ask him for more. Dana, you have to promise me."

That brief hope flared and died. "I promise."

Chase shook his head, half bending down before straightening. "What am I supposed to say to you?"

"Nothing."

He leaned toward me, and I flicked my gaze over him, frowning at the seeming incongruity between his words and his actions. "I can see it now, the questions you asked, how interested you always were in my family. I told you so much, and I didn't even realize I was doing it."

I had no defense, so I made none. "Chase." I breathed his name. "I'm so sorry for all of it."

More staring and breathing. "You did hurt me. You hurt someone I care about more than myself."

I tried to press back farther into the car. "I know." I was staring at his neck, unable to lift my eyes higher. I lowered them to where his open hand still held my door closed. "Then let me go." It was starting to hurt more standing there with him than it would to leave.

The tendons in his forearm shook. His voice lowered, and it sounded painful. "I can't."

The keys slipped through my fingers and hit the ground again. My gaze rose to his and held.

"I usually know what I want," he said. "I decide, and that's it. I don't look back."

"I'm not asking you to." I wasn't, not anymore. "I knew the first time we went out that I was making a choice. Just because it was the wrong choice doesn't mean I get to undo it."

"Tonight..." He stopped and started again. It was the first display of nerves I'd ever seen from him. "Tonight wasn't about us. That's not why I came—"

"You came for Brandon."

"All week I've been thinking about it, talking to Brandon and telling him about you. I thought it would make walking away easier if I could see you through his eyes." Impossibly, he was closer. "But he ended up seeing you through mine."

It was like my heart cracked wide open, this lump in my chest that had been slowly petrifying from all the lies and secrets I'd pumped through it. Freed, but hardly daring to beat.

"And what I see is a girl who made a lot of mistakes in an impossible situation. A girl who tried to stay away from me even as I tried everything I could not to let her. A girl who got me off a couch and helped me have the first honest conversation I've had with my mom in years. A girl who tonight gave my cousin hope for something he never let himself want. A girl who I started to fall for the second she handed me a bat to break a window, and a girl I did fall for when she showed me that I could play a piano I wouldn't have wanted to look at before her." Chase glanced down, not because he needed to break eye contact, but so that he could find my hand with his. "You told me that the day we met, I offered you something you couldn't walk away from, and now I'm saying it to you. It's not neat or easy, the way I feel, but watching you walk away—no. I don't want that."

I looked up, my eyes swimming with tears. "But Brandon—"

"Yeah, Brandon," Chase said, his head lifting to lock eyes with me. "That's not neat or easy either, but he'll be all the way on the other side of the country. Uncle Bran too." His other hand slipped into mine. "You and your family—especially your mom—showed him people can love something even as it hurts them. And I think, maybe sooner than Brandon will admit to himself, he'll want to talk to his dad about all of this. And when that day comes, I know my uncle will want to meet his son's sisters."

My heart hardly dared to beat in my chest. It was too much, thinking we might have more, my whole family. And Chase was still holding my hand.

"So...say it one more time."

My emotions were so close to the surface that I couldn't hide them if I wanted to. And I didn't want to hide anything from Chase ever again. "I'm sorry."

He smiled, one side of his mouth lifting. "Okay, that. You can say that, but I meant the other. Dana..." I would never get tired of hearing him say my name, especially when it sounded like he felt the same way. "Tell me it's real. And then stay, see what we're like when it's not about him at all."

I didn't tell him it was real, I showed him. As soon as I rose up and pressed my lips to his, it was like surfacing from deep underwater and drawing in that long-denied breath of air, of Chase, and knowing that, this time, I could keep him.

His arms encircled me, pulling my body against his until I could feel his heartbeat thumping against my chest. My hand slid up to twine around his neck. There was no sting to bitter the sweetness of that kiss, no guilt to mar the gladness. There was just us, and every part of me tingled back to life.

Nothing was neat or easy. I wasn't, and because of Brandon, Chase and I would never be. But that night, as the stars were beginning to pierce the darkening sky around us and the last of the sun glowed amber across the field, I thought maybe we all deserved a second chance.

★ ★ ★ ★ ★

ACKNOWLEDGMENTS

I can't believe I'm getting to do this for the second time. Nobody pinch me if I'm dreaming.

I poured myself into another book and it wouldn't have happened without the help and support of all these amazing people:

My literary agent, Kim Lionetti. Signing with you continues to be the best decision I've ever made as an author.

My editor, Tashya Wilson. Thank you for pushing me to dig deep again, and then deeper still. I couldn't ask for a better editor.

The whole team at Harlequin TEEN, including Lauren Smulski, Siena Koncsol, Shara Alexander, Amy Jones, Bryn Collier, Evan Brown, Aurora Ruiz, Olivia Gissing, Linette Kim, Erin Craig, Gigi Lau and Kristin Errico.

The fantastic HarperCollins children's sales team.

My brother, Sam Johnson. Your coaching and baseball/softball knowledge are staggering. Thanks for not letting me say *Hit!* Anything that sounds off is 100 percent your fault.

My sisters, Mary Groen and Rachel Decker. Mary, thanks for loving this book before it was even a book, and for loving me even when we were kids sharing a bed and you woke up with my gum in your hair. More than once. Rachel, thanks for all the stories from when you worked at "Jungle Juice," and for all the emoji-filled texts because you live stupid far away.

Thank you to my parents, Gary and Suzanne Johnson. Dad, thanks for the idea behind this book and for passing out my bookmarks to just about every person you meet. Mom, thanks for being the biggest fan of my life. I have no idea how I keep writing these dysfunctional families when I grew up with the complete opposite.

Thank you to Ken Johnson, Rick and Jeri Crawford, and the Depews—the "fame" hasn't changed me yet, Dan, but check back after the next book. Thank you for your unfailing love and encouragement.

To Sadie, Ainsley and Ivy. None of your other aunts named book characters after you. Just saying.

To Grady, Rory, Gideon and Dexter. Your names will be in future books. Promise.

Thank you to the best critique partners a girl could have, Sarah Guilory and Kate Goodwin. Love you both!

Thanks to all the amazing authors from the AZ YA writers group, especially Stephanie Elliot, Kate Watson and Kelly deVos. What would I do without you guys?

Thank you to Susan Moore and your Greek mythology class. I wouldn't have started writing without you.

Thank you to Aprilynne Pike for everything.

Thank you to Gabriella Morales and Christina Medrano

for reading early versions of this book and offering invaluable feedback. Any mistakes are my own.

And thanks to YOU, whoever and wherever you are reading this book. I have no words for how grateful I am.